I0669036

The Promise

Finding purpose in the circle of life

Ryan Gross

ISBN: 978-1- 970970-01-2

DEDICATION

To every caregiver who has walked beside someone through their final

journey. Whether it was a family member, friend, or professional job.

You are seen and appreciated.

The work you do in the quiet hours.

The small acts of comfort you provide.

The weight you carry while others sleep.

We thank you for this sacred work. You hold the space for both life and

death, for grief and grace, for fear and love. You are the steady hand,

the gentle voice, the bridge between worlds.

Thank you for your strength when exhaustion threatened your patience.

When despair tempted your resolve. But mostly for your presence when

it would have been easier to look away.

You teach us how to love in the hardest moments, how to honor the

circle of life, and how to say goodbye with dignity.

This story honors you.

Author Note

In the 5th century BC, the Greek physician Hippocrates coined the terms

karkinos and *carcinoma* to describe tumors he observed in his patients.

The word *karkinos* means "crab" in Greek. He chose this name because

the swollen veins surrounding a tumor resembled a crab's legs

extending from its body. From this ancient word comes our modern

term "cancer." Hippocrates understood, even then, that cancer in its advanced stages was largely incurable. He advised physicians, "It is better not to treat those who have internal cancer, since if treated, they die quickly. But if not treated, they survive for a long time."

Twenty-five hundred years later, despite remarkable medical advances, cancer still invades families without warning. It still makes impossible choices. It still asks the question that echoes through every diagnosis. How much would you sacrifice for the ones you love? This story begins with that question. And with a man who found an answer that defied medicine, logic, and mortality itself.

***

I have added reference materials at the end of this book for readers who wish to know more about the impact cancer can have on families, statistical data on breast cancer, tree burial along with the Palo Verde Nuclear Power Plant.

A heartfelt thank you to my wonderful wife. For without her steady voice, I could not have created such literary works of art.
I will always be grateful

Prologue

The desert was still dark when Manny Chavez pulled onto State Route 85, his truck's headlights carving tunnels through the pre-dawn emptiness at 4:45 AM. The road stretched ahead like a held breath, straight and certain through the Sonoran Desert. On either side, saguaros stood sentinel in the darkness that was ancient, patient, indifferent to the man driving past at seventy miles per hour.

Manny's coffee sat cooling in the cup holder. His third since three AM, when he'd given up on sleep and drifted downstairs to the kitchen. Karen's breathing had been labored last night. He'd stood in the doorway of her room... their room, relocated downstairs when the stairs became too much. He listened to the mechanical rhythm of her rest. The rise and fall of her chest. The small sounds of discomfort that even sleep couldn't erase.

He hadn't gone in. He didn't want to wake her. That's what he told himself, anyway. Now, driving through the dark, he tried not to think about the medical bills on the kitchen counter. Three thousand four hundred dollars that was still outstanding. The insurance covered most of it, they said. Most wasn't all. Most translated to still leaving you with numbers that climbed and climbed while your wife faded and faded.

He shifted his grip on the steering wheel trying to contain the stress. His hands were scarred from years of maintenance work, back before he'd been promoted to shift supervisor. Hands that knew how to fix things. Pumps, valves and cooling systems. Things with procedures. Things with solutions, not cancer. The eastern horizon was beginning to gray when he saw them... the three cooling towers of Palo Verde Nuclear

Generating Station rising from the desert floor like monuments to something he couldn't name. They were massive concrete structures, each over five hundred feet tall, releasing their endless plumes of steam into the sky. From a distance they looked almost graceful but up close, they were just industrial monoliths. Functional and impressive in their scale but not in their beauty.

Manny had been making this drive for twenty-six years. He wasn't sure when it had started feeling like surrender. The security guard at the entrance checkpoint waved him through with a familiar nod. "Morning, Chavez. Early as always."

"Morning, Tom." Manny held up his badge to be scanned, waited for the mechanical click and the rising gate. "Long night?"

"Something like that."

Tom's expression shifted slightly. It looked like sympathy was creeping around the edges as Manny looked away. He didn't want any sympathy. Sympathy was soft and it required him to acknowledge things he couldn't afford to acknowledge. The gate rose and he drove through.

The parking lot sprawled before him, a sea of vehicles under harsh orange security lights. Thousands of employees worked here. Engineers, technicians, operators and support staff. The largest nuclear power plant in the United State with three reactors. Four million people across the Southwest depending on the electricity generated here every single day.

Manny parked in his usual spot, turned off the engine, and sat in sudden silence. Through the windshield, the plant complex stretched across the desert. Buildings and towers, security fences, and lights blazing in the darkness. Somewhere inside was spent nuclear fuel rods that sat submerged in cooling pools, their radioactive decay generating heat that would persist for thousands of years. Some isotopes such as plutonium 239 had half-lives of twenty-four thousand years.

Long after his great-great-great-grandchildren's descendants were dust, this material would still be deadly. He kept it contained and kept people safe. But what legacy was that, really? Manny rubbed his eyes. He was too tired for philosophy. He grabbed his dosimeter badge from the passenger seat, clipped it to his chest, and stepped out into the desert heat. Even at five-thirty AM, the air was warm. By noon, it would be over a hundred degrees. He walked toward the entrance just like any other day.

Inside, the plant was a different world. Sterile white hallways with colored lines painted on floors to guide workers through the maze of corridors. The ventilation system hummed constantly, a white noise that became invisible after a few minutes. The temperature was controlled at sixty-eight degrees. Cold enough that Manny always kept an extra jacket in his locker. He moved through the second security checkpoint, passing through metal detectors and badge scanners with the muscle memory of repetition. Other workers flowed past, the night shift leaving as the day shift was arriving. The familiar pleasant nods exchanged along with brief greetings. Everyone looked tired or maybe that was just him.

The cooling pool observation deck was located in the heart of the facility, accessed through a series of locked doors that required both badge clearance and biometric verification. Manny pressed his palm to the scanner, waiting for the green light, as he heard the magnetic lock release with a heavy clunk.

The observation deck overlooked Reactor Cooling Pool #2. The pool itself was enormous at forty feet deep, filled with water so pure it was almost invisible. Except it wasn't invisible, it glowed with Cherenkov radiation. The eerie blue luminescence of particles moving faster than the speed of light in water. It was beautiful, deadly but mesmerizing. Below the surface, the spent fuel rod assemblies sat in carefully arranged racks, their radioactive cores cooled by the constant circulation of water. If the water stopped flowing or if the temperature rose too high... if any one of a dozen systems failed...it could be a serious concern. But they didn't fail... That was Manny's job along with everyone's job here. It had been five years without an incident as Gerald Reed liked to remind them.

Manny approached his control station. It was a bank of monitors displaying temperature readings, flow rates, radiation levels and system diagnostics. Everything was nominal... Everything was always nominal. Until it wasn't.

He logged in, beginning his shift checklist. Temperature: eighty-two degrees Fahrenheit. Flow rate: three thousand two hundred gallons per minute. Radiation levels: within acceptable parameters. He documented each reading, his fingers moving across the keyboard with practiced efficiency. "You good, Manny?"

He looked up in response. James Chen stood a few feet away, coffee in hand, his round face creased with concern. "Yeah." Manny managed something approximating a smile. "Just tired."

James nodded slowly. He'd worked at the plant for thirty-one years, longer than almost anyone except the old-timers counting down past retirement. He was a senior technician, competent and unflappable. The kind of guy everyone liked because he actually gave a damn. "Karen doing any better?" James asked quietly.

Manny's throat tightened. "She's fighting."

James held his gaze for a moment it was long enough to communicate what words couldn't. Then he nodded. "Let me know if you need anything, man."

"Thanks."

James walked away, back to his own station, leaving Manny alone with the glowing water and the constant hum of machinery. *Let me know if you need anything….* What did he need? A miracle. A cure. Time with his daughter before she became a stranger completely. Some sleep that actually brought rest. Or just to have his wife back the way she used to be... not the woman in the hospital bed downstairs, but Karen. The woman who laughed at his terrible jokes and dragged him on hikes through the desert and taught Maya about the names of plants. He needed his life back. But that wasn't an option on any checklist.

The morning crept forward as Manny moved through his routines on autopilot. Monitoring readings, documenting variances and coordinating with his crew. At some point, James brought him coffee without being asked. At some point, the sun rose outside, though you couldn't tell from inside the plant. Time became elastic in the plant, measured only by the shift clock and the rotation of tasks. Around eleven hundred hours, Gerald Reed appeared.

Manny saw him coming before he arrived. The crisp uniform, the military bearing, and the clipboard in hand like a weapon. Reed moved through the facility with the same purposeful efficiency he'd learned in the Navy. Nothing was wasted, everything measured and every interaction transactional. "Chavez."

"Mr. Reed."

Reed stopped at his station, pale eyes scanning the monitors. "You were twelve minutes late logging yesterday's temperature variances."

Manny kept his expression neutral. "Variances were within acceptable range. I logged them before end of shift."

"Protocol states real-time logging." Reed's gaze shifted from the monitors to Manny's face. "I need you focused, Chavez."

"Yes, sir."

A pause. Reed's eyes narrowed as they were slightly assessing, calculating. "Are you fit for duty today?"

"Yes, sir."

Another pause that was longer this time. The question Reed wasn't asking hung between them, *What's wrong with you?* The question Reed would never ask because it required acknowledging that people were more than their job performance. "See that you are," Reed said finally. "We've had five years without incident. I intend to keep it that way."

"Understood, sir."

Reed moved on to interrogate someone else. Manny exhaled slowly, forcing his shoulders to relax. Five years without incident. That's what mattered to Reed. Numbers and records with measurable outcomes. Not people.

But Manny understood, even if he resented it, that the record mattered. One mistake here and people died. Radiation didn't forgive exhaustion nor mistakes. It didn't care that your wife was dying. So, he compartmentalized. He had to... work stayed at work. Home stayed at home. Except he couldn't remember how to be at home anymore.

Hours later... time had become slippery again and Manny found himself staring at the control monitors, not really seeing them. The temperature reading flickered, just for a second. Then it returned to normal. It was probably a sensor glitch... it happened sometimes. He logged it and made a note for maintenance to check the sensor during the next scheduled inspection. But something felt like it was off. He couldn't name it or point to any specific reading or indicator. It was just a feeling, deep in his gut, that something was wrong.

He looked through the safety glass at the cooling pool. The water glowed its impossible blue. Everything looked normal and everything was normal. Wasn't it? He rubbed his face, he was so tired. Too tired... seeing problems where there weren't any. He needed a break.

The employee bathroom was empty when Manny entered. Its fluorescent lights humming their monotonous drone. The design was simple with institutional tile, industrial fixtures, the faint smell of industrial cleaner trying and failing to mask decades of use. He approached the sink, turned on the cold water, and let it run for a moment before cupping his hands beneath the stream. The water was shockingly cold. He splashed it on his face once, twice, three times. The shock of it helped. It made him feel present in his own body for the first time in hours. The water dripped from his face as he reached for the paper towel dispenser. His hand paused halfway there. He looked up back in the mirror and he saw a stranger looking back. The man in the reflection was older than Manny remembered being. Deep circles hollowed out his eyes... when had they gotten so dark? His skin looked gray under the fluorescent lights. His face had thinned, cheekbones sharper than they should be. His hair was more gray than brown now, though he couldn't remember when that had happened either. Water dripped from his chin as he gripped the edge of the sink. *When did I start disappearing?*

For a moment, just a brief, terrible moment he thought... *What if I just didn't go back out there? What if I got in my truck and drove away? Not home. Somewhere else. Anywhere else. Just... away.*

The thought horrified him. *What kind of man thinks about abandoning his dying wife?*

A coward or monster would. A man too weak to face what he'd been given to carry. He turned off the water and dried his face with paper towels. He looked in the mirror one more time. The stranger was still there wearing his face and drowning. He left the bathroom walking back through the sterile white hallways, following the colored lines on the floor back to his station. Back to work where he could forget. The work he could do. The work that made sense.

Twelve hours later, the shift ended. Manny logged his final readings, handed them off to the next supervisor with a brief summary of the day's non-events, and walked back through the plant toward the exit. His legs felt heavy along with his mind. Outside, the sun was setting. He'd arrived in darkness and was now leaving as the sun was setting, the way he did every shift. The desert sky was painted orange and purple, beautiful in that way desert sunsets were, but he barely registered it. He got in his truck and started the engine. He pulled out of the parking lot and toward State Route 85 as it stretched ahead of him, empty and straight. In the rearview mirror, the cooling towers of Palo Verde receded, their steam plumes glowing pink in the sunset light.

The thirty-five minute commute passed in a blur. His mind tried to shift gears from work mode to home mode, but the transition felt impossible. It was like trying to translate a language he'd forgotten how to speak. What would he find when he got there? Would Karen be awake? Would she be in pain? Would Maya talk to him, or would she retreat to her room with the door closed?

Would they eat dinner together, or would he heat something up and eat it standing at the counter while the medical equipment beeped softly from the downstairs bedroom?

Would he know what to say to either of them? Would they even want him to try? His truck turned onto West Desert Bloom Lane Buckeye AZ automatically, muscle memory guiding him home. At home the world felt wrong. He pulled into the driveway of 14762. The house was dark except for one light glowing in the downstairs bedroom window. It was Karen's room. Maya's window upstairs was dark. Either she was asleep at eight PM...unlikely or she was sitting in the darkness doing whatever fourteen-year-olds did when they didn't want to be found. Manny sat in his truck, engine idling, unwilling to go inside. Unwilling to face it... unwilling to put on the mask he wore at home that was somehow heavier than the mask he wore at work. *How did it come to this?*

The question had no answer. Or too many answers he couldn't afford to examine because examining them might break him completely. *Compartmentalize,* he told himself. *Work stays at work. Home is home.*

But he couldn't remember how to be at home anymore. He couldn't remember who he was supposed to be there. He couldn't remember the last time he'd felt like anything other than an intruder in his own life. He turned off the engine. The silence was immediate and suffocating.

Through the windshield, his house waited. His wife was inside, dying by increments. His daughter was inside, disappearing into grief and anger. And he was outside in the truck, unable to bridge the gap between the parking lot and the front door. *Get out of the truck,* he told himself. *Just go inside. Be there...*

His hand reached for the door handle, almost hesitating. Then, finally, he opened the door and stepped into the desert heat. The air was still warm even after sunset, carrying the scent of creosote and dust along with the faint mineral tang of the shared well water when someone ran their sprinklers. He walked to the front door and put his key in the lock. Turned it. Inside, the house was quiet except for the white noise hum of the air conditioning. He closed the door behind him while having absolutely no idea what to do next.

At the plant, problems have solutions. Water temperature rises... you adjust the flow. Radiation levels spike... you follow protocol. Everything has an answer. Everything makes sense. At home, nothing makes sense anymore. And Manny Chavez who had worked twenty-six years at Palo Verde, as a shift supervisor, responsible for systems containing enough radioactive material to poison a city... had no idea how to fix his own life.

He doesn't know that his life is about to change in ways he can't imagine. He doesn't know about the promise he'll make on a dark desert road. He doesn't know that some transformations can't be stopped once they begin. He doesn't know that the end of his human life is getting closer. He only knows that right now... in this moment, he's standing in his own house feeling like a ghost. And he has no idea how to be anything else.

Chapter One – The Promise

The couch had left its mark on Manny's back. It was a dull ache that radiated up his spine as he sat up at six am, his phone alarm cutting through the silence of the living room. He'd slept there again. This was the third night this week. He told himself it was to avoid waking Karen when he came home late from his shift, but the truth sat heavier than that. He silenced the alarm and sat in the darkness for a moment, listening to the house. The air conditioning hummed its constant white noise. From the bedroom downstairs, Karen's room, he could hear nothing. Either she was sleeping peacefully, or she was awake in the dark, managing her pain alone. He should have checked on her, but he didn't move.

Eventually, his body made the decision for him. He stood, his joints protesting, and walked into the kitchen. The coffee pot still held last night's burnt dregs. He'd forgotten to turn it off again. He dumped it, started fresh, and stood waiting for it to brew while the sky beyond the window began its slow shift from black to gray.

Six-fifteen. Maya's alarm would go off in fifteen minutes. Karen might be awake by now. He should make breakfast. His hands moved through the motions… eggs from the fridge, butter in the pan, bread in the toaster. Three plates from the cabinet. He set them on the counter in a row and tried to remember the last time all three plates had been used at the same table at the same time. He couldn't.

He made scrambled eggs as the toast popped. The coffee finished brewing with a final hiss and gurgle. Manny plated everything carefully trying to make it look like he cared, like this was normal, like families still did this. It was six-thirty and he waited.

Maya appeared at six forty-five, and Manny knew immediately this wasn't going to go well. She came down the stairs with her backpack already on, earbuds in, music loud enough that he could hear the tinny percussion from across the room. She didn't look at him. Didn't acknowledge the breakfast on the counter. Just headed straight for the front door. "Morning," Manny said. His voice came out rougher than he intended. "I made you breakfast."

Maya stopped, pulled out one earbud. Glanced at the eggs and toast with something that might have been contempt or might have been exhaustion. It was getting harder to tell the difference.

"Not hungry."

"You need to eat something."

"I'm fine."

The word hung there between them. Fine. Nobody in this house was fine. The word was a lie they all kept telling each other and themselves.

"How's school going?" Manny tried, searching for solid ground. "You have that biology test, this week, right?"

Maya pulled out the other earbud. Her expression shifted... something hardening behind her eyes. "What?"

"The biology test. You mentioned it last week. Or... maybe two weeks ago?"

"That was three weeks ago, Dad. I already took it."

Silence. The coffee pot dripped one last drop into the carafe. "How'd it go?" Manny asked quietly.

"Does it matter?"

"Of course it matters. I'm asking, aren't I?"

Something broke in her expression... not tears, not yet, but the prelude to them. "You're asking *now*. Three weeks late. Because you just remembered I exist."

"That's not fair. I'm here, aren't I?"

"No, you're not." Her voice was rising now, fourteen years old and cracking under the weight of grief she didn't know how to carry. "You're never here. Even when you're standing right in front of me, you're not *here*."

"I'm working. I'm paying the bills. I'm keeping this family..."

"You're hiding!" The words came out like an accusation. Like a wound. "At work, in the garage, wherever you can avoid..." She stopped herself.

"Avoid what?"

"This... us.... Mom! Everything."

Manny felt something in his chest constrict. "Maya..."

"You don't understand what it's like."

"What what's like?"

"Being here... watching her die." Her voice cracked. "While you get to leave every day and pretend that we don't exist."

"Maya..."

"You don't get it! You don't understand anything!"

She grabbed her backpack, turned toward the door. Manny moved to follow, his hand reaching for her shoulder.

"Maya, wait..."

The front door opened. A car horn honked from the driveway, it was her friends, Emma and someone else, waiting in a silver Honda. Maya didn't turn back. "I have to go."

"We need to talk about this..."

"I'm done talking."

She was almost crying now, but she wouldn't let him see. She never let him see anymore. The door slammed and Manny stood alone in the kitchen, his hand still half-raised, reaching for a daughter who was already gone. The breakfast sat on the counter. Three plates. He'd eat alone. Again. The slam of the door still echoed. But his daughter's words echoed louder: *You don't understand anything.*

He stood there for a long moment, frozen between going after her and staying. Between being a father and being a coward.

A soft sound from the hallway made him turn. Rosita stood in the doorway. Her weathered hands folded in front of her medical scrubs. She must have been in Karen's room, but he hadn't heard her arrive. She had that way about her... appearing like morning light, quietly but completely aware. "Señor Chavez," she said softly, her accent giving warmth to his name. "The eggs, they smell good."

Manny looked at the untouched plates. "Nobody wanted them."

"Ah." Rosita moved into the kitchen; her steps were unhurried. She'd been coming three times a week for the past two months, ever since Karen's condition had worsened. She was a professional caregiver recommended by the hospice nurse. But she felt like more than that. Like a grandmother who'd always been there, even though she hadn't. "Maya, she is angry," Rosita observed, picking up one of the plates.

"She has every right to be."

"Sí... But anger, it is like a plant, no? It grows from seeds we do not always see."

Rosita set the plate down and looked at him with dark eyes that had seen too much life to judge. "She is not angry at you, Señor Chavez. She is angry at what she cannot control. At the dying."

Manny felt his throat tighten. "I don't know how to talk to her anymore."

"Because you try to fix. But some things, they do not need fixing. They need..." She touched her heart. "Companionship."

Before he could respond, Karen's voice came from down the hall, weak and hoarse. "Manny?"

Rosita smiled slightly. "Go. I will clean these dishes. Your wife needs you."

Manny nodded, grateful for her presence, and turned toward the hallway. As he walked away, Rosita called softly after him. "Señor Chavez has your wife... has she made her plans? For after?"

Manny stiffened. "I don't want to talk about that."

"I know. No one does." Rosita's voice was gentle but firm. "But this is a gift you can give her. To let her tell you what she wants. Where she wishes to be buried. What kind of service and who should speak. These things are important."

"It feels like giving up."

"No." Rosita shook her head. "It is the opposite. It is taking away the burden of guessing. When the time comes, and it will come for all of us. The family is left with so many decisions. And they are paralyzed by grief, trying to guess what their loved one would have wanted. 'Would she want this music? Would she want cremation or burial? What would make them happy?'"

She looked at him steadily. "But if you talk about it now, while there is still time, then you will know. You don't have to guess. You don't have to carry that extra weight of wondering if you honored her wishes. You simply do what she asked. This is love, Señor Chavez. To talk about the hard things so the people we love don't have to suffer more than they already will."

Manny's throat was tight. "I'll talk to her. About... about what she wants."

"Good. And you, you should think about these things too. We all should. It is not morbid. It is wise. It is caring for the people we will leave behind. In my village, we say: 'El círculo de la vida no tiene esquinas donde esconderse.' The circle of life has no corners to hide in. We all walk it. All of us. Better to walk it with eyes open than closed."

Manny watched her for a moment, not quite understanding but feeling something shift inside him. He'd never asked where she came from or what life she'd lived before becoming a caregiver. But at that moment, he understood she'd walked this circle many times before. And she was asking him to do something he'd been avoiding, actually talk to Karen about death. He closed his eyes and breathed, "Coming."

The bedroom door was cracked open. Manny knocked softly out of habit. It was some vestige of privacy they still pretended mattered. "Come in."

He pushed the door open. The room had been a guest bedroom once. When they'd first moved in, they'd joked about turning it into a home office or maybe a craft room for Karen. That was before the stairs became too much. Before the hospital bed and before the oxygen tank that sat in the corner like a monument to what was coming. The curtains were drawn. Karen's eyes were sensitive to light now. Just another side effect of the medications, or the cancer, or both. The lamp on the nightstand casting a dim yellow glow that made the room feel smaller than it was.

Medical equipment crowded the space along with pill organizers, water bottles, tissues, a blood pressure cuff, and that oxygen tank. Photos on the nightstand tried to maintain normalcy. Their wedding day in Sedona, Maya as a baby and a family hike from five years ago when they'd all been whole. Karen was propped up on pillows, awake but barely. She looked so small against the white hospital bed linens. "Morning," Manny said quietly.

"I heard Maya leave. She sounded upset."

Manny sat carefully on the edge of the bed, trying not to jostle her. "We had a... disagreement."

"About?"

"Me and my failures as a father. Just the usual honey."

Karen's expression shifted to sadness, understanding, but exhausted by the weight of holding this family together from a hospital bed. "She's scared."

"I know."

"She needs you."

"I know."

"Do you?"

Before he could answer, Karen coughed... a deep, rattling sound that shook her whole frame. Manny reached for the water bottle on the nightstand and held it while she took small sips. She waved him off after a moment, breathing labored with her eyes closed. He waited... there was nothing else to do but wait. Finally, her breathing evened and she opened her eyes. "I need to talk to you about something."

Manny's body tensed up. He knew that tone. "Okay."

"I need you to promise me something."

"Karen..."

"Please. Just listen."

She looked at him with devastating clarity. "When I die..."

Manny flinched at the word. "Don't..."

"When I die, I need you to promise me that you'll move on."

"I don't want to talk about this."

"I know. But we have to."

Manny stood, turning away. He couldn't look at her. Couldn't sit still. "You're not dying. You're fighting. We're fighting."

"Manny. Look at me."

He turned back to look at her. She was looking at him with eyes that had already accepted what he refused to. "I'm dying. The doctors said six months, maybe a year. We both know it. We've known it for weeks."

"They've been wrong before..."

"They haven't been wrong." Her voice was gentle but firm. "I'm getting worse. You can see it. I can feel it."

Another coughing fit took her. Worse this time. Her whole body convulsed with it. Manny moved to her side, helpless, his hands hovering over her shoulders, wanting to help but not knowing how. The coughing subsided. She lay back against the pillows, exhausted, struggling to breathe. "I need you to promise me you'll move on," she said when she could speak again. "Find someone. Be happy. Don't spend the rest of your life mourning. I want you to live and be happy with Maya."

"I can't promise that."

"You have to."

"How am I supposed too just..." His voice broke. "You're my wife."

"I'll always be your wife, but I won't be here. And I can't leave knowing you're going to be alone forever."

"I don't want anyone else."

"I know. Not now. But eventually. Maya will need to know someone is going to be with you. She needs to live her life too. Promise me you'll try."

Karen shifted slightly in the bed, gathering strength. "And Maya. I need you to make her the priority."

"She is..."

"No. The plant is the priority. Work is the priority... overtime is the priority."

"I'm doing that for..."

"I know... for us and the bills. But Manny, she doesn't need money. She needs her father."

"I'm here."

"Are you?"

The question hung in the air between them, but Manny had no answer. Karen continued, her voice soft but relentless. "You're drowning in work because it's easier than being here. I understand. I do. But after I'm gone, you won't have me as an excuse anymore."

"That's not..."

"It is and I'm not blaming you. I'm just asking you to promise me that when I'm gone, you will be there for her. Actually, be there. Not working overtime, not hiding in the garage."

Something in Karen's words, maybe the mention of being scared, or maybe the weight of what she was asking. It triggered a memory Manny had been trying to suppress for three years. *The doctor's office. Sterile walls. The smell of antiseptic and fear. The mammogram had shown something. They'd need a biopsy. Manny had taken the day off work... one of the only times in twenty-six years he'd called in for something other than the flu.*

They'd sat in those uncomfortable chairs, holding hands, waiting. The doctor had come in with a folder. Her face had told them everything before she opened her mouth. "The biopsy confirmed our concerns. It's cancer. Invasive ductal carcinoma."

Karen's face had contorted into absolute terror. It was her worst nightmare crystallizing into reality in that single sentence. "How bad?" Her voice had been so small.

"Stage II. We caught it relatively early. Treatment will be aggressive, but you have options."

Karen had looked at Manny. Her eyes asking a question he couldn't answer: Am I going to die? He'd taken her hand. "We'll fight this. Together."

She'd nodded. But they both knew the statistics. Breast cancer, even caught early, could come back and metastasize. It could kill you slowly over the years while you watched your life slip away. Her terror had become his terror. Then it had become Maya's terror. The Chavez family had shattered that day. They'd been living in the aftermath ever since.

Manny blinked, the memory receding like a wave pulling back from shore. Karen was watching him. "You're thinking about it, aren't you? The day we found out."

"Yeah."

"I was so scared."

"So was I."

"I still am."

Karen took a shaky breath. "We need to talk about the practical things too."

"Karen..."

"I'm serious. The bills. The death benefit and Maya's college fund."

Manny sat back down on the edge of the bed, defeated. "Okay."

"The life insurance will pay out two hundred and fifty thousand dollars. It should cover the outstanding medical bills and leave enough for Maya's college."

"I don't want to talk about life insurance payouts."

"You have to. You need to know where everything is. The policy documents are in the file cabinet, top drawer. There's a folder labeled 'Important Documents.'"

"I'll find it."

"Promise me you'll use it for Maya and not keep working overtime to pay off bills. Not to avoid dealing with things. For *her*."

Manny nodded, unable to speak.

"She wants to study biology or environmental science, maybe. Like me."

"I didn't know that."

"Because you haven't asked her."

The accusation stung because it was true. "She applied to NAU and ASU. She hasn't told you because she doesn't think you care."

"Of course I care."

"Then show her. When I'm gone, you need to show her."

Guilt sat in Manny's chest like a stone. The guilt that he hadn't been present and that he'd been using work as an escape. It was a guilt that part of him... some terrible, shameful part. It was already imagining life after Karen died and hating himself for it. How do you raise a teenage daughter alone? How do you navigate grief with bills and a house that's too empty? How do you become the father you should have been all along when you don't even know where to start?

Karen saw it in his face. "I know this is hard."

"That's an understatement."

"But you're stronger than you think. And Maya needs you to be strong."

"I don't feel strong."

"I know. But you will be. You have to be."

Karen's breathing was labored now, the conversation taking its toll. "So, promise me. Say the words."

"Karen..."

"Say it... promise me you'll move on. Promise me you'll make Maya the priority. Promise me you'll actually *live* after I'm gone."

Manny was silent for a long moment. The weight of what she was asking pressed down on him like the roof might collapse. "I don't know if I can."

"You can... You have to."

Karen shifted slightly, gathering her remaining strength. "It's a promise both ways."

"What do you mean?"

"I promise you the same thing. If the situation were reversed... if you were the one dying... I'd move on. I'd prioritize Maya. I'd live."

"Karen..."

"I would. Because that's what love is. It's not holding on when you need to let go. It's not drowning together. It's making sure the people you love survive, even if you don't."

She paused, her eyes finding his. "I'm asking you to do the same. Not because you don't love me but because you *do*."

Manny's voice broke. "I don't want to lose you."

"I know... but you're going to. And when you do, I need to know you'll be okay. That Maya will be okay."

"Rosita told me to ask about your last wishes... what type of funeral... and I don't know what else."

"I know, she asked me too. I wrote it down for you. You don't have to ask. It's in the documents folder with everything else. You can read it later ok."

Karen reached for his hand. Her fingers were cold and thin, trembling slightly. "It's a shared burden, Manny. That's what we agreed to when we said 'I do' all those years ago in Sedona. Remember? For better or worse. In sickness and in health we would carry each other."

Manny remembered the red rocks glowing in the sunset. Karen in her simple white dress. The vows they'd made when the future had seemed infinite and death had seemed like someone else's problem. "I need you to carry this for me. After I'm gone. Can you do that?"

But it's not shared, Manny thought. *Not really. She's asking me to carry something alone. She's dying, and I'm the one who'll be left holding this impossible weight. It feels one-sided and unfair. I don't want to carry this. I can't lift this weight. Not in my mind, nor in my heart. The burden is too heavy.*

Another coughing fit took her. This one was worse... deeper, wetter, shaking her frame. Manny helped her sit up slightly, held the water bottle as he waited helplessly for it to pass. When it finally subsided, she lay back exhausted, her breath coming in shallow gasps. "Please," she whispered.

Manny looked at his wife. At the woman who had taught him to slow down, to see beauty and to understand that presence mattered more than productivity. The woman who was asking him to promise something he didn't know if he could keep. But she was asking and he loved her.

"Okay."

"Say it."

Manny took a breath. "I promise. When you're gone, I'll move on. I'll make Maya the priority. I'll... try to live."

"Not try... You will."

"I will."

Karen reached for his hand again. He took it. Her hand was so small now, fragile, cold. "Thank you."

They sat together in the dim light of the bedroom. The oxygen tank hissed softly as the air conditioning cycled on. Outside, the desert sun was rising, heating the world. Manny had made a promise. A vow. A covenant with his dying wife that he would survive her death. That he would live. He didn't know it was a promise he wouldn't be able to keep. He didn't know that the roles would reverse. He didn't know that in a few short hours, he'd make another promise on a dark desert road. A promise that would transform everything. He only knew that right now, in this moment, he'd sworn to his wife that he would live after she was gone. And Manny Chavez always kept his promises.

Karen fell asleep sometime around eight am, exhausted from the conversation, the coughing and the weight of what she'd asked. Manny sat with her for a while, watching her breathe. Counting the breaths. Afraid that if he stopped counting, one of them might be the last and he wouldn't notice until it was too late. Eventually, he had to leave. His shift started at noon today. It was a once-a-month routine that broke up his normal early shift. He needed to shower, change, get his head in the right space for work.

He stood carefully, not wanting to wake her. He walked quietly from the room, pulling the door almost closed behind him. Upstairs, he showered in the bathroom that still had both their toothbrushes in the holder even though Karen hadn't been upstairs in months. He changed into his work uniform. Clipped his dosimeter badge to his chest. He paused at Maya's closed bedroom door. She was at school but he thought about texting her an apology. Tell her he was sorry for not remembering the test, for not being there, for all of it. He pulled out his phone, opened the text thread staring at the blank message box.

What do you say? How do you apologize for disappearing while still being physically present? How do you tell your daughter you're sorry for failing at the one job that mattered? He closed the phone without typing anything. No messages from Maya either.

Downstairs, he grabbed his keys, his wallet, his thermos of coffee. He stood in the kitchen as Rosita was already cleaning up from him cooking. Looking at the three plates of cold breakfast still sitting on the counter. She just waved him on to work as she always did. Rosita was someone that they didn't know they needed but couldn't live without. He walked out to his truck in the already-brutal morning heat. Got in and started the engine. He looked back at the house; it seemed small and tired like him. It was holding two people, he was failing. The promise he'd just made to Karen sat in his chest like lead. Heavy. Immovable. *How do you promise to live when you don't remember what living feels like?* He didn't have an answer. But he put the truck in reverse and backed out of the driveway anyway.

The drive to Palo Verde took longer with traffic during the day, forty-five minutes. Manny barely registered the miles. His mind cycled through the morning on an endless loop: Maya's anger: *You don't understand anything.*

Karen's request: *Promise me you'll live.*

The memory of the diagnosis, *It's cancer.*

The weight of the promise, *I will.*

He tried to compartmentalize. Work was work. Home was home. That's what Gerald Reed would say. That's what a good shift supervisor did. They left the personal shit at the door and focused on the job. But the walls were crumbling and by the time he pulled into the Palo Verde parking lot, he felt hollowed out. A scraped clean shell going through the motions. He parked in his usual spot. Turned off the engine. Once again sat in silence getting ready for the shift.

Through the windshield, the cooling towers rose against the blue desert sky, steam plumes climbing into the heat. He checked his dosimeter badge on his chest. Got out of the truck and walked toward the entrance. He had promised Karen he'd live after she died. He had no idea how. But he'd keep the promise. He always kept his promises. That's what would doom him.

Chapter Two – Answered Prayer

The day after making the promise to Karen, Manny arrived at Palo Verde. He'd barely slept. Maybe three hours on the couch before giving up and staring at the ceiling in the dark. The promise sat in his chest like a stone. *I'll move on. I'll make Maya the priority. I'll live.*

How? He had no answer. It was a new day as security waved him through. He parked in his usual spot, went through the motions... badge scan, metal detector, dosimeter clipped to his chest. The familiar routine of entering the plant usually brought him a measure of calm. At least here, he knew what to do. Today, it felt like walking into a cage.

His station overlooked Reactor Cooling Pool #2, the water glowing its eerie blue beneath the observation deck. Manny logged in and began his shift checklist. Temperature: 82°F. Normal. Flow rate: 3,200 gallons per minute. Normal. Radiation levels: within acceptable parameters. Normal. Everything was fine, but he wasn't fine.

His fingers moved across the keyboard, documenting readings he'd documented a thousand times before. But his mind was elsewhere. It drifted to home and into Karen's bedroom and then towards sitting beside Maya's closed door, wondering what to say and finding nothing. *I'll make Maya the priority.* But he didn't know how to talk to her. He didn't know how to bridge the gap or how to be a father when being a father required being present, and presence was the one thing he couldn't figure out how to give. "You okay, man?"

Manny looked up. James Chen stood a few feet away, coffee in one hand, concern on his face. "Just tired."

"You say that a lot."

"Yeah."

James hesitated, shifted his weight. "Look, if you need to take some time off..."

"I'm fine. I need to be here."

James's expression said he didn't believe it, but he nodded anyway. "Alright. Let me know if you need anything."

"Thanks."

James walked away, back to his own station. *But Manny wasn't fine. And he didn't need to be here. He needed to be at home. But home was unbearable compared to here.*

Not long after settling in, Gerald Reed appeared on the observation deck. Manny saw him coming as usual. The crisp uniform, the military bearing, and that dam clipboard in hand like a weapon. He tensed automatically. "Chavez."

"Mr. Reed."

Reed stopped at his station, pale eyes scanning the monitors. Looking for something to criticize. He always found something. "You logged the morning check-in four minutes late."

"Yes, sir. Traffic was..."

"Excuses don't prevent incidents. Punctuality does."

"Understood."

Reed's eyes narrowed, assessing. "You look unwell. Are you fit for duty?"

"Yes, sir."

A pause. Reed's gaze lingered on Manny's face... cataloging the exhaustion, the weight loss, the hollowness. Building a file in his mind.

"See that you remain so."

Reed moved on to interrogate someone else, making his daily rounds. Manny exhaled slowly, his shoulders relaxing by degrees. *Another eight hours of this. Monitoring systems that don't need me while avoiding Reed. Thinking about Karen and Maya. Thinking about the promise I made and have no idea how to keep it.*

The shift stretched ahead like a prison sentence. Time stood still and Manny took a break. He couldn't focus or think. The walls of the plant felt like they were closing in. The sterile hallways, the fluorescent lights, the constant hum of ventilation systems.... He needed air. But there was no air here, just recycled climate control. He went to the employee bathroom instead. The fluorescent lights hummed their monotonous drone. The institutional tile matching the industrial fixtures was blurring his emotions. The smell of industrial cleaners running up his nose. Manny approached the sink, turned on the cold water, and let it run. The sound was almost soothing. Almost... He cupped his hands beneath the stream and splashed his face a few times. The shock of cold water helped briefly. He looked up at the mirror. The same stranger from days ago looked back. Hollow eyes with gray skin who was disappearing. For a long moment, Manny just stared at his own reflection. At the ruin of what he used to be. Then something broke. "God..." His voice came out hoarse, barely above a whisper. He gripped the edge of the sink as water dripped from his face. "I know... I know people say you only give us what we can carry."

His reflection stared back, accusing. "But I can't carry this. I can't."

His voice cracked. He was talking to a bathroom mirror. Talking to God in a bathroom at a nuclear power plant because he had nowhere else to go. "Karen needs me to be strong. Maya needs me to be there. And I don't know how."

Silence. Just the hum of fluorescent lights and the running water. "If you have time..." The absurdity of it... asking God if He had time. "If you're listening..., can you send an angel? Someone to help me. Please."

He waited as if expecting an answer. As if the mirror might speak back. Nothing. "I'm drowning here. I don't know what to do."

Still nothing. Manny turned off the water and dried his face with paper towels. He looked at himself one more time and felt foolish praying to a bathroom mirror. *But what else is there?* He left the bathroom, returning to his station. Back to the monitors, the glowing water and the routine that meant nothing. The prayer sat unanswered in his chest until the shift ended.

Manny logged out, handed off to the next supervisor with a brief summary of the day's non-events, and walked through the plant toward the exit. An end to another looped event day, matching yesterday. Outside, the sun was setting painting the desert sky in shades of orange and purple it did on most days. Beautiful, in that harsh way desert sunsets were. Manny barely registered it. He got in his truck and started the engine, pulling onto State Route 85, heading home. Thirty-five minutes through empty desert. The highway stretched straight and certain, cutting through the Sonoran landscape. Saguaros stood out as an ever present sentinel against the dying light. Manny's mind was blank void of peace... Just empty. He was hollowed out, driving on autopilot, the way he always did now.

About ten miles from the plant, he saw it. An old pickup truck pulled off on the shoulder, hazards blinking weakly in the dusk. Someone moving around the back of the vehicle. Manny's first instinct was to keep driving. It was dangerous to stop on open roads in Arizona. It could be a setup or a carjacking. People got shot for less out here. It was not his problem, but as he passed, he caught a glimpse. He saw an old man, gray hair, hunched over, struggling with something at the rear wheel. Manny's foot eased off the gas. *What if it were you? What if it were Karen, stranded? What if Maya broke down and nobody stopped?*

He pulled onto the shoulder a hundred yards ahead of the old truck. Sat for a moment, engine idling, while debating. *Keep driving. You have enough problems.* But he turned off the engine and got out.

Manny approached slowly, hands visible, keeping his distance. The desert was quiet except for the wind. The truck looked ancient. It was a 1970s model with faded green paint and more rust than metal in places. The old man looked up as Manny approached. "You need help?"

Manny stayed back, ready to retreat if necessary. The old man smiled. It was genuine and relieved. "That'd be mighty kind of you, if you don't mind."

He was older, maybe in his seventies. Gray hair, weathered face and kind eyes. He was wearing worn jeans and a faded plaid shirt with cowboy boots. Something about him felt... warm and non-threatening. Almost familiar in a way, though Manny had never seen him before. Manny came closer. "Flat tire?"

"Afraid so... and my hands aren't what they used to be." The old man held up the tire iron, gnarled fingers trembling slightly. "Can't get these lug nuts loose."

"I can help with that."

They worked in companionable silence for a few minutes. Manny loosened the lug nuts. His hands remembered this work from his years in maintenance. The old man watched, holding the spare tire. Something about helping out... actually fixing something. It felt good. Finally, a problem with a solution. "You're good at that," the old man said.

"I used to do maintenance before I got promoted into management. I spent years fixing things."

"That's an important skill. Fixing things that are broken."

Something in his tone made Manny look up. The old man was watching him with kind, knowing eyes. Manny went back to work, jacking up the truck, removing the flat tire. The old man handed him the spare without being asked. They worked like a team, like they'd done this before. When the spare was on and the lug nuts tightened, Manny lowered the jack and stood, wiping his hands on his pants. "Should be good now. Drive safe."

"I will. Thank you, son."

They stood there in the fading light, not quite ready to part ways yet.

"You look exhausted," the old man said quietly. "If you don't mind me saying."

Manny wasn't surprised. Everyone had been telling him that lately. "Long day. Long year, really."

The old man nodded. "I can see that. Are you carrying something heavy?"

Manny paused, considering. Something about this man felt safe. Something about standing in the desert at sunset with a stranger made it easier to tell the truth. "My wife is dying of cancer. I made her a promise that I don't know how to keep."

"What kind of promise?"

Manny looked at the horizon, at the sun bleeding orange into purple. "That I'll move on after she's gone. That I'll make our daughter the priority. That I'll live." He laughed, bitterly. "I don't even know what that means anymore."

The old man was quiet for a moment. Then he walked to his tailgate that was already down, sat down heavily, and gestured for Manny to join him. "Can I tell you a story?"

Manny hesitated, then sat. "Sure."

"Long time ago, I was in a place like you are now. I was desperate. I didn't know which way was up. I asked God for help."

"Did He answer?"

The old man smiled, sad and knowing. "He did but not the way I expected. Not the way I wanted, at first. But He answered."

The desert wind blew warm across them. "Sometimes God's help doesn't look like help. Sometimes it looks like something else entirely. But it's always what we need, even if it's not what we asked for."

Manny felt something in his chest loosen. The first glimmer of something that might have been hope. "This promise you made to your wife," the old man said. "Do you want to keep it?"

"Of course. I love her. But I don't know if I can."

"Why not?"

"Because she's the strong one. She's the one who held us together all of these years. I'm just... I'm just the guy who works and pays bills and doesn't know how to talk to his own daughter."

"Well, I'm sure you're more than that."

"Am I?"

Silence. The sun sinking lower, shadows growing long. The old man asked quietly: "If you could do anything... anything at all... what would you do?"

Manny didn't hesitate. "I'd switch places with her."

"Your wife?"

"Yeah. Let me be the one who's dying. Let her live. She can carry this burden better than I can. She can be there for Maya. She's stronger, smarter, better at all of it."

He'd never said this out loud before. But it was the truth he'd been thinking for months. "I want to be the foundation for my daughter to grow from. But I don't know how to do that alive. Maybe... maybe I can do it another way."

The old man watched him carefully. "You're sure about that?"

"Yes."

"Because some people ask for things they really don't understand. They think they know what they want, but they don't see the whole picture."

The old man's tone shifted. He was still kind, but serious. Warning. "Careful what you wish for, son."

A pause. "You just might get it."

Manny smiled at his response. It was the first real smile in days. Something about the old man's words felt like permission. Maybe this impossible thing was possible. Maybe someone heard his bathroom prayer after all. "God willing," Manny said.

The old man smiled back... sad, knowing, resigned. "God willing indeed. And if that happened you would be ok with it?"

"Yep, no second thoughts about it. I'd be grateful that my prayer was answered."

They sat together for another moment, the desert growing dark around them. Then the old man stood, extended his hand. "Thank you, son. You've helped me understand more than you know."

Manny took his hand. It was warm, firm and solid. The handshake lingered a moment longer than normal. Something passed between them. A warmth that spread up Manny's arm, into his chest. He felt... lighter, better, like maybe things would be okay. The old man released his hand. "Take care of yourself... And remember... sometimes the answer to prayer looks different than we expect."

"I'll remember."

"I believe you will."

The old man got in his truck and started the engine. It sounded better than it should for a vehicle that old. It was smooth, strong and reliable. He pulled back onto the highway. Manny watched the taillights disappear into the dusk. He stood alone on the shoulder of State Route 85, feeling... good. Better than he'd felt in months. The weight in his chest had lifted. The desert looked beautiful. He noticed the sky painted in the impossible colors, the air warm and clean. The world suddenly felt full of possibility.

Maybe the old man was right. Maybe God does answer prayers. Maybe help is coming. Maybe I can keep the promise after all.

Hope bloomed in his chest for the first time since the diagnosis years ago. Manny got back in his truck, started the engine, and pulled onto the highway heading home. Everything felt different. The sunset was stunning as the oranges and purples were bleeding into deep blue, stars beginning to appear in the darkening sky. The desert stretched around him, beautiful and harsh... but alive. Life seemed brighter, clearer and possible. He couldn't wait to tell Karen about this. The old man on the side of the road. The conversation they had along with the story about asking God for help and maybe receiving it. How he'd helped someone... he finally fixed something. How he'd prayed in the bathroom and maybe, just maybe, someone had answered. She'd be glad he stopped. She'd be proud of him for helping. She always was. Maybe this was the turning point. Maybe this was where things started to get better.

Maybe I can do this. Maybe I can keep the promise. Maybe we'll be okay. The warmth from the handshake still lingered in his chest. A gentle heat, like standing in sunlight after being cold for too long. He felt at peace. Twenty minutes later, Manny pulled into the driveway of 14762 West Desert Bloom Lane in Buckeye.

The house was lit. There was a warm light glowing from the windows. Karen's room and Maya's room were on. It looked like home for the first time in months. He turned off the engine and sat for a moment, smiling. Through the windshield, he could see the backyard. The empty space beyond the patio where Karen had planted native species when they'd first moved in. The yard looked peaceful in the dusk, bathed in the last light of day. Manny got out of the truck. The desert air was still warm, carrying the scent of the desert and dust. He walked to the front door with something like peace in his heart. He put his key in the lock and turned it, opening the door. Inside, the house was quiet as the air conditioning hummed. Somewhere, he could hear the faint sound of Maya's music from upstairs. He walked down the hall toward Karen's room, ready to tell her about the old man and the prayer and the hope he'd found on the side of the road. Ready to tell her that maybe, just maybe, everything would be okay.

Manny didn't know that the handshake had sealed it. He didn't know that his wish had been granted. He was unaware that his dosimeter badge, the small device clipped to his chest that measured radiation exposure had just malfunctioned, its internal mechanisms quietly failing in ways that wouldn't be discovered for days. He didn't know that he'd traded his life for Karen's at that moment on the desert highway. He didn't know that the old man was exactly what he'd asked for... an angel. He also didn't know that starting tomorrow, his exposure to radiation levels was far beyond safe limits, with no warning, no alarm, no protection. That in dying, he would make one final choice. He only knew that for the first time in months, he felt hope. And that was enough. For now.

Chapter Three – It Begins

Manny knocked softly on Karen's door, the warmth from the handshake still lingering in his chest like banked coals. "Come in."

Her voice was clear, stronger than it had been that morning when he'd made the promise. Stronger than it had been in weeks. He pushed the door open. Karen was sitting up against her pillows, the bedside lamp casting soft light across her face. She was awake, alert, looking at him with something that might have been curiosity or might have been relief. "You're home. How was your day?"

Manny sat on the edge of the bed, carefully, the way he always did. He took her hand and her fingers felt... different. Less cold and fragile. There was warmth beneath the skin that hadn't been there this morning. "Something happened on the way home," he said. "I need to tell you about it." Karen squeezed his hand. "I'm listening."

Manny told her about the old pickup truck with its hazard lights blinking on the empty highway. About his hesitation. The danger of stopping on Arizona roads and the decision to pull over anyway. About the old man with gray hair and kind eyes, struggling with a tire iron his hands couldn't manage anymore. "I helped him change the tire. We talked."

"What did you talk about?"

"About you. About the promise we made."

Karen's expression softened. "And?"

"He told me a story. About a time, he was desperate, when he asked God for help. He said God answered. Not the way he expected, but He answered."

The warmth in Manny's chest pulsed gently as he spoke. He didn't notice it at all. He didn't feel the way it was beginning to move. As it was spreading down his arm, flowing into their joined hands. "He asked me what I would do if I could do anything." Manny's voice was quiet. "I told him I'd switch places with you. Let you live and let me be the one who..." He couldn't finish.

Karen's eyes filled with tears. "Oh, Manny..."

"He warned me. He said to be careful what I wish for. That I might get it." Manny managed a small smile. "I said 'God willing.'"

The warmth left his chest completely as it moved into Karen's body. Neither of them noticed the moment it happened. The subtle shift, the exchange of the invisible transaction. "That was kind of you," Karen said quietly. "To stop and help."

"It felt good. To fix something... To help someone."

They sat together in the dim light, hands joined in silence. Something was different between them. Something had changed but neither of them could name it yet.

Karen spoke first. "He sounds special. Like he was meant to find you."

"Or I was meant to find him."

"Maybe both."

She shifted slightly against the pillows, and Manny noticed. He really noticed that she seemed more comfortable than usual. She was less careful with her movements. Less like every shift in position might trigger pain. "Are you feeling okay?"

Karen paused, considering. "Actually... yeah. I feel better. The best I've felt in weeks."

"Really?"

"Really." She sounded surprised. "I don't know why. Maybe it's the new medication finally kicking in. Or maybe..." She looked at him, smiled. "Maybe it's hope."

They talked for a while longer about the old man and the story he'd told, along with his boring day at work. And as they talked, Manny realized something remarkable. Karen hadn't coughed once. Not once since he'd entered the room. Usually, she couldn't speak for more than a minute or two without those terrible rattling coughs that shook her whole frame. But now... nothing. Just her voice, steady and clear, the way it used to be. "Karen," Manny said slowly. "You haven't..."

"I know." She looked as surprised as he felt. "I noticed."

They stared at each other, afraid to acknowledge it fully. Afraid to hope too hard. "Maybe it's a good day," Karen said finally.

"Maybe it is."

They left it at that. They were too afraid to examine it too closely. They were afraid to jinx it.

The next day after school Maya came home to find Rosita in the backyard, kneeling by the struggling desert garden Karen had planted years ago. The older woman's hands moved carefully through the dry soil, pulling weeds that had taken over. "Your mother loved this garden," Rosita said without looking up. Maya had learned that Rosita always seemed to know when someone was watching. Maya dropped her backpack on the patio. "It's all dying."

"Mmm... That is what it looks like, sí?" Rosita sat back on her heels, wiping her forehead. "But look here." She pointed to a brittle-looking ocotillo. "See these tiny buds? Life, waiting."

"Waiting for what?"

"Rain and the right time. These desert plants, they are very wise. They know when to sleep and when to wake." Rosita pulled another weed, gentle despite the stubborn roots. "They look dead, but they are only resting. Saving their strength."

Rosita was quiet for a moment, her hands still in the dirt. "I have been a caregiver for many years, mija. Thirty-two years. I have seen many people die." She looked up at Maya, her eyes gentle but direct. "And I have seen a few miracles. Not many, but a few."

"You think my mom could receive a miracle?"

"I think... your mother is still here. That is what matters." She pulled another weed. "In my village, we believed that sometimes... not always, but sometimes when the love is strong enough to hold someone here. When they are loved so much, so completely, that the universe... it listens."

Maya felt tears in her eyes. "Dad barely even talks to her. He's never home."

"Ah, but you are wrong, mija." Rosita's voice was firm but kind. "Your father, he talks to her in ways you do not see. He works those long hours to keep the roof over your heads, the medicine in the cabinet. He sleeps on that uncomfortable couch so your mother can rest undisturbed. He makes the breakfast nobody eats." She smiled sadly. "These are love letters, Maya. Just written in a language you have not learned to read yet."

Maya wiped her eyes. "I'm so angry at him."

"Because he is still here to be angry at. That is okay." Rosita stood, her knees creaking, and sat beside Maya on the step. "Let me tell you something about the circle of life. When I was a girl, my grandfather, he raised me after my parents died. He taught me about the desert. He said, 'Rosita, in the desert, everything has its season. The cactus blooms, then the bloom dies. The monsoon comes, then the drought. The rabbit is born, the rabbit dies, and feeds the hawk. The hawk dies, and feeds the earth. And from the earth, the cactus grows again.'"

She put a warm hand on Maya's shoulder. "Death is not the end of the circle, mija. It is part of the circle. And right now, your mother... she has been given more time in her season. But all seasons change. That is the way."

"I don't want her to die."

"Of course not. That is because you love her." Rosita squeezed her shoulder. "But when the time comes, and it will come for all of us. The love does not die. Love, it stays. It becomes part of everything. Part of you. You carry it forward, and that is how the circle continues."

They sat together in the desert heat, looking at the garden that looked dead but wasn't. "Do you think the ocotillo will bloom?" Maya asked.

"When the rain comes," Rosita said. "When it is time."

Later that eveing, Karen heard footsteps in the hallway. Light and quick. Maya's familiar rhythm with her headphones in, head down, moving past the door toward the kitchen. She saw her through the open doorway. "Maya?" Her voice was strong enough to carry. "Honey?"

The footsteps stopped. Manny turned to see Maya standing in the hallway, frozen, one earbud pulled out. Staring at the doorway with an expression caught between shock and something that might have been hope.

It had been so long since Karen had called out to her. Months of hushed voices and tiptoeing past the sickroom. Months of her mother too weak to raise her voice above a whisper. "Come sit with us?" Karen's voice was warm and inviting. Maya hesitated. She looked from her mom to her father and back again. Her face was uncertain, guarded, but something in her eyes was cracking. "Please?" Karen patted the bed beside her.

Maya pulled out her other earbud and slowly moved into the room. She sat carefully on the opposite side of the bed from Manny, like she wasn't sure she was allowed to be there. She wasn't sure this moment was real. "Hi, baby," Karen said softly.

"Hi, Mom." Maya's voice was timid.

For a moment, none of them spoke. They just sat there... the three of them together in Karen's room. All of them were uncertain how to navigate this unexpected territory. Then Karen asked, "How was school?"

Maya blinked. "It was... fine."

"Just fine?"

"Yeah. Normal."

Karen smiled. "Tell me about normal."

And slowly, carefully, Maya did. She talked about her biology class, about the lab they'd done on plant cells. About Emma being dramatic over some boy. About the essay due next week in English that she hadn't started yet. Small things that were normal things. Things they hadn't talked about in months. Manny listened, watching his daughter's face slowly relax. He was watching Karen lean forward slightly, engaged, asking questions and really listening. He saw them connect in a way they hadn't been able to since the diagnosis had shattered their lives. "Dad said you applied to NAU and ASU," Karen said. "I'm so proud of you."

Maya glanced at Manny, surprised. "You told her?"

"Of course I did."

Maya looked at him for a moment... something unreadable in her expression. She then turned back to Karen. "Yeah. I applied. I don't know if I'll get in."

"You will," Karen said with certainty. "You're brilliant."

"Mom..."

"You are."

For a few minutes, they were just a family. Talking, listening and present with each other. The way they used to be. The way they hadn't been in years. Manny felt something in his chest that might have been peace. Or might have been exhaustion. He ignored it because this moment was too important to interrupt. Karen shifted against her pillows, and a strange expression crossed her face. "You know what?" She sounded almost surprised. "I'm hungry."

Silence followed. Manny and Maya both stared at her. Karen hadn't had an appetite in months. Eating had been a chore, a necessary misery to maintain some semblance of strength. They'd been forcing her to eat small amounts. Broth, crackers, anything she could keep down. But *hungry*? Actually wanting food? "You're hungry?" Manny couldn't keep the disbelief from his voice. Karen laughed. It was a real laugh, light and surprised. "I know. I can't believe it either. But I am... starving, actually."

Manny stood immediately, purpose flooding through him. This was something he could do. This was helping. This was hope. "I'll make you something. What do you want?"

"Anything. I don't care. Whatever we have."

"I'll find something. I'll be right back."

He moved toward the door, energy in his step despite the strange heaviness creeping into his bones. He ignored that too. Karen was hungry and wanted to eat. That was all that mattered. "Thanks, Manny," Karen called after him. He turned back, smiled. "Of course."

Alone in the kitchen, Manny opened the refrigerator and surveyed the contents. Not much... He'd been meaning to go grocery shopping but kept putting it off. There were some eggs, some wilted vegetables, and leftover meatloaf from two nights ago. Nothing fancy, but it would do. He pulled it out, put a portion on a plate and slid it into the microwave. He waited while it hummed and turned, warming the food back to life. His mind was spinning. Karen was better, actually better. Sitting up, talking, no coughing, and now hungry. It didn't make sense. Cancer didn't just... improve. Not like this.... Not in a matter of hours. But maybe... maybe the new medication was finally working. Maybe she was having a good day. Maybe...

Maybe the old man was right. Maybe God does answer prayers.

The thought was absurd. The wish he'd made on the side of the road to switch places with Karen. They were just words. Just desperate fantasy. Wishes didn't come true. Angels didn't grant miracles. Did they? A wave of dizziness hit him. Manny gripped the counter, closed his eyes, breathed. He was just tired. He had a long day and an emotional evening. The microwave beeped interrupting his denial. He shook off the dizziness, grabbed the plate, found a fork, and headed back toward Karen's room.

While Manny was in the kitchen, Karen turned to Maya. "I'm glad you came in."

Maya's expression was guarded. "I'm glad you called."

A pause while the air conditioning hummed. "I missed you." Maya's voice was small, almost childlike. "I'm right here, baby."

"No, I mean... I missed *this*. You...talking and being..." She couldn't finish. Tears threatened her speech. Karen reached for Maya's hand. "I know. I've missed it too."

They sat together for a moment, hands clasped. Then Maya's expression hardened slightly. "He's never here. Even when he's here, he's not."

Karen knew who she meant. "He's trying."

"I don't think he is..."

"Yes. He doesn't know how, but he is."

Maya pulled her hand away. "You always defend him."

"Because I know him. And I know you." Karen's voice was gentle but firm. "You know, relationships are a two-way street."

Maya looked at her, defensive. "What's that supposed to mean?"

"I'm not saying this is your fault. But you're shutting him out too."

"Because he shut me out first."

"I know. But if you both keep waiting for the other one to reach first, you'll never connect."

Maya crossed her arms. "So, I'm supposed too just... what? Pretend everything's fine?"

"No. But you could try talking to him. Really talking. Not fighting or shutting down. *Talking.*"

"He doesn't want to talk to me."

"He doesn't know how to talk to you. There's a difference."

Maya was silent, jaw tight, as the tears were brimming. Karen softened. "He's scared, Maya. He's terrified of losing me. And he's terrified of losing you."

"He has a funny way of showing it."

"Men do. Especially your father. But that doesn't mean he doesn't feel it."

Karen waited, letting her words settle. "Give him a chance. Try... Please. For me."

Maya looked at her mother. She was pale, thin, but more alive than she'd been in months. She looked at the woman who might not be here much longer, who was asking one last thing of her. "Okay," Maya said quietly.

"Thank you."

Manny returned carrying a plate with reheated meatloaf and a fork. Nothing fancy. But it was food, and Karen was hungry. He handed it to her. Karen took the fork, speared a piece of meatloaf, brought it to her mouth. Chewed and swallowed.... They all waited in suspense but there was no nausea or pain. No difficulty as she took another bite. "Oh my God."

Manny tensed. "What? Is it bad?"

Karen looked up at him, eyes wide, and then she laughed. "No. I just... I can't believe how good day-old meatloaf tastes."

For a moment, Manny just stared at her. Then Maya started laughing. Then Manny was laughing too. It was genuine, surprised, relieved laughter that filled the small bedroom. The absurdity of finding joy in reheated leftovers. But it wasn't about the meatloaf. It was about Karen eating and about being together. Hope was blooming in the darkest places as Manny sat back down on the edge of the bed. He watched Karen take another bite, then another. He was overjoyed as he watched Maya lean against her mother's shoulder, smiling. The three of them together. Happy and whole. For this moment, everything was perfect.

Karen finished half the portion. It was more than she'd eaten at one sitting in weeks as she set the plate aside with a satisfied sigh. "That was exactly what I needed."

They lingered together, none of them wanting to break the spell. Just sitting in the warm light of the bedside lamp, comfortable in the silence. Eventually, Karen yawned. It was a normal, satisfied yawn, not the exhausted half-conscious drifting that usually claimed her. "I should probably rest."

Manny stood and took the plate. "I'll clean up."

Maya stood too. "I should do homework."

But neither of them moved immediately. As if leaving might shatter whatever magic had made this evening possible. Before she left, Maya leaned down and kissed her mother's forehead. "I love you, Mom."

"I love you too, baby."

Maya glanced at Manny. Met his eyes for a brief moment. "Night, Dad."

"Goodnight, Maya."

Not warm, but not hostile either. A truce and a beginning. She left, closing the door softly behind her. Manny sat back down on the edge of the bed and took Karen's hand one more time. "That was nice."

Karen smiled. "It was. Thank you."

"For what?"

"For stopping to help that old man. For telling me about it. For..." She paused, searching for words. "I don't know. Today just felt different. Better."

"It did."

Karen's eyes were already drifting closed. "Maybe things are finally looking up."

Manny watched her face relax into sleep. He watched her breathe steady, even and peaceful. No gasping or pain etched in the lines around her eyes. "Maybe they are," he whispered.

He kissed her forehead gently. "I love you."

She was already asleep as Manny turned off the lamp and walked quietly to the door. He stepped into the hallway and pulled the door almost closed behind him, leaving it cracked in case she needed him in the night. In the hallway, Manny stood for a moment, letting his eyes adjust to the darkness. He felt... tired. More tired than usual. A deep, bone-level exhaustion that made his limbs feel heavy. A slight ache in his joints. A chill that the air conditioning couldn't quite account for. He shook it off. Nothing a good night's sleep wouldn't fix. He looked back at Karen's door. The light was off, peaceful and quiet. She was better. Maya had talked to them. They'd laughed over day-old meatloaf. They'd been a family again, even if just for an hour.

The warmth from the handshake was completely gone now. But he didn't need it anymore. He had something better. He had hope. Manny walked upstairs, past Maya's closed door where he could hear faint music playing. He went to the bathroom, brushed his teeth, and looked at his reflection in the mirror. The same tired face he'd been seeing for months. Nothing was different or changed. He didn't notice the slight pallor of his skin or the way his eyes looked a little more hollow. There was a faint discoloration beginning at his fingertips that was occurring. It was a subtle darkening, like faint bruising, almost invisible in the bathroom light. He turned off the light moving to the couch. It was his usual spot these days and he laid down. Sleep claimed him almost immediately. It was a deep and dreamless sleep.

He didn't know that Karen's cancer cells were dying inside her body. That her tumors were shrinking, her blood clearing, and her organs healing. He didn't know that the trade had been made. That the wish had been granted. That he'd given her his health and taken her place as the one who was dying. He didn't know that tomorrow, the symptoms would begin. That by next week, they would be undeniable. That within weeks, he would be diagnosed with acute radiation syndrome. It would be fatal and irreversible.

He didn't know that this was one of their last normal evenings. A lasting moment of innocent hope. He only knew that his family had been together and that they'd laughed. That Karen had eaten, and Maya had smiled for a few perfect minutes. They'd been whole again and that was enough for tonight.

Chapter Four – Simple Pleasures

Manny woke to sunlight streaming through the living room window, warm on his face. For a moment, he lay still on the couch, eyes closed, letting the morning settle around him. No alarm had awoken him. He'd simply opened his eyes, naturally, peacefully. He couldn't remember the last time that had happened. The house was quiet, and it was Saturday. He sat up slowly, feeling the stiffness in his back and shoulders. Sleeping on the couch was taking its toll. His joints ached in a way that made him feel older than his forty-seven years. He rolled his shoulders, stretched his neck, and dismissed the discomfort. A hot shower would fix it. But first, coffee.

As he stood, he glanced down at his hands and paused. The tips of his fingers looked... off. Slightly discolored, almost bruised. He flexed them, turning them over. It was probably nothing... maybe he'd banged them on something at work without noticing. The plant was full of hard edges and metal surfaces. He made his way to the kitchen, filled the coffee maker, and leaned against the counter while it brewed. The memory of last night drifted through his mind. Karen laughing over day-old meatloaf, Maya sitting with them, the three of them together like they hadn't been in months. Years, maybe. *She's getting better.*

The thought filled him with something close to hope, and hope was dangerous. He'd learned that over the past year. Every good day had been followed by three bad ones. Every moment of improvement was crushed by another setback. But last night... last night had felt different.

The coffee maker gurgled its final breath, and he poured himself a cup.

He stood by the kitchen window, looking out in the backyard. A few birds hopped along the fence line, their small bodies dark against the morning sky. He couldn't remember the last time he'd stood still long enough to watch birds. A sound from down the hall made him turn. Movement, coming from Karen's room. He set down his coffee and walked quietly toward her door. It was slightly ajar, light spilling into the hallway. He knocked softly. "Karen? Are you up?"

"Yeah." Her voice came through clear and strong. No rasp, no struggle for breath. "Come in."

He pushed the door open. Karen was sitting up in bed, pillows propped behind her, hair loose around her shoulders. The morning light caught her face, and Manny stopped in the doorway. She looked... good. Better than good. The gray tone that had settled over her skin for months was gone, replaced by something that almost resembled color. Her eyes were bright, focused. She was awake in a way she hadn't been in so long. "Did I wake you?" he asked.

She shook her head. "No. I just... woke up." A small smile. "I feel good, Manny. Really good."

He moved to the edge of the bed and sat down, taking her hand. It was warm. Not cold and fragile like it had been. It was warm, solid and *there*. "You look good," he said quietly. "Better than you have in..." He couldn't finish. He didn't want to jinx it. Karen squeezed his hand. "I know. I can feel it. Something's different."

They sat in silence for a moment, both afraid to name what they were hoping for. Remission felt like too big a word and healing felt impossible. But *better*... better was safe. "I don't want to just lie here," Karen said suddenly. "Can we... do something?"

Manny blinked. "What do you want to do?"

"I don't know. Anything. Can we sit in the living room and watch something, maybe look out the window." She looked at him, and her eyes held something he hadn't seen in months, eagerness. "Just... be together. Normal things."

Manny felt his throat tighten. "Yeah. Yes. Let me make you some tea or coffee. Whatever you want."

Karen laughed. A real laugh, that was light and easy. "You're already doing too much. Just help me to the living room."

"Are you sure you're up for it?"

"I'm sure."

He helped her stand, his arm around her waist, but she didn't lean on him as heavily as she had before. She was steadier and somehow stronger. They walked slowly down the hall and into the living room, where the morning light was even brighter, filling the space with a golden glow. Karen settled onto the couch with a soft sigh, and Manny draped a blanket over her lap. He went back to the kitchen, retrieved his coffee, and made Karen a cup of tea chamomile, the way she liked it. When he returned, she was looking around the room like she was seeing it for the first time. "I missed this room," she said softly.

Manny set the tea on the coffee table and sat beside her. "It missed you."

She leaned against him slightly, and he put his arm around her shoulders. They sat like that for a while, not talking, just being. The house creaked and settled around them. Outside, the birds sang. "This is nice," Karen murmured. "Yeah," Manny agreed. "It is."

Karen's gaze drifted to the window. "Look! The birds are out."

Manny followed her eyes. Several small birds were hopping along the windowsill, their movements quick and jerky, their chirping loud and insistent. "I forgot how nice that sound is," Karen said. "Chirping. Like little alarms saying, 'Wake up, the world is beautiful.'"

Manny smiled. "You always loved birds."

"When Maya was little, we used to sit on the porch and watch them. Remember?"

"Yeah. You'd try to teach her the different species."

"She never cared about the names." Karen's voice was warm with the memory. "She just liked the sounds."

They watched the birds fly from the sill to the small tree in the yard, their songs overlapping, chaotic and joyful. The morning light caught their wings, making them flash dark and bright. Then Karen gasped softly. "Oh! Look, Manny... a bunny!"

A small cottontail rabbit had hopped into view near the bush at the edge of the yard. It froze, ears alert, nose twitching as it sensed them watching. Karen's voice was full of childlike delight. "Did you see it?"

Before Manny could answer, the bunny darted forward and disappeared under the bush in one quick motion, there one moment, gone the next. Karen laughed. "Did you see how fast it went? One second there, next second gone."

"Like it was never there," Manny said.

"Magic." Karen kept watching the bush, as if willing the bunny to reappear. It didn't, but she didn't seem to mind. She leaned her head against Manny's shoulder. "I could watch this all day."

"Then let's watch," Manny said.

They sat in comfortable silence, the tea steaming on the table, the birds continuing their morning symphony. Manny couldn't remember the last time they'd done this. The last time they just sat together, watching the world outside, not rushing to appointments or treatments or anywhere else. Just being together. After a while, Karen shifted beside him. "You know what I want to do?"

"What?"

She looked at him with a playful smile. "Watch a movie. Something silly. A romantic comedy. One of those stupid ones we used to watch."

Manny grinned. "You mean the ones I used to complain about?"

"Yes. Those exact ones. And you're going to watch it with me and you're not going to complain."

"Deal."

Manny reached for the remote and handed it to Karen. They scrolled through the options together, Karen pointing at titles and Manny making exaggerated groaning sounds until she swatted his arm. "That one," she said finally, pointing at the screen. "The one with the guy and the girl who hate each other and then fall in love."

"That's literally every romantic comedy."

"Exactly. Perfect."

Manny pressed play. The opening credits rolled with bright music, attractive people in a picturesque city, all the predictable markers of a film that would ask nothing of them except to feel good for ninety minutes. Karen tucked herself more snugly under his arm, her head on his shoulder, and pulled the blanket over both of them. The tea sat forgotten on the table. The birds continued singing outside. And for the first time in longer than Manny could remember, everything felt... normal.

The movie played out exactly as expected. The characters were cute, argued constantly, slowly realized they were perfect for each other despite their differences. Karen laughed at the jokes, even the dumb ones, and Manny found himself laughing too, not at the movie, but at the sound of her laughter. He'd missed that sound. He wasn't really watching the screen, he was watching her. The way her eyes crinkled when she smiled, the way she leaned into him, the way she was *here*. Present and alive. She caught him looking. "What?"

"Nothing," he said. "Just... I love you."

Her expression softened. "I love you too."

She kissed him, brief and tender, and they turned back to the movie. On screen, the couple was having their inevitable third-act breakup, the misunderstanding that would be resolved in the final ten minutes. Karen sighed contentedly, as if she knew exactly what was coming and was perfectly happy about it. "I love a good happy ending," she murmured.

"Me too," Manny said quietly.

The movie wrapped up exactly as promised. The couple reunited, the kiss in the rain, the swell of music along with the final shot of them laughing together as the credits rolled. Karen sighed again, this time with satisfaction. "That was perfect."

Manny smiled. "It was pretty formulaic."

"That's what made it perfect."

They sat in the glow of the television, neither of them moving to turn it off, just holding each other as the credits scrolled by. Manny felt something in his chest. Not the warmth from the handshake, which had faded days ago, but something else. Gratitude, maybe. Or just... peace.

Thank you, he thought, not sure who he was thanking. *Thank you for this.*

Footsteps on the stairs made them both look up. Maya appeared, still in pajamas, her hair a messy halo around her face. She stopped when she saw them on the couch together. "Mom? You're... out here?"

Karen smiled. "Good morning, sweetheart."

Maya blinked, processing. Her mother, sitting on the couch. Not in bed. Looking healthy and *happy*. Sitting with her father like it was the most natural thing in the world. "Are you feeling okay?" Maya asked carefully.

"I feel great, actually."

Maya's eyes moved between them, uncertain. Manny patted the couch beside him. "Want to join us?"

Maya hesitated. "ok... maybe for a minute."

She crossed the room and sat on Karen's other side, close but cautious, like she was afraid the moment might shatter. Karen shifted to make room, and Maya leaned against her mother's shoulder. For a moment, none of them spoke. They just sat there. The three of them together, like they used to be, like Manny had almost forgotten they could be. Maya's voice was small. "This is nice."

"It is," Karen agreed, wrapping her arm around her daughter.

Manny watched them, his wife and daughter pressed together on the couch, the morning light falling across their faces, and felt his chest tighten with something too big to name. After a few minutes, Maya pulled out her phone to check the time. "I should get ready, I have plans with Emma today. We are going to the mall."

"Okay, honey. Have a good day."

Maya stood, but she looked back at them, her expression softer than it had been in weeks. "I'm glad you're feeling better, Mom."

"Me too, sweetheart."

Maya's eyes flicked to Manny for just a second. not hostile, not warm, but not closed off either. It was a new beginning. "See you later, Dad."

"Have a good day, Maya."

She disappeared up the stairs, and Manny heard her bedroom door close. Karen leaned back against the couch, looking tired now but satisfied. "I think I wore myself out."

"You want to go back to bed?"

"Not yet. Just... let me sit here a little longer."

"As long as you want."

She closed her eyes, her head resting on his shoulder again, her breathing slow and even. Manny watched the window, where the birds were still hopping along the sill, where the bush still hid the bunny, where the world continued its small and beautiful routines.

He looked down at his hands, resting in his lap. The discoloration at his fingertips seemed a little more pronounced now, spreading slightly past the tips. He flexed his fingers and they felt stiff. Probably just age or he was just sleeping wrong. Eventually, Karen stirred. "What time is it?"

Manny checked his phone. "Almost ten."

"You have to go to work soon."

"Nope, it's Saturday. I'll be here when you wake up."

"Promise?"

"Yep, that's a promise."

He stood, offered her his hand, and helped her to her feet. She was steady but clearly tired. He walked her back to the bedroom, helped her settle under the covers, and pulled the blanket up around her shoulders.

"Thank you for this morning," she said, her eyes already drifting closed.

"Thank you," Manny replied.

"For what?"

"For being here. For watching birds and bunnies and bad movies with me."

She smiled without opening her eyes. "Anytime."

He kissed her forehead gently. "Get some rest."

"You too. You look tired."

"I'm fine."

She was already half-asleep, her breathing evening out. Manny stood there for a moment, watching her, then quietly left the room. In the bathroom, he showered quickly, the hot water doing little to ease the ache in his joints. He dressed and paused in the living room before going to the garage and doing his normal chores around the house. The blanket was still on the couch. The mugs still sat on the coffee table. The television screen was dark. The morning light had shifted, slanting through the window at a different angle now. *I want more of this,* Manny thought. *More mornings. More simple things.*

He looked at his hands again. The darkening at his fingertips was definitely spreading... past the tips now, toward the first knuckles. He should probably mention it to someone. Maybe James would know what it was. Probably just a rash. He headed out the door to cut the grass and edge the sections by the sidewalk. Outside, the day was bright and clear. The birds were still singing. Somewhere, the bunny was probably still hiding under the bush. The world was continuing, indifferent and beautiful.

As he pushed the lawnmower, cutting the grass he looked at the window of Karen's bedroom, curtains open, light streaming in. *Thank you,* he thought again. *For bringing her back to me. Please... let it last.*

He didn't know yet that his prayer had already been answered. And that the cost was already growing within him, darkening his fingertips, spreading through his bones. He kept pushing the lawn mower, still hopeful, still grateful, and still believing they might finally have more time together. Still not knowing that time was the one thing he no longer had.

Chapter Five – The Pianist

Manny woke before his alarm again. The couch had become very uncomfortable, and his body was starting to protest. His back ached, his joints felt stiff and swollen. There was a deep tiredness in his bones that sleep didn't seem to touch at all now. He sat up slowly, rubbing his face, and checked the time. 6:47 am. Early enough...

He stood, stretched, and felt the familiar pull of discomfort through his shoulders and lower back. Getting old, he thought. Or maybe just sleeping on a couch for too many nights in a row. He should probably go back to sleeping in the bedroom, but the couch had become easier somehow. It was less distance to cross when Karen needed him. A smaller disruption to her rest.

In the kitchen, he started the coffee maker and filled the kettle for tea. The morning ritual was becoming automatic now...coffee for him, chamomile tea for Karen. He stood by the window while he waited, watching the early light spread across the backyard. The birds were already out, hopping along the fence, calling to each other. He wondered if they were the same birds from yesterday, or if all small brown birds just looked the same to him. Karen would know. She'd always been better at noticing things like that. The kettle whistled. Manny poured the tea, let it steep, then carried both mugs down the hall. He knocked softly on Karen's door. "Karen? You awake?"

"Come in."

He pushed the door open with his shoulder, both hands holding the mugs. Karen was already sitting up in bed, pillows propped behind her, looking out the window. The morning light caught her profile, and Manny paused in the doorway. She looked even better than yesterday. The change was subtle but undeniable. There was more color in her face, more clarity in her eyes. She turned to him and smiled. "I thought you might want this," he said, offering her the tea. "You're spoiling me."

"You deserve it."

He sat on the edge of the bed, his own coffee warming his hands. Karen took a sip of her tea and sighed contentedly. "The birds are back," she said, gesturing to the window. "I've been watching them."

Manny looked out and saw three or four small birds were perched on the feeder Maya had hung years ago. Back when she still did things like that, back before everything got hard. "I forgot how much I love mornings," Karen said softly.

"I could get used to this," Manny said.

"Me too."

They sat in comfortable silence for a moment, sipping their drinks, watching the light change. It felt right... like something they should have been doing all along but had somehow forgotten how. Karen set her tea on the nightstand. "I really do feel so much better. It's... strange."

"Strange good, or strange bad?"

"Strange miraculous." She looked at him. "Like I turned a corner I didn't know was there."

Manny felt hope rise in his chest, dangerous and fragile. "Maybe the treatment's finally working."

"Maybe." Karen paused, her gaze distant. "Or maybe... I don't know. When I was going through treatment, I met so many people. Other patients." She looked at him again, something shifting in her expression. "You learn things about life when you're that close to death."

Manny set his coffee down. "What kind of things?"

Karen seemed to be choosing her words carefully. "People who are dying... they change. Or maybe they just become more themselves." She folded her hands in her lap. "They stop caring about the small things. The petty things. They reach out for connection and peace."

Manny listened, quietly.

"There was this man," Karen continued, "he was older, always so angry at the nurses. But one day, near the end, he started thanking them. Holding their hands. Apologizing for being difficult." She smiled sadly. "And there was a young woman who couldn't stop crying at first. Then one day she was just... calm. She spent her last weeks writing letters to everyone she loved."

"That sounds... hard to watch," Manny said.

"It was. But it was also beautiful, in a way. Like when you know time is short, you finally see what matters."

"What matters?" Manny asked quietly.

Karen met his eyes. "Love. Connection. Leaving something beautiful behind."

The room fell silent except for the soft sounds of the house settling and the distant chirping outside. Manny reached for Karen's hand, and she took it. "There was one woman I'll never forget," Karen said, her voice softer now. "She played the piano."

"At the hospital?"

Karen nodded. "It was over six months ago. I was there for treatment. They had this common area, sort of a waiting room. Nice, for a hospital. Big windows, some chairs, a couple of magazines." She paused. "And in the corner, there was a piano. A beautiful baby grand. I'd never seen anyone play it."

Manny squeezed her hand gently, encouraging her to continue. "I was sitting there, waiting for my name to be called. I was feeling like hell. I was tired, nauseous, just... done." Karen's gaze was distant now, seeing the memory. "And this woman walked in the area. They had these small hotel rooms where patients could stay during prolonged treatment. She came from one down the hall. She was moving slowly ya know..."

"What did she look like?"

"Middle-aged. Maybe forty. Thin, like we all were." Karen's voice grew quieter. "She was wearing a scarf... a beautiful silk scarf, white with light pink patterns. But you could see underneath... she'd lost her hair. The scarf covered most of it, but there were bare patches at the edges."

Manny could picture it... the sterile hospital corridor, the fluorescent lights, the woman trying to hold onto her dignity with a beautiful scarf. "She looked exhausted," Karen continued. "But also... determined. Like she'd come there with a purpose. She walked all that way with her IV holder trailing right beside her. She pulled it in a dreading way."

"What did she do?"

"She walked straight over to the piano. She didn't look at anyone, nor did she say anything. She just sat down on the bench." Karen's eyes were bright with the memory. "And she adjusted the scarf, like she was preparing. Getting ready for something important."

"There was maybe a dozen of us there. Patients mostly, a few family members. A nurse at the desk. A doctor passing through. Everyone was in their own world. Reading, staring at their phones, just waiting."

Karen paused, and Manny waited. "And then she started playing."

"What did she play?"

"A Chopin concerto..." Karen's voice filled with awe. "I didn't know which one at the time, but I looked it up later. It's a long piece. It was difficult and you could tell from the first notes... this wasn't an amateur playing. She was a master.

People looked up. The sound was so unexpected, so out of place in a hospital. But also... perfect. Like it was exactly what we all needed to hear."

Manny could almost hear it. The sudden music cutting through the antiseptic quiet, the notes spilling out into a space filled with fear, pain and waiting. "Her hands moved across the keys like they'd been doing it her whole life," Karen said. "She played confidently and yet gracefully. Her eyes were closed. She wasn't playing for us... she was playing for herself. But we were all transfixed."

"Time stopped in that moment Manny... the nurse stood up from her desk. She just stood there, listening. The doctors who'd been passing through stopped in the doorway. They didn't move. Patients put down their phones, their magazines and just stopped. We all just... watched in amazement."

Karen's voice grew thick with emotion. "It was beautiful... and heartbreaking. There were these fast, complicated passages where her fingers flew. And then slow, aching parts that felt like grief made into sound."

"She played the whole thing. Every note. It was perfection."

Manny realized he was holding his breath.

"When she finished," Karen whispered, "the last note just... hung in the air. Nobody moved. Nobody breathed. Then someone started clapping and then everyone did."

"What did she do?"

Karen's eyes glistened. "She opened her eyes. Stood up from the bench but she didn't acknowledge it. She didn't smile, nor did she bow, she didn't even look at us. She just adjusted her scarf and walked out."

"Just like that?"

"Just like that. I remember feeling almost hurt. Like, we were all so moved, and she didn't even care." Karen wiped her eyes. "But then I realized... it wasn't about us."

Manny waited, knowing there was more. "The next day, I was back for another treatment. I overheard the nurses talking." Karen's voice broke slightly. "She'd passed away...That night."

"The same woman?"

Karen nodded, tears slipping down her cheeks. "The same woman."

Manny pulled her into his arms, and she let herself cry against his shoulder for a moment before pulling back and wiping her face. "She knew," Karen said. "She had to have known. That was her last time. Her last chance to play. She didn't do it for the applause. She did it because... that's who she was. A pianist... And she wanted to be that one more time."

Manny felt his own throat tighten. "That's incredible. She was incredible."

"She was. But also... she was just someone with cancer, like me, who knew her time was running out." Karen looked at him intently. "People near death, they know... deep down, they know. And they reach for what matters. For her, it was music." She squeezed his hand. "For me, it's this. You... Us.... These mornings."

They sat in silence, the weight of the story settling between them. Manny understood now why Karen had told him about this woman. She had shown her something about how to face death. How to choose beauty even in the end. But then Karen's expression shifted, growing darker. "Cancer takes everything from you. You know that, right?"

"I know it's been hard."

"No, I mean... *everything*. Your dignity. Your privacy. Your control." Her voice was firm, almost angry. "Strangers see you naked. Doctors prod you. They scan you and sometimes cut you open. You throw up in front of people. You can't control your body. You lose your hair, your strength, your ability to do the simplest things."

Manny listened, his heart breaking. "You become a patient. A diagnosis. A case number." Karen's hands were trembling. "You stop being a person. You're a collection of symptoms and test results. People talk about you like you're not there. 'How is she doing?' 'What did the doctor say?' Like you can't speak for yourself."

"I'm sorry," Manny said. "I didn't realize..."

"You couldn't have. Nobody can, unless they go through it." She looked at him, and her expression softened. "But you've been there. You've stayed. That matters."

"I never would have left."

"A lot of people can't handle it. Partners leave. Friends disappear. Because it's too hard to watch." Karen's voice dropped to a whisper. "You didn't leave."

Manny felt tears fill up his eyes. "I love you."

"I know." She smiled, sad and grateful. "But here's the thing. Even when cancer takes your dignity, you can still choose how you face it. That woman playing the piano... she chose beauty. Other people choose love. Or faith. Or just... presence."

"What do you choose?" Manny asked.

Karen looked at him for a long moment. "I think that's what I've been missing. Choice... I've been so focused on fighting, on surviving, I forgot too just... live. In the time I have." She leaned her head against his shoulder. "These mornings... this is me choosing. This is me, living."

Manny wrapped his arm around her and held her close. He didn't know what to say. Everything felt inadequate. "I've been so afraid of losing you," he finally said. "I think I forgot to just... be with you."

"I know. But you're here now. That's what matters."

They sat like that for a while, holding each other in the morning light. The birds continued their singing outside. The world continued turning. And for this moment, they were together. Karen pulled back slightly and looked at him, her eyes narrowing with concern. "You look tired."

"I'm okay."

"No, really. Are you feeling alright? You've been working so much."

Manny felt the ache in his bones, the exhaustion that never quite left, the strange darkness spreading across his fingertips. But he smiled. "I'm fine. Just... emotional. This conversation."

Karen didn't look entirely convinced. "Promise me you'll take care of yourself."

"I promise."

She touched his face gently. "I need you, Manny. I can't do this without you."

The words hit him harder than they should have. "You have me. Always."

Manny glanced at the clock on the nightstand. "I should get ready for work."

"Already?"

"Yeah. But I'll be home tonight."

"I'll be here."

He stood, leaned down, and kissed her forehead, letting his lips linger there for a moment longer than usual. "Thank you for listening," Karen said. "For being here."

"Always," he repeated.

Before he could move toward the door, Karen caught his hand. "Manny?"

He turned back. "Yeah?"

"When this is all over... when I'm better, let's do something. Go somewhere. Even just... a weekend away. Something normal."

Manny smiled, though it hurt. "I'd like that."

"Me too."

He left her there, resting against the pillows, and walked to the bathroom. In the mirror, his reflection looked haggard. Paler than yesterday. The dark circles under his eyes had deepened, and his skin had taken on a more grayish cast. He looked down at his hands, turning them over. The discoloration had spread past his fingertips now, creeping further up his knuckles. The skin looked damaged somehow. It was rougher, darker, like a bruise that wouldn't heal. He flexed his fingers and they felt stiff and swollen.

He should say something to someone. James, maybe a doctor but Karen was getting better. That was what mattered. He splashed cold water on his face, trying to wake himself up, and got ready for work. Twenty minutes later, he was in his truck, pulling out of the driveway. He looked back at the house. He saw the window of Karen's room, curtains open, light streaming in. She was probably watching the birds again or resting. Either was she was getting stronger. *Thank you for these mornings,* he prayed silently. *Thank you for bringing her back to me. Let me have more time with her. Please.*

He didn't know that he was praying for the impossible. That she was healing because he was dying. The wish already granted. There was no turning back. All he knew was that his wife was alive, and she'd shared something profound with him this morning. A story about a woman who chose beauty in her final moments. A woman who played Chopin and then walked away, content with one last time.

He wondered what he would choose, if he knew his time was running out. But he didn't know, not yet. He put the truck in drive and headed toward Palo Verde, toward his shift, toward the radiation that was already killing him cell by cell. And in the house behind him, Karen lay in bed, feeling stronger than she had in months, feeling like herself again.

Feeling like maybe, just maybe, everything was going to be okay. Neither of them knew the truth.

But the pianist's song still echoed in Karen's memory. She had heard it on the radio since then and on each occurrence, it stopped time at that moment again... A gift given freely, a final act of beauty, a choice made in the face of death. And somewhere, somehow, it meant something. Even if they couldn't see it yet.

Rosita found Karen sitting in the living room, staring out the window at the birds. It had been a week since the miraculous change, and Karen was still growing stronger each day. "You are thinking very loudly today," Rosita said, settling into the chair across from her.

Karen laughed softly. "Is it that obvious?"

"After many years, I know the sound of a mind that cannot rest." Rosita folded her hands in her lap. "You want to tell me what troubles you, or should I guess?"

"I'm getting better, Rosita. Really better. And I don't understand why."

"Does it need understanding? Or does it need accepting?"

Karen turned from the window. "But what if it's temporary? What if this is just... a pause before everything gets worse again?"

Rosita nodded slowly. "This is possible. Or maybe it is permanent. Or maybe it is something in between. We do not know. So, the question has become... what do you do with not knowing?"

"I'm scared to hope."

"Ah." Rosita leaned forward. "Let me tell you about my abuela. My grandmother. When I was a little girl, she was dying of the cancer, like you. The doctors said three months. But she lived two more years. Two years of pain, yes, but also two years of sunsets. Two years of teaching me to make tortillas. Two years of stories. Two years of love."

"What happened after two years?"

"She died. On a Tuesday afternoon, with her whole family around her, in the home she loved." Rosita's eyes glistened. "And when she died, we grieved. But we also celebrated. Because those two years... they were a gift. She did not waste them being afraid of when they would end."

Karen felt tears slip down her face. "I feel like I'm dying while Manny is still here, and he's disappearing while I'm still alive. We're missing each other."

"So, stop missing each other." Rosita's voice was gentle but firm. "You have been given time, señora. I do not know how much. Nobody does. But you have today. And maybe tomorrow. Do not waste today being afraid of when tomorrows run out."

"It's not that simple."

"No. It is exactly that simple. We make it complicated." Rosita stood, walked to the window, and gestured at the birds. "Do you think they worry about winter? They do not. They sing today. They eat today. They fly today. And when winter comes, they fly south or they stay and endure. But today, they sing."

She turned back to Karen. "This is what I have learned, after holding many hands as they go. The people who die at peace are not the ones who lived the longest. They are the ones who lived the fullest in whatever time they had. They are the ones who said, 'I love you.' Who forgave. Who made peace. Who chose presence over worry."

Karen wiped her eyes. "I'm scared I won't know how."

"You already know. You have always known." Rosita returned to her chair. "Talk to your husband. Really talk. Not about bills or Maya's school or doctor appointments. Talk about your love and tell him what you need...ask him what he needs. You can experience the bridge between you before it is too late."

"And Maya?"

"She is learning from you. She watches how you face this. You are teaching her how to be strong, how to love and how to endure." Rosita smiled. "And she is teaching you how to receive care, how to be vulnerable and how to let others carry you sometimes. This is the circle we must teach, and in turn so will they."

They sat together in the morning light, the birds singing outside, the house peaceful around them. "Rosita?" Karen asked. "Do you believe in miracles?"

"Sí. But not the kind in movies. The real miracles, they are quieter. A day without pain. A conversation that heals. The choice to love when it would be easier to close your heart."

She met Karen's eyes. "You are living a miracle, señora. Whatever time you have been given, a week, a month or years... it is more than you had. Do not question the gift. Just unwrap it."

Karen nodded slowly. "Thank you."

"De nada. Now, I will make us lunch, and you will tell me about that pianist you cannot stop thinking about. The one who played Chopin."

Karen smiled. "How did you know?"

"Because I overheard you my dear. That and you have the look of someone who has seen death choose beauty. That look, it changes a person. Come, we will talk about it. Tell me with your eyes closed, let me relive it with you in your heart."

Chapter Six – Tables Turn

The alarm on Manny's phone screamed at six am. He fumbled for it, nearly knocked it off the coffee table, finally silenced it. For a moment, he just lay there on the couch, staring at the ceiling, trying to remember why his body felt like it had been beaten. Then he tried to sit up. Pain lanced through his joints. It was in his knees, hips, shoulders, and elbows. A deep ache in his bones that reminded him of the flu, but worse. It was sharper and more invasive. He gripped the couch arm and pulled himself upright, breathing hard from the effort. I *Just didn't sleep well. This couch is killing my back... I need coffee.*

His internal rationalizations sounded hollow even to himself. The shower didn't help. Usually, the hot water woke him up and cleared his head. Not long ago it loosened his muscles and prepared him for the day. But standing under the spray, he felt cold. The water was hot and he could see the steam but his skin felt clammy and cold. He struggled with it, he couldn't quite reach the warmth. He turned the temperature up hotter and then up again. The bathroom filled with steam as his skin turned red from the heat. But he still felt cold. He gave up, turned off the water, dried himself with shaking hands. In the mirror, he looked worse than he felt. His whole body seemed pale. The dark circles were still there under his eyes like bruises. His cheekbones seemed more pronounced than yesterday. He asked himself if had he lost weight? In one night?

He thought it was stress, exhaustion due to him not sleeping. Not sleeping was the new normal. He dressed in his work uniform, clipped his dosimeter badge to his chest, and headed downstairs.

Before leaving, Manny paused at Karen's door. It was cracked open, the room was dark and quiet. He pushed it open slightly, peered inside. Karen was asleep, lying on her side, breathing easily. He noticed full color in her cheeks. Her face was peaceful, relaxed and free of the pain-lines that had been carved there for months. It was a small miracle. *At least she's better. That's what matters.*

He closed the door softly, grabbed his keys, and left. He didn't check on Maya, she was probably still asleep. He should check on her, but he was running late. Another small failure to add to the pile.

The drive to Palo Verde was difficult. Manny kept drifting... not physically, but mentally. His attention was wandering. The highway stretching ahead of him, empty but straight. He'd blink and realize he'd driven three miles without conscious thought. He gripped the steering wheel harder hoping it would force him to focus. The exit to the plant came up fast. He almost missed it; he had to brake hard and swerve onto the off-ramp. The truck behind him honked. Manny's heart hammered. *Pay attention. Good God man, pay attention.*

By the time he reached the security checkpoint, his hands were shaking. "Morning, Chavez." The guard leaned out of the booth, then frowned. "You okay? You look rough."

"Just tired."

The guard hesitated, eyes scanning Manny's face. Then nodded slowly. "Alright. Have a good shift."

The gate rose up and Manny drove through. *Everyone keeps saying that. I look tired. I feel tired. I AM tired. But this is more than tired.*

The walk from the parking lot to his station felt like miles. Each step required conscious effort. His legs were heavy and his balance was slightly off. The fluorescent lights in the hallways were too bright, stabbing into his eyes. The temperature-controlled air was too cold, seeping into his bones. By the time he reached his station overlooking Reactor Cooling Pool #2, he was breathing hard and sweating despite the chill. He sat down at his control station and logged in. The monitors swam in and out of focus. He blinked hard, rubbed his eyes, and tried again. Temperature: 82°F. Normal. Flow rate: 3,200 gallons per minute. Normal. Radiation levels: within acceptable parameters. Normal. Everything was fine. He was not fine and he knew it...

He started his shift checklist, typing with trembling fingers. He made three typos in the first entry, deleted it and started again. On his next try he made two more typos. *Focus. Just focus man.*

But the nausea was building. It was a slow, rolling wave in his stomach. The cold sweat on his forehead along with his skin felt clammy and wrong. He gripped the edge of his desk, closed his eyes, and breathed. *You can do this. You've done this a thousand times. Just get through the shift.*

"Hey, man. You don't look good. For real this time dude."

Manny opened his eyes. James Chen stood beside his station, coffee in hand, concern etched across his round face.

"I'm okay."

"No, seriously. You look like you're about to pass out."

Manny tried to stand up to prove he was fine, to demonstrate control... and the room tilted. James's hand shot out, caught Manny's arm, steadied him. "Whoa. Easy buddy. Sit down."

Manny sat down, his breath coming in short gasps. The monitors in front of him swam out of focus again. The floor felt unsteady. "When's the last time you ate?" James asked.

"I... this morning. I think."

He hadn't or he couldn't remember when he'd last eaten. Yesterday?

"You need to go to medical or go home."

"I'm fine. Just give me a minute."

"You're not fine. You're shaking."

Manny looked at his hands. They were trembling... not slightly, but visibly. Like his body was vibrating at the wrong frequency. "I just need... I need a minute."

James looked at him for a long moment. "Alright. One minute. Then we're calling medical."

Then the nausea hit like a freight train. Manny stood abruptly, the chair rolling back behind him. "I need..."

He didn't finish. He just moved, stumbling slightly, toward the hallway. "Bathroom's that way," James called after him. "I got your station."

Manny barely heard him. He was focused entirely on reaching the bathroom before... He made it, barely.

In the privacy of the stall, Manny's body rejected everything. Over and over, violent and uncontrollable, until he was shaking and gasping. There was nothing left as he sat on the floor for a moment. It was disgusting, the tile cold and grimy against his legs, but he couldn't stand up. He couldn't move. *What is happening to me?*

Eventually, he pulled himself upright and stumbled to the sink. He turned on the cold water and splashed it on his face. He looked up at the mirror and the man looking back was barely recognizable. He was so messed up... Gray skin with Hollow eyes. His lips were pale, almost colorless. The dark circles under his eyes looked like bruises, deep and purple. And his hands... Manny held them up, staring. The discoloration he'd noticed yesterday had spread. The tips of his fingers were dark... not bruised, but something else. Something that looked almost like burns. The skin was damaged, rough when he rubbed his thumb across his fingertips. It had spread past his fingernails now, already creeping past his knuckles. *This isn't exhaustion. This is something else.* Fear crept in, cold and insidious. *This isn't normal.* He returned to his station slowly, still shaking, and pale. James looked up from monitoring Manny's screens. "You good?"

"Yeah. Thanks."

The lie tasted bitter. Manny sat down, he tried to focus on the monitors. Everything swam together. He tried to type a log entry. Too many typos. He deleted it and tried again but it was worse. His hands wouldn't cooperate. His eyes wouldn't focus. His body was betraying him. And then he heard the footsteps. Crisp and purposeful with military precision. Gerald Reed.

Manny looked up as Reed approached, clipboard in hand, pale eyes already scanning him with clinical assessment. "Chavez."

Manny tried to straighten in his chair. "Sir."

Reed stopped two feet away. Looked at Manny the way someone might look at a malfunctioning piece of equipment. "You do not look fit for duty."

"I'm fine, sir. Just..."

"You are dismissed for the remainder of the day."

"Sir, I can..."

Reed cut him off with a raised hand. "That was not a request. You are unfit. Leave now!"

The words landed like a slap. Manny opened his mouth to protest, but Reed had already turned to James. "Mr. Chen, take over his duties and call in support as needed."

"Yes, sir."

Reed looked back at Manny one last time. "Go home. See a doctor and do not return until you are fit for duty."

He walked away without waiting for a response. Manny sat there, stunned. He was dismissed like a child sent home from school. As if he was someone who couldn't be trusted to do his job. But Reed was right. He couldn't do his job. He could barely stand or think. He was unfit for duty. James helped him gather his things... his jacket, his thermos, his keys. "Don't take it personally," James said quietly. "Reed's an ass, but he's right. You need to go home."

"I know."

"You going to be okay to drive?"

"Yeah. I'll be fine."

Another lie. They both knew it. "Listen," Manny said, needing something, anything positive to hold onto. "Karen had a good morning. First time in weeks, she had energy. She ate breakfast and smiled."

James's expression softened. "That's great, man. Really."

"Yeah." Manny managed a weak smile. "My exhaustion must have finally caught up with me. But at least she's doing better."

"That's what matters. Now, go home. Rest and take care of yourself."

Manny nodded and left. Behind him, James watched him go, worry was etched across his face.

The parking lot stretched before Manny like a desert. The sun too bright, its heat oppressive even at nine in the morning. His vision tunneled. His steps were uncertain and he reached his truck, fumbled with the keys while dropping them. He had to bend down to pick them up. He nearly fell over when he straightened up. I *just need to get in the truck and rest for a minute.*

Inside, the air-conditioned interior felt good after he started the car. He sat in the driver's seat, and closed his eyes. *Just for a second. Then I'll drive home.*

Tap tap tap.

Manny jerked awake, disoriented. Where was he? What time was it? A face at the window. It was an older man in a security uniform with a stern expression. Manny rolled down the window, groggy and confused. "You can't sleep in the lot, sir. Leave or report for duty. Those are the options."

"I... what time is it?"

The guard checked his watch. "Fourteen hundred hours. You have been here a while."

Manny looked at his phone. 2:00 PM. *Five hours. He'd been unconscious for five hours.* He was lucky the truck hadn't run out of gas. Panic spiked through him, cutting through the fog. "I'm sorry. I don't know what happened. I was just... I must have dozed off."

"You need to leave. Or I have call it in."

"I'm leaving. I'm sorry."

Manny rolled the window back up with shaking hands. The guard watched him until he put the car in gear. Manny pulled out of the parking lot, barely functional, the terror sitting cold in his chest. *What the hell is wrong with me?*

The drive home was a nightmare of forced concentration. Manny gripped the steering wheel, forcing himself to watch the road, the lines, and the other cars. Every mile felt like ten. Every moment he expected to drift, to crash or black out again. *Five hours, I lost five hours.* This wasn't exhaustion. It wasn't stress. This was something wrong, deeply, fundamentally wrong. Karen was getting better. Miraculously better and he was falling apart... *Is it connected?* The thought came unbidden, irrational. *No... That's crazy.*

But he looked at his hands on the steering wheel. The darkening at his fingertips. The rough texture. The way his skin didn't quite look like skin anymore. *Isn't it?*

He made it home somehow. Pulled into the driveway and turned off the engine. It was early afternoon. Karen might be awake but Maya was still at school. He should check on Karen. He should tell her what happened. Maybe she could help? Instead, he went inside and collapsed onto the couch. Sleep took him before he could even remove his shoes.

The dream world was waiting for him. Manny stood on State Route 85 at dusk. The sky painted orange and purple, stars beginning to appear. The highway was empty except for one vehicle... The old pickup truck on the shoulder with its hazards blinking. The old man standing beside it, looking at Manny with kind, sad eyes. "Hello again, son."

Manny moved toward him, his feet carrying him without conscious thought. Everything felt sharper than reality. More real than real. "What's happening to me?"

The old man smiled. "You're getting what you asked for."

"I didn't ask for this." Manny gestured at himself... his trembling, failing body. "Didn't you?"

The old man extended his hand. Manny watched himself reach out like observing from outside his own body and shake it. But this time, he saw. He saw the light. It was golden, warm, and alive. Flowing from the old man's hand into Manny's. The light drifted up his arm and into his chest. Spreading through his entire body like liquid fire. "God let me give you what you needed to make your wish come true," the old man said.

"What wish?"

"To switch places with her. Your life for hers."

The light pulsed inside Manny's chest. He could feel it now. It was hot and terrible. Everything was changing. "You're carrying what she carried," the old man continued. "And the result is what you are experiencing now."

"What did you give me?" Manny's voice was desperate, pleading. "What's happening to me?"

The old man smiled in a sad, knowing, unchangeable way. "You'll understand when the time comes."

The dream began to fade and Manny reached for the old man. He tried to hold onto him, and demand answers. But the light was fading, the highway dissolving, the old man's face receding into darkness. "Wait... please!"

Manny awoke with a gasp. Disoriented and sweating. His heart hammering against his ribs. The living room was dim in the afternoon light filtering through the blinds. The house was quiet. The air conditioning humming its constant white noise. *It was Just a dream.... It was just a dream.*

But he could still feel it. The light spreading through his body. The old man's sad smile. The words echoing: *"You're getting what you wished for."*

Manny sat up slowly, his body protesting and he Looked down at his hands. The discoloration had spread. Well past his knuckles now. Creeping toward his wrists. The texture undeniably rough, damaged... wrong. He touched his right hand with his left. He felt the roughness, the wrongness of it. *It's not possible.* But the dream had shown him the truth. The light transferring. The wish being granted. The old man giving him something.

Something that was changing him. *This isn't possible. The old man was just an old man. That's insane.* But his hands told a different story. And the dream was so vivid, more real than reality. It had shown him the moment it happened. The handshake. The transfer... The light... *What did you give me?*

No answer. Just the hum of the air conditioning and the evidence of his own changing body. Manny sat on the couch in the dimming afternoon light, staring at his hands. Trying to rationalize and explain it away. Trying to convince himself this was a simple medical concern... a rash, an infection, something a doctor could treat. But the dream lingered. The old man's words echoed: *"Careful what you wish for..."*

The house was silent. Karen resting and Maya was still at school. He was alone with this, whatever this was. Alone with the knowledge that something had been transferred to him. Something supernatural. Something he didn't understand and his body was changing in ways that couldn't be explained. It seemed that it couldn't be stopped nor couldn't be undone. Manny whispered into the empty room: "What have I done?"

There was no answer, only the slow, inexorable process of dying. Only the darkening of his hands and the rough texture of damaged skin spreading up his arms. Only the memory of golden light and an old man's sad smile. He was left with the certainty that he'd wished for something he didn't understand. And now he was getting exactly what he'd asked for.

Manny went into the kitchen and found Rosita still there, even though her shift should have ended hours ago. She was sitting at the kitchen table, a cup of tea cooling in front of her, waiting. "Señor Chavez. Sit."

It wasn't a request and so he sat down. Rosita studied his face for a long moment, her eyes seeing more than he wanted them to. "You are sick."

"Naw, I'm just tired."

"No." She shook her head. "I know tired and I know sick. And I know dying. You have the look of the third."

Manny's hands started shaking. He pressed them flat on the table. "Karen is better."

"Sí, she is... A miracle, no?" Rosita reached across the table and covered his hands with hers. They were warm, calloused, gentle. "But miracles, they have a cost, don't they. Everything has a cost."

"I don't know what you mean."

"I think you do." Her eyes held his, dark and knowing. "I have been a caregiver for many years. I have seen many things the doctors do not or cannot see. Because they look at bodies and diseases. I look at souls and sacrifices."

Manny felt tears come to fill his eyes. "I met someone. On the road.

An old man with a broken truck."

"Tell me."

Manny did just that... he told her about the prayer in the bathroom, about the old man on the desert highway, about the conversation and the handshake and the wish he'd made. To trade places with his wife. To let Karen live and he would take her place as the one dying. Rosita listened without interrupting. When he finished, she sat back in her chair, her expression sad but not surprised. "Mi abuelo... my grandfather, he told me stories when I was young. About angels who walk among us. About prayers that get answered in ways we do not expect. About love so strong it can change fate." She paused. "I did not always believe him. Until I became a caregiver. Until I saw the things I have seen."

"So, you think... you think it's real? That this is actually happening?"

"I think Karen was dying. Now she is not. I know you were well. Now you are not." Rosita's voice was gentle. "I think you made a trade, Señor Chavez, and the universe, it accepted."

Manny put his head in his hands. "What have I done?"

"You have loved completely and without condition. This is not selfishness." She stood, walked around the table, and put her hand on his shoulder. "In my village, we tell a story about the mother corn plant. You know this story?"

He shook his head no. "The mother corn, she grows tall and strong. She makes the ears of corn that feed the family. But to make those ears, she must give everything... all her energy and life force. When the corn is ready, the mother plant, she dies. She becomes dry and brown. But her children, they live. They feed the family. And from those seeds, new corn grows."

She squeezed his shoulder. "This is the circle of life, Señor Chavez. One generation gives everything so the next one can grow. The mother plant does not regret becoming the dry stalk. She does this with joy, because her children live. No one wants to die. That is human and is okay."

Rosita knelt beside his chair so she could look him in the eye. "But you have been given a gift, not the gift of dying, but the gift of knowing. Most people die suddenly, with words unsaid, with love unexpressed, with nothing prepared. You have time. Not much, maybe. But some."

"Time for what?"

"To say what needs saying. To make the peace and teach your daughter who you are. To love your wife with all that you have left."

She touched his face gently. "To become the father, you wish to be. You are the roots and earth of the family. A permanent presence for them. This is the way things are, Señor Chavez."

Manny was silent but Rosita knew from his face that he was uncertain of how things would turn out. "If you did not love them so much, dying would not scare you." She wiped his tears with her thumb. "But listen to me. You do not walk this path alone. I will be here for Karen, Maya, and for you. I will help them understand and remember. I will help them continue the circle after you are gone."

"Why would you do that?"

"Because this is why I became a hospice caregiver. Not to keep people alive, but to help them die well. To help families love each other through the hardest thing they will ever face." She smiled sadly. "You gave Karen life. I will help her live it. That is my part of the circle."

They sat together in the quiet kitchen, the weight of death and love and sacrifice filling the space between them.

"Señor Chavez," Rosita said finally. "You asked God for an angel. He sent you one. And that angel granted your prayer. Do not curse the answer because it costs you. Accept it and walk into it with courage. Show your family how to face death without fear and how to choose love even when it costs everything."

"I don't know if I can."

"Then I will teach you. That is what elders are for, no? To teach the young how to walk the hard roads." She stood, pulled him to his feet. "Now, you will go to your wife. You will hold her. You will be grateful for today, because today she is alive because of you. And tomorrow, we will face tomorrow."

Manny nodded, unable to speak. Rosita walked him to Karen's door, then paused. "One more thing. In my village, we do not fear death. We prepare for it. We honor it. We understand it is part of the circle. When your time comes, you will not be alone. I promise you this. You will be surrounded by love. And after... after, you will become something beautiful but still you will remain the roots and earth. The foundation of this family and journey into next life. That is not an ending, Señor Chavez. That is transformation."

She left him at the door, disappearing back into the kitchen, a quiet presence who had seen this circle turn many times before. And Manny understood, finally, that he was not alone. That the circle of life included not just birth and death, but also witnesses. Guides in the form of elders who had walked the path and could light the way for others. He opened the door to Karen's room and spent some time with her.

Chapter Seven - Good with your hands

Maya knelt on the bathroom floor, her phone propped against the wall, playing the YouTube video for the third time. The guy in the video made it look easy... unscrew the old P-trap, clean the threads, screw on the new one, done. But he wasn't lying on his back in a cramped bathroom with a leaking pipe dripping cold water onto his face. She wiped her forehead and rewound the video to the part about tightening the slip nuts. Left hand or right hand thread? She couldn't remember.

The sink had been leaking for over a week now. A slow, persistent drip that pooled under the cabinet and soaked through the towel she'd stuffed there. She'd mentioned it to her dad twice. Once in passing, once directly but he'd just nodded and said he'd get to it. He never did but she couldn't really blame him. Between work and Mom being sick along with whatever else was going on with him lately, fixing a leaky sink probably didn't make the priority list. But Maya was tired of emptying the bowl she'd put under the drip every morning. Tired of waiting for someone else to handle it. So, she was handling it herself.

She grabbed the adjustable wrench from her dad's toolbox. It was dusty and half-forgotten in the garage. She positioned herself under the sink. The P-trap was right there, a curved piece of PVC pipe with two connections. Simple enough... she fit the wrench around the first slip nut and turned. It didn't budge. She then repositioned, braced her feet against the cabinet frame, and tried again. This time it moved, just barely, with a groan of protest. "Come on," she muttered, twisting harder.

The nut loosened suddenly, and dirty water gushed out, splashing her face and soaking her shirt. "Shit!"

She scrambled backward, wiping her eyes, then grabbed the bucket she'd set nearby and shoved it under the drain. The water slowed to a trickle. She lay back down, wrench in hand, and kept working.

Twenty minutes later, the old P-trap was off, lying in the sink like a defeated opponent. She found the replacement parts in a dusty box in the garage, probably purchased months ago and forgotten. She held it in her hands now. She lined it up carefully, threading the slip nuts by hand first, just like the video said. Then she tightened them with the wrench, slow and steady, feeling the resistance as the rubber gaskets compressed. She turned the water back on with no drips.

She waited, watching the connections, but they stayed dry. Maya sat back on her heels and allowed herself a small smile. She'd done it. She fixed the damn sink on her own, with no help on her first try. She just needed to clean up the mess and put the tools away. She left the old P-trap in the sink as evidence. Not that anyone would notice.

Manny woke up on the couch wondering how he got there. Things were becoming a blur. He recalled talking to Rosita after driving home from work but then nothing... The ache in his bones had deepened into something almost unbearable, and the discoloration on his hands had spread past his knuckles, creeping up toward his wrists.

He sat on the couch for a moment, gathering the energy to move. The house looked quiet. Karen was probably still resting and Maya was probably in her room. He thought of making dinner, doing something useful. He forced himself off the couch and into the kitchen, the air was cool and still. He stood there for a moment, trying to remember what he was supposed to do next. His mind felt foggy, slow. Check on Karen. That was it.

He walked down the hall, moving carefully, and glanced into her room. She was asleep, curled on her side, breathing soft and even. She looked better every day. She had more color, more life. Whatever was happening to him, at least she was improving. He closed her door quietly and turned toward the bathroom. He needed to splash cold water on his face, wake himself up. That's when he saw it. The bathroom door was open; tools scattered on the floor. The old P-trap sitting in the sink. A bucket of dirty water. The cabinet under the sink was still open.

Manny stopped in the doorway, confused. Had he fixed this? He didn't remember fixing it. But the tools were out, the work was done. Maybe he had and just... forgot? His memory had been unreliable lately. Gaps and fog where clarity used to be. "Oh. Yeah. I fixed the sink."

Manny turned and Maya was standing in the hallway, phone in hand, looking at him with a mixture of defiance and uncertainty. "You fixed it?" she said. "The leak. The one I told you about. Twice. I fixed it..."

The words landed like a quiet accusation. He had forgotten. She'd asked, and he'd nodded and done nothing. "Can I see?" he asked.

Maya shrugged and stepped aside. Manny moved into the bathroom, crouched down... slowly, his knees protesting. And then he looked under the sink. The new P-trap was installed cleanly, the connections tight, the threads properly sealed. He reached up and tested the slip nuts. Solid. He stood, turned on the faucet, and watched. No leaks. Not even a drip.

He looked at Maya, who was still standing in the doorway, arms crossed. "This is good work," he said.

She blinked, surprised. "Yeah?"

"Really good. You replaced the whole P-trap?"

"YouTube video," she said, relaxing slightly. "It wasn't that hard."

"Still. A lot of people wouldn't even try. They'd just call a plumber."

Maya smiled a little. "We don't really have plumber money."

The truth of that hit Manny harder than it should have. "No," he admitted. "We don't."

He looked at the tools, at the evidence of her competence, and felt something twist in his chest. It was pride, mixed with guilt. She shouldn't have had to do this alone. "I'm sorry kiddo. I didn't fix this," he said quietly. "You told me, and I just... I forgot."

"You've been busy."

"That's not an excuse."

Maya shrugged, but her expression softened. "I didn't mind. I kind of liked it, actually. Figuring it out was part of the fun."

Manny studied her... really looked at her, for the first time in what felt like months. When had she grown up? When had she become capable and self-reliant and able to fix a sink on her own? "You know," he said, "you get that from me."

Maya raised an eyebrow. "What?"

"Being good with your hands. Figuring things out and fixing things."

She scoffed lightly. "You haven't fixed anything around here in months."

It stung because it was true. "I know. But I used to. Before everything got... complicated."

He gestured to the bathtub. "You mind if I sit for a second?"

Maya hesitated, then sat on the closed toilet lid. They faced each other in the small bathroom, tools still scattered on the floor between them. "I grew up doing this kind of stuff," Manny said. "My dad... your grandpa. He made sure I knew how to fix things. Cars, engines, anything mechanical."

Maya's expression shifted. She rarely heard him talk about his father. "I didn't know that."

"Yeah. He was a diesel mechanic. Master mechanic, actually. Worked for Detroit Diesel for thirty years."

"What's Detroit Diesel?"

"Big engine manufacturer. They made diesel engines for trucks, buses, and heavy equipment. Industrial stuff." Manny smiled at the memory. "My dad was... incredible with engines. He could hear something wrong just by listening. He knew every part, every system. People would bring him engines that nobody else could fix, and he'd figure it out. Always."

Maya leaned forward slightly, interested. "What was he like?"

Manny thought about it. "Tough... Quiet. He was the kind of guy who didn't talk a lot, but when he did, you listened. He used to say, 'If a man built it, a man can fix it.'" He paused. " And 'A person who can fix things will never be helpless.'"

"That's kind of cool," Maya said.

"It was. I grew up in his garage. Every weekend, he'd have me out there, handing him tools, watching him work. He'd explain everything. 'This is the crankshaft. This is the piston. This is how combustion works.' I was like eight years old, learning about diesel compression ratios."

Maya smiled. "Did you like it?"

"I loved it. There was something... satisfying about taking something broken and making it work again. It was like solving a puzzle, except the puzzle was real, so it mattered."

"So why didn't you become a mechanic?"

Manny paused. It was a fair question. "I thought about it. But being a diesel mechanic... it's hard on your body. My dad's back was destroyed by the time he retired. His hands were a mess. Scars, arthritis, constant pain."

He looked down at his own hands, darkened and damaged now for different reasons. "I wanted something stable," he continued. "Something with benefits, retirement, and security. So, I went into nuclear operations. It's stable work, good pay and I could support a family." He met Maya's eyes. "But I never stopped being good with my hands. I just used them differently."

Maya was quiet for a moment, processing. Then she said, "I've been thinking about maybe taking auto shop next semester."

Manny's face lit up. "Yeah?"

"I don't know. My counselor says I should focus on college-prep classes. But I kind of want to learn how cars work."

"You should take it," Manny said firmly.

"Really?"

"Absolutely. Knowing how to work on cars and how to fix things... that's a life skill. You'll always need it. And honestly?" He leaned forward. "If you've got the interest and the aptitude, you should pursue it. Don't let anyone tell you it's not academic enough or not for girls or whatever."

Maya looked down, a small smile playing on her lips. "Thanks."

"You did good work here," Manny said, gesturing to the sink. "I'm proud of you."

The words hung in the air between them. Maya looked up, surprised, and for a moment neither of them spoke.

"Thanks, Dad," she said quietly.

The word Dad. It felt fragile and warm at the same time. Maya pulled out her phone, checking the calendar. "Oh. Um. I have a parent-teacher conference next week."

"Yeah?"

"It's not a big deal. Just a check-in. You probably don't need to come."

Manny straightened. "I want to come."

Maya looked up, genuinely surprised. "You do?"

"If you want me there, I'll be there."

She hesitated. She wasn't used to this... to him offering and being present. "Mom usually goes."

"I know. But if she's not feeling up to it, I can go. Or we can both go."

"She's feeling better, actually. A lot better."

"Then we'll both go," Manny said. "If that's okay with you."

Maya studied him for a moment, then nodded slowly. "Yeah. Okay."

"When is it?"

She told him the date and time. Manny pulled out his phone and added it to his calendar right there, in front of her. She watched him do it, and something in her expression softened. They stood, and Maya started gathering the tools. Manny bent to help, moving slowly, and she noticed. "Dad? What's wrong with your hands?"

Manny looked down. The darkening had spread past his wrists now, creeping up his forearms like a bruise that wouldn't heal. The skin looked rough, and damaged. He pulled his sleeves down quickly. "Nothing. Just... irritation from work. Chemicals or something."

Maya frowned. "That doesn't look like nothing."

"I'll get it checked out. Don't worry."

But she did worry. He looked pale, exhausted, and older than he should. "Are you okay? Like... really okay?"

Manny forced a smile. "I'm fine. Just tired... long shifts."

She didn't believe him, but she didn't push. Not yet. They carried the tools out to the garage together, working in silence. Manny showed her how to clean the wrench properly before storing it, wiping it down with an old rag. "Dad would've killed me if I put dirty tools back in the box," he said. Maya smiled. "Noted."

They put the toolbox back on its shelf, and Manny paused, looking at it. It had been his father's once. It was battered metal, scarred from decades of use. Now it was his and someday, maybe, it would be Maya's. "If you ever want to work on something together," Manny said, "fix something, build something... let me know."

"Yeah," Maya said. "Maybe."

It wasn't a commitment, but it wasn't a rejection either.

They headed back inside. Maya paused at the stairs, her hand on the railing.

"Hey, Dad?"

Manny turned. "Yeah?"

"Thanks. For noticing. The sink, I mean. And... the other stuff."

Manny felt his throat tighten. "Thanks for taking care of it. And for giving me a chance to show up."

Maya nodded and headed upstairs. Manny watched her go, listening to her footsteps fade, then her door close softly. He stood alone in the hallway, exhausted and aching, but feeling something else too. It was a rebuilding of a connection. Perhaps small and fragile, but real.

He looked down at his hands again. The damage was spreading. He could feel it in his bones, in the way his body was slowly failing. But he'd shown up for Maya today. He'd connected with her, praised her, made a promise to attend her conference. That had to count for something. In the garage earlier, standing beside the toolbox, he'd had a thought that came from somewhere deep and instinctive: *She's got it. She's got what Dad gave me. She'll be okay.*

He didn't know why he'd thought it in those terms... *she'll be okay* as if he wouldn't be there to see it. But the thought had come anyway, unbidden and certain. *Even when I'm gone, she'll be okay.*

He shook his head, dismissing it. He was just tired. Just worn down. He wasn't going anywhere. But as he walked to the kitchen to see about dinner, his hands trembling and his vision blurring at the edges, part of him wondered if his body knew something his mind didn't want to accept. That time was running out. That he was dying so Karen could live. And Maya was capable, resourceful, good with her hands. She would have to learn to be okay without him. He braced himself against the counter and closed his eyes, willing the dizziness to pass. Not yet, he thought. Not yet. I still have things to do and promises to keep. The parent-teacher conference and showing up for Maya. Being there for Karen. Just a little more time but the darkness spreading across his hands whispered a different truth. Time was the one thing he no longer had.

Chapter Eight – Medical Evac

Manny barely remembered the drive home from Palo Verde. The thirty-five minutes on State Route 85 blurred together... highway lines, desert landscape, the setting sun bleeding orange into purple. His hands gripped the steering wheel so tightly his knuckles ached, but it was the only thing keeping him conscious. *Just make it home. Just get there. He had avoided Mr. Reed and ignored James's pleas to stay home sick.*

By the time he pulled into the driveway, his entire body was shaking. He was cold despite the desert heat. Exhausted beyond anything he'd ever experienced. He turned off the engine and sat for a moment, gathering what little strength remained. The house looked warm. The lights were on in the windows. Karen's room. Maya's room. Home. *I made it.*

He got out of the truck slowly, carefully. Each movement was deliberate. Walking to the front door felt like climbing a mountain. The familiar routine... Place the key in the lock, turn, push. Inside, the air conditioning hummed. Somewhere upstairs, he could hear the faint sound of Maya's music.

Manny stopped in the hallway, listening. It was television audio. Not the medical equipment sounds he'd grown accustomed to or the labored breathing in silence. He heard actual TV voices, a laugh track, the sound of a show playing at normal volume. Karen hadn't watched TV by herself in months. Manny moved toward her room, the door partially open, warm light spilling into the hallway. He pushed it open and stopped. Karen was sitting up in bed. Not propped against pillows at a careful angle. Actually, sitting upright, back straight, remote control in her hand, eyes focused on the television mounted on the wall. She looked... God, she looked *alive*.

Color in her cheeks, not even a hint of the gray paleness he'd seen for months. Not the exhausted translucence of someone fading. It was real and healthy color. Her eyes were bright, alert, engaged with what she was watching. She turned when she heard the door, and her face lit up. "Manny! You're home."

Then her expression shifted. Concern replacing the smile. "Honey, are you okay? You look terrible."

Manny opened his mouth to respond, but before he could speak, Maya appeared behind him in the hallway. "Dad! Did you see? Mom's up! She's been up all afternoon!"

Maya was practically glowing. She was all smiles, energy radiating from her. The kind of happiness he hadn't seen in her face in years. Then she really looked at him. Her smile faltered. "Dad?"

Manny couldn't make it any further. His legs gave out... not dramatically, just a slow failure of strength. He stumbled toward the living room, made it to the couch, and collapsed onto it. The shaking got worse. He was freezing. The house was temperature-controlled, comfortable, but he felt like he'd been left in a freezer. "Dad, what's wrong?"

Maya rushed over, grabbing the blanket from the back of the couch and throwing it over him. "I'm fine," Manny managed. "Just... tired."

"You're freezing." Maya's hands touched his arm through the blanket, and she pulled back slightly. "Dad, you're shaking."

From her room, Karen's voice carried. Stronger than it had been in months, able to project now. "Maya, bring me the phone."

Maya hesitated, torn between her father shivering on the couch and her mother's request. "Go ahead," Manny said, forcing the words out. "I'm okay."

Maya looked at him for another moment with doubt written all over her face. She then hurried toward Karen's room. Manny closed his eyes, pulled the blanket tighter, and tried to stop shaking. I *just need to rest. Just for a minute.*

In Karen's room, Maya found her mother already sitting on the edge of the bed, preparing to stand. "Your dad's phone. It should be in his jacket pocket."

Maya retrieved it from where Manny had dropped his jacket by the door and brought it to her mother. Karen took it, scrolling through the contacts with steady hands. "Who are you calling?"

"James Chen. Your dad's coworker."

"Why?"

Karen found the number, pressed dial. "Your father won't make it to work tomorrow. Someone needs to know."

The call connected. Karen put it on speaker so Maya could hear. "Hello?"

"Mr. Chen? This is Karen. Manny's wife."

A pause. Then James's voice, careful: "Mrs. Chavez. Is everything okay?"

"Not really. Manny just got home and he's really sick. I wanted to let you know… he won't be able to come in tomorrow."

"How sick?"

Karen glanced at Maya, then toward the living room where Manny lay shivering under the blanket. "He can barely move. He's shaking. He looks awful."

Another pause. When James spoke again, his voice was heavy with something that sounded like guilt. "He looked real bad today. Real bad. I was worried."

"I think he needs to see a doctor," Karen said.

"I think so too." James was quiet for a moment. "Tell your mom..." He paused, realizing he was talking to Karen. "Mrs. Chavez, I'll stop by after my shift. Around eight. I want to check on him."

"Thank you, Mr. Chen."

"And Mrs. Chavez? It's good to hear your voice. Manny said you were having a good day."

Karen smiled slightly. "I'm having an amazing day."

"I'm glad. I'll see you tonight."

The call ended. Maya stared at her mother. "You're calling his work? Making decisions?"

Karen looked at her daughter. "Someone has to and I can now."

Maya sat with her mother for a while after the call, watching her change channels, sip water from the glass on her bedside table without assistance, adjust the pillows behind her back with easy movements. It was surreal. Days ago ... *days...* her mother could barely lift her head. Eating was a struggle and speaking more than a few words triggered coughing fits that shook her entire frame. Now she was sitting up, alert, functional and *present*. "Mom, how are you feeling?"

Karen considered the question. "Better. So much better. I don't understand it, but I feel... good."

"This is a miracle."

Karen's expression softened. "Maybe it is."

Maya glanced toward the living room. Through the doorway, she could see her father buried under the blanket, barely moving except for the occasional shiver. Back to her mother, glowing with health. The contrast should have been obvious. But Maya didn't see it. She couldn't see it. Too focused on the joy of her mother's recovery to notice the pattern. Too relieved to question the timing. Miracles happened, right? Maybe the new medication worked. Maybe prayer worked. She didn't see they were trading places.

James Chen arrived at eight pm sharp, carrying a container of soup his wife Linda had made. Maya let him in, led him to the living room where Manny still lay on the couch. "Hey, man. How you feeling?"

Manny's eyes opened. "Been better."

His voice was hoarse, weak. James set the soup on the coffee table and crouched beside the couch, studying his friend. "You're burning up." James touched Manny's forehead briefly. "You have a fever."

"I'm cold."

"That's the fever. You need a doctor."

"I'll be fine."

"You're not fine."

Manny didn't argue. He didn't have the energy. James stood, turned to Maya. "Your mom...she's really up? Doing better?"

Maya nodded. "Do you want to see her?"

James glanced at Manny, who waved a weak hand. "Go ahead."

Maya brought James to Karen's room and James stopped in the doorway. He'd expected... well, he wasn't sure what he'd expected.

Manny had told him this morning that Karen was having a good day. But James had known Karen Chavez for years, had watched her decline over the past few months. He'd expected to see a dying woman having a slightly better afternoon. Instead, he saw Karen sitting up, alert, smiling, *healthy*. "James. It's been a long time."

She extended her hand. James shook it, stunned by the firm grip, the warmth. "Mrs. Chavez. You look... really good."

"I'm feeling really good. For the first time in months."

James didn't know what to say. The contrast was staggering. Manny falling apart in the living room. Karen recovered and vibrant in here. Both happening simultaneously. It didn't make sense. But he wasn't going to question a miracle. "I'm glad," he said finally. "Really glad."

Five days later

Manny had stayed home. He was too sick to work, too weak to argue. And in those five days, the exchange became undeniable.

Day 2

Karen got out of bed unassisted and walked to the bathroom on her own. She came back smiling, marveling at the simple act of walking without pain. Maya watched with tears in her eyes, filming it on her phone, texting friends about the miracle. Manny slept eighteen hours and woke up worse. He had nausea, chills, with every joint aching.

Day 3

Karen went upstairs for the first time in months. She actually descended the stairs, gripping the railing but not needing support. She sat at the kitchen table and ate a full meal of eggs, toast, orange juice. She finished everything as Maya cried with joy. Manny had tried to get up from the couch to join them, but he could only manage two steps and he had to sit back down. His hands were worse. The discoloration was spreading up his forearms now, the skin rough and damaged, and peeling in places.

Day 4

Karen took a short walk in the backyard. It was just five minutes, but she stood in the desert sun, breathed the warm air, and smiled at the sky. Maya took photos, captured the moment, texted them to relatives with messages of hope and gratitude. Manny had nightmares, feverish, disorienting dreams. The old man appeared, light transferring, and the warmth spreading. In the dreams, he saw himself becoming roots, spreading deep into earth. Becoming foundation. Becoming a tree. He woke covered in sweat, confused, terrified. *Am I dying or changing? Which is worse?*

Day 5

Karen talked about scheduling an oncology follow-up appointment. She wanted to see if the scans would show improvement. She was hopeful... more than hopeful. She felt *healed*. Maya scheduled it eagerly, already imagining the doctor's shock, the confirmation of the miracle.

Manny woke with severe nausea. He couldn't eat much. But he was hiding it well. He forced himself up. "I need to go back to work."

Day 6. Morning.

Karen tried to stop him. "Manny, you're not well."

"I'll be fine. I can't miss any more time."

He dressed slowly, each movement requiring focus. Clipped his dosimeter badge to his chest out of habit, even though he barely registered the motion. Maya watched from the kitchen, worried. "Dad, maybe you should listen to Mom."

"I have to go. I'll be okay."

He wasn't okay. Everyone could see it. But he went anyway, driven by some desperate need to be functional, to be working, to be *something* other than the dying man on the couch.

Palo Verde Nuclear Generating Station looked the same as always. Imposing, industrial, and secure. Manny parked in his usual spot, walked slowly toward the entrance. The security guard barely recognized him.

"Chavez? You sure you should be here?"

"I'm cleared for duty."

He wasn't. He'd just shown up. The guard hesitated, then waved him through. "Alright. But you look rough, man."

Manny nodded and kept walking. Each step was a monumental effort. Other workers stared as he passed, whispered to each other. He ignored them, focused on reaching his station. James saw him coming from across the observation deck. His face fell. "Manny, what are you doing here? You shouldn't be here."

"I'm fine."

"You look like hell."

Manny sat down at his station, logged in with shaking hands. The monitors swam in and out of focus. He tried to type a log entry... gibberish appeared on screen. He deleted it and tried again. It was worse. His hands wouldn't cooperate. His eyes wouldn't focus. His body was betraying him.

Alicia, one of the engineers, approached. "Chavez, your hands... what happened?"

She was staring at his forearms where the sleeves had ridden up slightly, revealing the dark, damaged skin, peeling in places. Manny pulled his sleeves down. "Nothing. I'm fine."

"That doesn't look like nothing..."

She didn't finish. Because Gerald Reed had appeared. Reed took one look at Manny and his expression hardened, not with anger, but with the clinical assessment of someone who recognized a medical emergency. His military training and the routine of the years spent doing it. He'd seen wounded soldiers and he knew what serious looked like. He yelled out loud... "Medic, stat."

He keyed his radio without taking his eyes off Manny. "Medical to Cooling Pool Observation Deck Two. Immediate."

To Manny: "Chavez, you are unfit for duty. Period."

"Sir, I can..."

Reed cut him off with a raised hand. Not harsh. Almost gentle.

"Soldier, you need help. Let them help you."

He turned to James. "Mr. Chen, take over his duties and call in support as needed."

"Yes, sir."

Reed looked back at Manny one last time. His voice softer, the military bearing giving way to something almost compassionate. "Go with the medics. That's an order son. Evac him out of my department."

Two medics arrived with a stretcher within minutes. Manny tried to protest. This was humiliating, he could walk but when he tried to stand, his legs wouldn't hold him. They helped him onto the stretcher. Strapped him in and checked his vitals. "Pulse is rapid. BP low. Temp 103."

One of the medics looked at Manny's hands, gently pushed up his sleeves. "These look like radiation burns. Severe ones."

Manny's voice weak: "I wear my dosimeter. I'm within limits."

The medic glanced at the badge clipped to Manny's chest. "We'll see about that."

They wheeled him away as James watched from his station, worry etched deep in his face. Mr. Reed stood with his clipboard, already documenting the incident, already thinking about safety reviews and investigations. And Manny lay on the stretcher, staring at the ceiling as they moved him through the hallways toward Medical, wondering how everything had fallen apart so fast.

The medical bay was sterile, bright, clinical. They transferred Manny to an examination table, and started running tests immediately. Dr. Hassan, the plant's head physician, examined Manny's arms carefully. "How long have you had these?"

"Few days. Maybe a week."

"And you didn't report them?"

Manny didn't have a good answer. Dr. Hassan checked Manny's dosimeter badge, reading the exposure levels. "Your badge reads within safe limits."

"So... I'm not...?"

"Your symptoms say otherwise." Dr. Hassan frowned. "Classic acute radiation syndrome. Nausea, fever, skin damage, weakness. But your badge says you haven't been exposed."

He looked at the dosimeter more carefully, then took it off Manny's chest. "Let me run a diagnostic on the badge itself."

Ten minutes later, Dr. Hassan returned with a grim expression. "Your dosimeter has been malfunctioning. Internal failure. It's been reading false low for..." He paused, checking the diagnostic report. "We can't determine how long. Could be days. Could be weeks."

Manny stared at him. "What does that mean?"

"It means you've been exposed to radiation well above safe limits, and your badge didn't catch it. It failed to alarm. It didn't warn you. You've been working in conditions that should have triggered immediate evacuation, and you had no way of knowing."

The words landed like blows. "How much exposure?"

"We're running tests now to determine that but based on your symptoms. I'd say significant, dangerous levels. Potentially..." Dr. Hassan paused. "This is serious, Mr. Chavez. Potentially fatal."

The room tilted. Manny gripped the edge of the examination table. "Fatal."

"Acute Radiation Syndrome. Your cells have been damaged at a fundamental level. We'll do everything we can, but I need you to understand the severity."

Questions followed. Where was he at when he was exposed? What areas had he worked in? When did the dosimeter fail? How much radiation? The doctor explained there would be an investigation... worker's comp, safety review, potential liability, union involvement. But Manny barely heard any of it. All he heard was... *fatal*. What he truly heard... *the wish was granted.*

They sedated him for further testing. As Manny slipped into unconsciousness, the dream returned. He was standing on State Route 85 at dusk. The old man beside his truck, watching Manny with sad, knowing eyes. "Well, son you seem to be on your way."

Manny's dream-voice trembling: "Am I... I'm really dying?"

The old man smiled gently, mournful. "You did it for them. You are the family's foundation of love."

Images flooded Manny's mind. He saw roots spreading deep into the earth. They were permanent, unshakable and holding firm. A tree standing for decades with shade and shelter. But also, a grave. An Earth. burial... "I don't understand," Manny said. "The burns, the sickness... is it radiation or...?"

"You wished to take her place. You are!"

"But what's happening to me?"

The old man's expression infinitely sad. "You're dying, son. That's what you asked for. To die so she could live."

"And the tree?"

"That's your choice. How you want to remain."

Understanding broke over Manny like dawn. Not transforming magically into a tree. Dying from radiation. The mechanism, the method, the natural consequence of a supernatural wish. But the tree... the tree could still be part of it. A choice. A request.

Bury me with a tree over my grave. Let my body decompose, become earth, nourish roots. Let the tree be the place Maya can visit. Let me be present that way. I can be a foundation... a permanent place to return to. Not magic but meaning. The old man began to fade. "The exchange is nearly complete. Her life for yours. You kept your promise. Now it's her turn."

Manny woke in the medical bay, groggy from sedation. Dr. Hassan stood beside the bed. "Mr. Chavez. We need to discuss next steps."

"What next steps?"

"Hospitalization. Radiation treatment. Supportive care. This isn't something we can handle here at the plant. You need to go to a hospital with oncology and radiation specialists."

"No."

Dr. Hassan blinked. "I'm sorry?"

"I want to go home."

"Mr. Chavez, this is serious. Potentially life-threatening. You need intensive care."

"I know what it is. I know what it means. I want to be with my family."

They argued. Dr. Hassan listed the risks, the dangers, the consequences of refusing treatment. But Manny was adamant. Finally, reluctantly, they released him AMA (Against Medical Advice). They gave him medication and instructions. They scheduled a follow-up appointment with specialists and warned him repeatedly that his prognosis was poor. Manny signed the paperwork with shaking hands, numb and overwhelmed. He understood now. He was dying and Karen was living. The wish had been granted.

James drove him home. They rode in silence for most of the drive. Finally, James asked quietly, "The dosimeter failure. How long?"

"They don't know. Weeks, maybe."

"Jesus, Manny."

More silence. Desert landscape passing outside the windows. The sun setting, painting the sky in impossible colors. "What happens now?" James asked. Manny looked at his hands. They were damaged, discolored, proof of what had happened. "I go home. I spend time with my family. And I... prepare."

James didn't ask what he meant. They both knew. James pulled into the driveway as dusk settled over the desert. "Thank you," Manny said.

"Call if you need anything. Anything at all."

"I will."

Manny got out of the car slowly, walked toward the front door. James waited until he was inside before driving away.

Inside, the house was warm and lit. Karen was in the living room... *in the living room*, not her bedroom. She was reading a book in the armchair. She looked up as Manny entered. Her face changed immediately. "Manny, what happened?"

Maya appeared from the kitchen. Saw her father's face. It was pale, devastated, exhausted beyond measure. "What did they do to you?"

Manny sat heavily on the couch. Every word cost him. "Radiation exposure. My dosimeter was malfunctioning. I've been getting exposed for... they don't know how long."

Karen stood, walked over to him, strong and steady and sat beside him. "How bad?"

Manny met her eyes. "Bad."

Silence as the air conditioning hummed. Outside, the desert evening settled into darkness. Karen reached for him. "Come here."

And for the first time in months, maybe years... she was the one strong enough to hold him. She was the one who wrapped her arms around him while he fell apart. The reversal was almost complete.

Maya watched from across the room, still not understanding. Mom better. Dad is sick. Both true but separate in her mind. They were not connected. Not yet anyways. Manny, was in Karen's arms, she sensed he was dying and she was living. Manny Knew the wish had been fulfilled and the promise kept. But how would he tell them? How would he explain that his death was saving her life? He didn't know yet. But soon, he'd have to. And soon, he'd make a request: *When I die, don't bury me in a traditional cemetery. Plant a tree. Let me be the roots. Let that be where Maya visits me.* But not tonight. Tonight, he just let Karen hold him. And tried to remember what it felt like to be held by his strong wife. Because soon... very soon that would be a memory too.

Chapter Nine – Truth be told

Manny sat on the couch in the living room, wearing long sleeves despite the Arizona heat, trying to summon the energy to move. Several days had passed since the diagnosis. He was on medical leave with worker's comp paperwork. An Investigation was ongoing at the plant. None of it mattered much. What mattered was that he was dying, and every moment felt borrowed.

He heard movement from Karen's room. The door opening, footsteps in the hallway and then she appeared. Manny looked up and felt his breath catch. Karen stood in the doorway wearing jeans. Real jeans and a soft blue sweater with shoes on her feet. Her hair was brushed and pulled back. The color had returned in her cheeks. No longer hospital gowns or pajamas. She wasn't wearing the clothes of someone confined to a sickbed. She was *dressed* like a person going out into the world. "Karen?"

She smiled, tentative and genuine. Then she did a small turn. "What do you think?"

Manny's eyes filled with tears. "You look beautiful."

"I feel good." She walked toward him, steady on her feet, no assistance needed. "Really good."

She sat beside him on the couch. The role reversal was striking. For months, he'd sat beside her bed and now she sat beside him on the couch. Karen took his hand gently. Her fingers were strong and warm. His were rough and damaged beneath his long sleeves. "Maya has parent-teacher conferences tonight," she said quietly. "I was thinking..." She paused, looked at him carefully. "Would you like to go with me?"

Manny stared at her. "You want to go?"

"I can. For the first time in years, I actually can."

"Yes." He didn't hesitate despite the exhaustion weighing on him like stones. "Absolutely yes."

"Are you sure? You're not feeling well."

"I'm on sick leave anyway. I want to do this."

I need to do this. While I still can. He didn't say it. But she heard it anyway. He could see it in her eyes. The understanding, the sadness along with the urgency. They both knew time was limited. Neither said it out loud.

Maya came home from school around four, backpack slung over her shoulder, earbuds in as she was already moving toward the stairs. Then she saw her mother in the living room. DRESSED. Sitting up and looking alive. Maya stopped dead. "Mom?"

Karen stood up, actually stood, walked over on steady legs and pulled Maya into a hug. A real hug with strong arms and no fragility. She was without pain. Maya started crying before she could stop herself. "You're up. You're actually up and dressed."

"I am." Karen pulled back, smiled through her own tears. "And we're going to your teacher conferences tonight."

"Both of you?"

Maya looked past her mother to where her dad sat on the couch. He looked terrible. He was pale, exhausted and barely able to hold his head up. But he was smiling. "Both of us," Manny said.

Maya's emotions tangled together... the joy that her mom could come and the terror about her dad. This was what she'd wanted for years. Both parents showing up, being involved, being *there*. But not like this. Not with her dad looking like he might collapse at any moment. "What time do we need to leave?" Maya asked quietly.

"Six," Karen said. "We have time."

They arrived at Maya's high school just before six o'clock. Karen walked steadily and confidently while Manny moved slowly, carefully, with one hand on the car door for support before straightening and following them toward the entrance. Maya walked between them, hyper-aware of the contrast. Other parents in the parking lot lightly stared. Some knew Karen had been sick for quite some time and were surprised to see her. The news traveled fast in their community. They saw her now and their faces registered shock, joy, the kind of wonder reserved for miracles. But Maya saw them glance at her father too, confusion crossing their features. Inside, the hallways were the familiar painted cinder block, fluorescent lights and bulletin boards covered with student work. They found the biology classroom first.

Mr. Patterson greeted them warmly. "Mr. and Mrs. Chavez. Good to see you both."

If he noticed Manny's condition, he didn't comment. "Maya is doing well. Solid B+ student. With a little more focus, she could push right into an A."

Manny leaned forward, listening intently. "What can she do to improve?"

His hand shook slightly as he pulled out a small notebook. Maya watched him struggle to grip the pen. "The lab reports are strong," Mr.

Patterson said. "But the written tests could have more detail added. I'd suggest reviewing the study guides more thoroughly before exams."

Manny wrote it down. His handwriting was shaky but legible. "I'll help her with that," he said.

Maya felt something crack in her chest. He was HERE. Finally, here. Asking questions and taking notes. He was caring about the details. This was what she'd wanted but he could barely sit upright in the chair.

English was next. As Ms. Rodriguez smiled when they entered. "Maya is a creative writer. Thoughtful analysis. She has a real voice."

"That's wonderful to hear," Karen said.

Manny asked, "What should she focus on for college applications? What would make her stand out?"

Ms. Rodriguez considered the question and answered. "Her personal essays will be strong as she writes from the heart. I'd encourage her to develop a portfolio, maybe enter some writing contests and submit some articles to literary magazines."

Manny nodded, writing again. His breathing was a little labored now. Math class and then History. Each teacher had feedback and in each conversation, Manny was engaged, present and asking questions. Maya watched him fight to stay focused, to stay upright, to be the father she'd needed him to be for years. And her heart swelled watching him be there tonight.

After the last conference, they sat in the school cafeteria. Most of the other families had already left. The space was quiet except for their voices. Manny looked at Maya across the table. "You applied to NAU and ASU. Have you thought about what you want to study?"

Maya shifted uncomfortably. "Maybe biology? I don't know yet."

"You don't have to know," Manny said. "But you should think about what excites you."

Karen added, "Follow what makes you curious."

Maya felt the weight of their attention. Both parents actually *listening* to her. Really listening. "Maybe environmental science," she said slowly. "Or maybe teaching... or research. I'm not sure."

"Whatever you choose," Manny said, his voice thick with emotion, "do it because it matters to you. Not because it's safe or expected."

He paused, meeting her eyes. "I spent too many years just going through the motions. Don't do that, try to live deliberately and make it count."

The urgency in his words hit her like a wave. "Dad, are you okay?"

Manny's eyes were wet. "I'm fine. I just... I'm proud of you. I don't say that enough."

Maya reached across the table and took his hand. His skin was rough, damaged, but warm. "I know," she whispered.

In the parking lot, Manny stopped. "Let's get dinner. My treat."

"Dad, you're on medical leave. We should save money."

"I'm on sick leave pay, and worker's comp is covering medical. We're okay." He looked at Karen. "Where do you want to go?"

Karen's face lit up. "Casa Mariachi... carne asada."

Her favorite Mexican restaurant. They hadn't been in over a year... she'd been too sick. Manny smiled, "Then that's where we're going."

At Casa Mariachi, Karen insisted on going inside. "I want to walk and use my legs."

Manny stayed in the car, too exhausted to move. Maya went with her mother inside the restaurant. It smelled like grilled meat, cilantro, lime. It was warm and familiar. Karen ordered at the counter, carne asada plates for three, chips and guacamole, horchata. The cashier, a middle-aged woman who'd worked there for years, recognized her. "Mrs. Chavez! So good to see you! You look wonderful!"

Karen beamed. "Thank you. I feel wonderful."

Maya stood beside her mother, watching her order food like a normal person. Standing in line, smiling, talking and alive. It was surreal, kinda like a miracle. But Dad was not doing well in the car outside. How could both things be true?

Back at the house, Karen set the table for dinner. She hadn't done this in years as Maya helped, still processing everything. The conferences, her dad's engagement, her mom's health and the impossible reversal of it all. Manny sat on the couch, gathering his strength to move to the table. When the food was ready, he joined them slowly. He sat down carefully while Karen opened the containers. The smell of carne asada filling the kitchen as she took a bite and closed her eyes. "Oh my God. I forgot how good this is."

She laughed. It was genuine, joyful, *living*. Maya watched her mother eat with appetite, with pleasure, with the kind of enjoyment that came from being denied something and finally having it again. Manny picked at his food. The nausea made eating difficult. But he smiled, watching them be *present* in the moment.

Maya talked about her friends, about school drama and college applications. Karen asked questions, engaged, interested. Manny added comments, made jokes. For a few minutes, they were just a normal family eating takeout and talking about nothing important. Which was everything important. Maya saw her father's hands tremble when he lifted his fork and the exhaustion in his eyes. She wasn't sure what she saw. It was almost like he was fighting to stay at the table, to not leave this moment.

After dinner, Manny stood to help clean up. "I'll get the dishes."

He took two steps toward the kitchen and swayed. His hand shot out, caught the wall. "Manny..." Karen was up immediately.

"I'm okay." He made it to the couch. "Just need to sit for a minute."

He lay down, exhaustion finally winning. "Just for a minute..."

His eyes closed and sleep took him instantly. It wasn't peaceful, he collapsed with labored breathing, his skin pale in the lamplight. Karen and Maya watched from the kitchen. "Is he okay?" Maya's voice was soft and frightened.

"He's exhausted. The doctors said the radiation exposure... it's taking a toll."

"How bad is it?"

Karen's face tightened. "Bad."

They cleaned up quietly, putting away leftovers and washing dishes. The clink of plates and running water the only sounds as Manny was asleep in the next room. Maya finally asked the question she'd been holding back. "What did the doctors say? Exactly?"

Karen chose her words carefully. "Acute radiation syndrome. From exposure at the plant."

"Will he get better?"

Silence. Karen wanted to protect her, to shield her from the truth for as long as possible. But Maya deserved honesty. Or at least as much honesty as Karen could give without breaking her daughter's heart completely. "We hope so," Karen said quietly. "Time will tell."

"What does that mean?"

"It means we make the most of the time we have."

Maya's voice dropped to almost a whisper. "How much time?"

"I don't know."

The truth and a lie. Karen didn't know exactly but she knew enough. She had seen enough in Manny's decline, in the way he looked at them, in the urgency of tonight. Maya sat down hard at the kitchen table as tears started. "This isn't fair. You were sick and you were dying. Now you're better and he's..."

She couldn't finish. Karen sat beside her, took her hand. "I know. It doesn't make sense."

She didn't know what to tell her. "But he's trying," Karen said. "Did you see him tonight? Really there, really present."

"Why now? Why when he's so sick?"

"Maybe that's when we finally figure out what matters." Karen squeezed Maya's hand. "He wants to know you. So, he's trying to give you everything he can, while he still can."

Maya started crying in earnest. "I don't want him to die."

"Neither do I."

They held each other in the quiet kitchen. The dishes were half washed and the leftovers put away. In the next room Manny was sleeping, his time was running out.

Later that night, after Maya had gone upstairs overwhelmed, processing, escaping to her room... Karen sat beside Manny on the couch.

She covered him with a blanket. Watched him sleep. She was healthy for the first time in years. She could breathe without pain. She could move without exhaustion. She could eat, walk, and *live* while it looked as though he was dying. The timing was too perfect. Her recovery was too miraculous. His decline was too sudden. The old man on the highway. Manny had told her the story. The wish... She wondered but dismissed it...

"I'd switch places with her."

Karen put her hand on Manny's chest, felt his heartbeat. Strong but labored. Fighting but failing. She whispered into the quiet: "What did you do, Manny?"

Karen sat in the dark beside Manny on the couch, tears streaming down her face, hand on his chest feeling his labored heartbeat. The moment was interrupted as the front door opened. Rosita appeared in the doorway, took one look at the scene... Manny asleep, Karen crying beside him and she understood immediately. "Señora," she said quietly. "Come. Let him rest."

Karen didn't want to leave Manny's side, but Rosita's gentle insistence pulled her to the kitchen. They sat at the table, the light dim, the house quiet except for Manny's breathing from the other room. Karen was beside herself with worry... "What is happening?"

"Señora, in time we will know more but for now we must wait. You must be careful with yourself as you are just beginning to feel better."

As they sat in silence, she could hear his breathing just above the hum of the air conditioning. The weight of understanding settling over her like a shroud. She knew something was wrong, she didn't want to believe it. But she knew. Had he'd wished to take her place. And somehow... impossibly, supernaturally the wish had been granted. She was living because he was dying. Karen sat, tears streaming down her face, and felt the full weight of what love could cost... what it had cost. What he'd paid for her.

Rosita sat quietly, her hands folded in prayer, asking God to give this family strength for the journey ahead. She had walked this road many times before. But each time, each family, each love story ending in death, it still touched her. Still reminded herself why she did this work. Not to prevent death, but to help families walk through it with grace. The circle continued. Always, the circle continued.

Chapter Ten - Investigation

James pulled up in front of the Chavez house at seven-thirty in the morning. The sun was already hot in the sky of Arizona blue that promised another scorching day. He killed the engine and waited. Inside, Manny would be getting ready. Slowly, painfully for the appointment with the radiation oncologist. The follow-up appointment that Karen didn't know the full purpose of. The appointment Manny had insisted James drive him to. "You just got better," Manny had told his wife. "Please rest, James will take me."

Karen had argued, of course she had but Manny had held firm. She was finally healthy and strong. He wanted her to stay that way.

The front door opened and Manny emerged, moving carefully down the steps, with one hand on the railing. He looked worse than he had two days ago. He was so pale and seemed more fragile. It was like something essential was being drained from him hour by hour. James got out and met him at the passenger door. "Morning buddy."

"Thanks for doing this," Manny said quietly.

"Of course, man. That's what friends do."

They both knew this wasn't a good news appointment. They both knew what the doctor would probably say. Neither of them spoke about it during the drive. The medical center sprawled across several acres. A complex of buildings connected by covered walkways, manicured desert landscaping along with signs directing patients to oncology, cardiology, and radiology. James found parking near the oncology wing. He helped

Manny out of the car, noting how much assistance he needed now, how his legs seemed uncertain beneath him. Inside, the corridors were clean, bright and cold with an overhead presence of the air conditioning working intently. The many staff footsteps echoed on polished floors. Manny checked in at the desk. He provided his paperwork, indicated that James was with him and his insurance cards, the formality of it all... "Have a seat. Dr. Nguyen will call you back shortly."

They sat in the waiting room surrounded by other patients in various stages of treatment. There were so many oxygen tanks and wheelchairs scattered about. The geography of illness mapped onto human bodies. James wanted to say something comforting but he was coming up short. He was trying to be hopeful, but everything that came to mind felt hollow. "James Chen?"

A nurse stood in the doorway. Middle-aged, kind face. "Gentlemen... Mr. Chavez? " Dr. Nguyen is ready for you."

James stood up as Manny followed him into the back office.

The examination room was small and functional. It was a typical room with an exam table with paper covering. A basic sink and a computer on a rolling cart. There were posters on the wall about radiation safety, cancer screening, and patient resources. Dr. Patricia Nguyen entered the room after that polite knock on the door. She was in her fifties, Vietnamese American, the gray threading through her dark hair pulled back in tied up fashion. She carried a tablet and wore an expression James recognized immediately. Doctors learned to school their faces, but there were tells. The set of the mouth and the way they avoided eye contact while settling into their chairs. This was not a good news face.

"Mr. Chavez." Dr. Nguyen shook his hand, then James's. "I've reviewed all your test results. The blood work, the scans and the tissue samples from your radiation burns."

She pulled up images on the computer. James saw bone scans, blood cell counts, as well as radiation exposure measurements. None of it looked good to his untrained eye. "Let me examine you first, then we'll talk."

Manny removed his long-sleeved shirt slowly. James heard his own sharp intake of breath. The radiation burns had spread. What had been contained to Manny's forearms and neck now extended up to his shoulders, across his chest. The skin was mottled red and purple, blistered in places, weeping in others. Dr. Nguyen's expression tightened, but she remained professional. Gently she examined the burns with gloved hands and checked his lymph nodes. They were clearly swollen. She then listened to his heart and lungs. Next, she looked at his gums that were bleeding, a sign James knew meant something bad about bone marrow. She took notes on her tablet. Asked about symptoms. "Do you experience a lot of nausea?"

"Constant."

"Fatigue?"

"I can barely stay awake."

"Any weakness?"

"I can't walk without holding onto something."

"Bleeding? Besides the gums?"

"Nosebleeds and some bruising that won't go away."

Dr. Nguyen nodded, adding each symptom to her notes. Finally, she set down the tablet and sat in the chair across from Manny. Not standing but sitting facing Manny. James's stomach dropped, he knew doctors only sat when they had something heavy to deliver. "Mr. Chavez," Dr. Nguyen began, her voice gentle but direct. "Is this someone you want present for this conversation?"

She glanced at James and Manny didn't hesitate. "He's, my friend. He can stay."

Dr. Nguyen folded her hands and Met Manny's eyes. "Based on your exposure levels and the progression of your symptoms, you have acute radiation syndrome. Stage four."

Silence followed as he tried to absorb it... "What does that mean?" Manny's voice was steady, despite everything. "It means your bone marrow has been severely damaged, and your body can't produce blood cells properly. Your immune system is failing, this in turn is impacting your organs. They are beginning to show signs of distress."

"Can you treat it?"

The pause that followed was answer enough. "We can try supportive care," Dr. Nguyen said carefully. "Blood transfusions to replace the cells your body can't make. Antibiotics to fight infections your immune system can't handle. Medications to manage pain and nausea. But, Mr. Chavez, the exposure was significant and prolonged. The damage is... extensive."

James gripped the armrest of his chair. His knuckles turning white. Manny leaned forward slightly. "Will I survive this?"

Dr. Nguyen met his eyes with compassionate honesty. "No, Mr. Chavez. I don't believe you will."

The words landed like stones dropped into deep water. That sinking Finality. Manny absorbed them without flinching. "How long?"

"It's uncertain but it could be weeks. Perhaps a month or two at most.

It's difficult to predict precisely as every case is different. But given the progression we're seeing..."

She trailed off... The implication was clear. Then she leaned forward, her voice gentle but firm. "Put your affairs in order, Mr. Chavez. You are on borrowed time."

The phrase hung in the air. *Borrowed time.* Manny nodded slowly, taking it in while processing. James wanted to scream and to demand another opinion. There had to be options, experimental treatments, anything that might offer hope. But in his mind, he knew better. He'd seen Dr. Nguyen's face and heard the certainty in her voice. This was real... it was happening. Manny was dying.

They walked out of the medical building in silence and found a bench near the entrance, shaded by a Palo Verde tree. Manny sat down to rest as neither spoke for a long time. Finally, James managed: "Manny, I'm so..."

"Don't. Please."

Another silence that was heavier now. James stared at the parking lot. The cars coming and going, people walking in and out of the medical center. Life was continuing around them while Manny's world had just ended. "Karen needs to know," James said finally.

"I know."

"When are you going to tell her?"

"I don't know. Soon."

Manny's hands were shaking, and he clasped them together to still them. "She just got better. I don't want to..." He couldn't finish the thought. James turned to face him, "You can't carry this alone."

"I have to be the one to tell her. To tell Maya."

"Manny..."

"Look if you are my friend, I need to be the one, James. You can't tell them. It has to come from me."

James felt the weight of it settling on his shoulders. The knowledge of the secret. The burden of knowing his friend was dying and having to pretend he didn't know. "Uh... yeah ok. It's just so...," James said quietly. "You shouldn't have to..."

"I need confirmation."

Manny's eyes pleaded. James exhaled slowly. "Yeah buddy. I got it, I'm following, you lead."

The words bound him in Manny's choice. They made him complicit. They sat together on the bench, two friends sharing a terrible secret, and James wondered how he was supposed to look Karen in the eye. How he was supposed to hide his sadness from Maya. How he was supposed to act normal when nothing would ever be normal again.

***

Karen was in the kitchen when they arrived home. She'd been cooking and the smell of something baking filled the house. She looked healthy, capable and alive. The contrast to Manny was devastating. She came to the door when she heard them. She was trying to read Manny's face, and James's hidden expression. "What did the doctor say?"

Manny made it to the couch before answering. He sat down heavily. "They're going to manage the symptoms and keep me comfortable."

It wasn't a lie, but it wasn't the whole truth either. Karen sat beside him, took his hand and studied his face. She knew there was more, and James could see it in her eyes. But she didn't press in front of him. "Okay," Karen said quietly. "We'll get through this."

James stood awkwardly in the doorway. "Call if you need anything."

"Thank you," Manny said. "For everything."

Their eyes met with the secret passing between them like a current. James nodded and left. Outside, in his car, he sat with his hands on the steering wheel and tried to breathe.

Weeks. Maybe a month or two.

His friend was dying. And he had to pretend he didn't know. Over the next day, Karen took over completely. She managed Manny's medications, a growing collection of pill bottles lined up on the kitchen counter. There was pain management, anti-nausea and antibiotics. She set up a schedule, a pill organizer with compartments for morning, noon, evening, bedtime. She brought him water when he needed it, food when he could keep it down and blankets when he felt cold despite the Arizona heat.

She helped him to the bathroom when he was too weak to walk alone. She changed the bandages on his radiation burns with gentle, steady hands. The sick room had relocated from her bedroom to the living room. Everything had shifted now. The role reversal was complete. Manny lay on the couch covered in blankets, watching his wife move through the house with strength and purpose. He was grateful and heartbroken. This was what he wanted. Karen healthy, capable and living. But the cost was crushing to her. He wanted to tell her everything about the dream. The wish and the old man being an angel. The exchange of light via the handshake but he couldn't find the words. Not yet.

Karen worked with quiet efficiency but worry gnawed at her. His decline was too rapid and too severe. And the timing of it... her miraculous recovery and his sudden collapse. The pattern was becoming undeniable. She just didn't want to believe what it meant. Maya watched from the edges. She didn't understand. Mom got better so fast and dad got worse just as fast. It didn't make sense. She sat beside the couch one afternoon while her dad dozed. When he woke, she asked, "Dad, what's really happening?"

"I'm just sick, sweetheart. The radiation exposure from the plant."

"But you'll get better, right? Like Mom did?"

The pause was too long. "Right, Dad?"

Manny forced a smile. "The doctors are doing everything they can."

It wasn't an answer and Maya knew it. Fear coiled in her stomach... it was cold and heavy. Late at night, she heard her parents talking through the walls, but she couldn't make out words, but the tone was enough. It was serious with sadness.

She saw her mom crying in the kitchen when she thought no one was watching. She watched her dad get weaker every day. His skin was worse. His breathing labored. His eyes were hollow. Something was very wrong, and no one would tell her the truth. She texted Emma, "I think my dad is really sick, like really sick."

Emma responded: "I thought your mom was the sick one?"

"She was. Now she's better and he's... I don't know what's happening."

Emma sent back a sad face emoji. It didn't help. Maya still felt alone. Terrified and helpless. Watching her father die by inches and unable to do anything about it.

***

At the Palo Verde Nuclear Generating Station, Gerald Reed sat at his desk staring at the incident report. The top of the report heading was labeled... Worker exposed to dangerous radiation levels. Dosimeter malfunction. It was under his watch and on his shift. His safety record... five years of perfect performance was over. The report had a status in bold letters. COMPROMISED. Reed's body tightened as he read it. This shouldn't have happened. This couldn't have happened, not in his department and not on his watch. He picked up the phone and called the radiation safety team.

"I want every area Chavez worked inspected. Every station, every corridor, every cooling pool access point. We must find the leak. We have to find the source. Now!"

Within the hour, teams were deployed with Geiger counters, dosimeters and radiation mapping equipment. They swept the Cooling Pool Observation Deck #2 and Manny's primary station. Then they left no area unchecked. The maintenance corridors, equipment rooms and the break areas. Everywhere Manny would have been. They scanned every surface, every fixture, looking for elevated readings as hours passed. The reports came back unconclusive. Nothing was found, all levels nominal with no leaks. All the readings were within normal parameters. No leaks, malfunctions or anomalies were detected. Mr. Reed was beside himself as he received the results of... No contamination was found. No source identified.

Reed called the team leader. "That's impossible. Chavez was clearly exposed. The dosimeter failed, but he WAS exposed. Where did it happen?"

"Sir, we're not finding a source. Everything reads normal."

"Then look harder. Expand the search."

The crew expanded the search, and they checked adjacent areas as well as nearby systems. Every place Manny might have walked through and still there was nothing. Two days into the investigation, Reed assembled his team in the command center. He paced in front of them, clipboard in hand. "Five years," he said, voice tight. "FIVE YEARS of perfect safety record with zero incidents. Zero exposure events. Zero failures."

His team stood silent. "And now this! On my watch. One dosimeter fails and one worker gets exposed to fatal levels of radiation. How?"

An engineer near the back shifted uncomfortably as Reed continued, "Corporate is going to audit us. The NRC will investigate. OSHA will crawl up our asses. All because of this."

"Sir," the engineer ventured. "About Chavez... do we know his condition?"

Reed waved it off. "Medical is handling that. Our job is to find the source and ensure this doesn't happen to anyone else."

"But sir, shouldn't we..."

"I can't share private health data. You know that it's against policy and a HIPPA violation. Let's focus on the investigation," Reed cut him off. "That's your job. That's all our jobs."

At the back of the room, James Chen stood with his arms crossed as he was listening. His disgust was growing with every word out of Reed's mouth. Manny was DYING and all Reed cared about was his stupid safety record. James walked out before he said something he'd regret. The investigation was stalled for lack of data.

Days had passed and still no radiation leak was found. No equipment malfunction was identified beyond the failed dosimeter. No contamination was detected and there was no explanation. Reed grew more frustrated. "How does a man get exposed to fatal levels of radiation with NO SOURCE?"

The team had no answers, but theories had developed. Maybe the dosimeter failed first or maybe Manny entered an area he shouldn't have. He got exposed without knowing it and left the area. That's how no trace remained. But it was speculation, water cooler gossip with no proof. Reed's conclusion formed gradually, inevitably to user error. Chavez must have violated protocol and gone somewhere he wasn't authorized. He must have made a mistake. Because the alternative... that the PLANT failed him, that the SYSTEMS failed was unacceptable. Reed wrote his initial report accordingly until more data became available. Dosimeter malfunction: confirmed. Radiation source: undetermined. Likely cause: worker error, unauthorized access to restricted area. He filed it with corporate and with the NRC. He protected the facility and his record while he threw Manny under the bus. James heard about the report secondhand. He read the conclusions, and his hands shook with rage. They were blaming Manny for his own death. They were making him responsible for the failure of their equipment, their systems, their safety protocols and there was nothing he could do about it.

***

Evening settled over the Chavez house. Maya was upstairs in her room. Manny lay on the couch. Karen sat beside him in the quiet. Finally, she spoke. "The doctor told you something you're not telling me."

Manny didn't respond. "Manny, please. I need to know."

He looked at her. This woman he'd saved, this woman he loved. Strong, healthy and alive because of what he'd done. He wanted to tell her everything. He knew he had to but not tonight. He wasn't ready. He didn't know how to find the words. "I'm tired," he said quietly. "Can we talk tomorrow?"

Karen studied his face and saw the deflection. The fear combined with the weight of whatever he was carrying. She wanted to push and demand the truth but she nodded. "Okay. Tomorrow."

She leaned down, kissed his forehead. "I love you."

"I love you too."

She went to bed, leaving him alone in the dark living room. Manny lay awake staring at the ceiling while Dr. Nguyen's words echoed in his mind.

Put your affairs in order. You are on borrowed time.

He had to tell them and explain what he'd done. He had to make his final requests just like Karen did. He needed to tell her about the tree burial. But how do you tell your wife you're dying? How do you tell your daughter you're leaving? How do you explain you chose this? Manny closed his eyes against the weight of it. It was borrowed time... Every moment from here was borrowed and he had to make them count.

Chapter Eleven – Truth Revealed

The house was quiet in the way it only could be on weekday mornings after Maya left for school. Karen stood at the kitchen sink, washing the breakfast dishes, her movements efficient and sure. Two months ago, she couldn't have stood this long without exhaustion pulling her down. Two months ago, lifting a coffee mug had felt like lifting weights.

Now she felt strong. Almost herself again. The cancer that had been eating her alive had simply... stopped. The doctors used words like "remission" and "inexplicable improvement," but Karen knew it was more than that. She could feel it in her bones, in her blood, in the way her body no longer betrayed her with every breath.

Behind her, Manny sat at the kitchen table. She could feel his eyes on her back. "Can we talk?" His voice was quiet. "Really talk. About the promise."

Karen's hands stilled in the soapy water. She'd known this conversation was coming. She had felt it building for days now, ever since he'd come home from Dr. Nguyen's office looking like he'd seen his own ghost. She dried her hands and turned. Manny had that familiar look she used to see in the mirror. It was terrible... the pale, hollow-eyed, skin carrying a grayish cast that made you look decades older. Manny's was worse and the discoloration on his hands had spread to most of his body. The skin was dark and mottled like old bruises. "Okay," she said. "Let's talk."

He gestured toward the living room. "Can you close the door?"

That small request told her everything. This wasn't a conversation for open spaces. This was something that needed containment, privacy and walls to hold it. She followed him into the living room and closed the door behind them. They sat on the couch together, and Manny took her hand. His skin felt rough, damaged, but his grip was gentle. "I need to tell you something," he said. "And I need you to just listen. All the way through. Can you do that?"

Karen's heart was already racing. "Manny, you're scaring me."

"I know and I'm sorry." He took a breath, steadying himself. "You know when I went to Dr. Nguyen's recently that she Looked at everything on the bone marrow, organ function, all of it."

Karen waited, her hand tightening around his. "She said I'm not going to survive this." The words came out flat, practiced, like he'd been rehearsing them. "The radiation exposure damaged my bone marrow too severely. My organs are starting to shut down. She said I have weeks. Maybe a month or two at most."

The words didn't make sense at first. Karen heard them, but they felt disconnected from reality, like he was reading from a script for someone else's life. "No," she heard herself say. "No, there has to be something they can do. Other treatments, trials, something..."

"There isn't." Manny's voice was gentle but firm. "I've accepted it. I need you to accept it too."

Tears were already sliding down Karen's face. She covered her mouth with her free hand, trying to hold back the sob rising in her throat. "She told me to put my affairs in order," Manny continued. "She said I'm on borrowed time."

"Borrowed time." Karen repeated the words like they were foreign.

"How can you just... how can you accept that?"

"Because I have to... And because..." He paused, gathering himself. "There's something else I need to tell you. About what I want. After."

Karen wiped her eyes, trying to focus through the tears. "After?"

"I saw something on TV a few weeks ago. An advertisement about tree burials... natural burials where they plant you under a tree. Instead of a traditional cemetery."

Karen blinked, trying to follow. "A tree?"

Manny's face softened slightly, and she saw something in his expression that looked almost like hope. "There's a place called Eternal Forest Memorial. It up north past Surprise, heading toward Wickenburg. They have acres of desert land with native trees... mesquite, Palo Verde, ironwood. You pick your tree, and they bury you naturally beneath it. No embalming, no concrete vault, just earth and tree."

He leaned forward slightly, trying to make her see what he was seeing. "The tree grows from your body, Karen. You become part of it and people can visit. It's not traditional like standing over a grave marker, but sitting in the shade. Being with their loved one in a living thing."

Karen stared at him, tears still streaming. "You've really thought about this."

"I have. And that's what I want." His eyes held hers. "I want Maya to be able to visit. To sit under the tree and talk to me. To tell me about her day, her life. A living memorial, not an empty stone."

Karen's throat was so tight she could barely speak. "If that's what you want, then that's what we'll do."

Manny pulled her close, and she let herself cry against his shoulder for a moment. But even through her grief, something was clicking into place in her mind. A pattern she'd been too close to see. Her impossible recovery. His impossible decline. The timing is too perfect, too synchronized. She pulled back, looking at him through her tears. "Manny... what did you do?"

His expression flickered, just for a second and she knew. She knew.

"What did you do?" Her voice was rising now. "Who was that old man? The one you helped on the highway?"

Manny's face went carefully blank. "I told you. His truck broke down, and I helped him fix it."

"Don't lie to me. Not now. Not about this." Karen stood abruptly, pacing to the window. Her mind was racing, connecting pieces she hadn't wanted to see. "I get better the same week you get sick. Miraculously better. And you get miraculously worse. That's not coincidence."

She turned back to him, her voice shaking. "Why did you do this? What did you do?"

Manny closed his eyes. When he opened them again, they held a resignation that terrified her. "I prayed for an angel," he said quietly.

Karen stared at him. "What?"

"I was desperate." His voice was steady now, like he'd been waiting to tell this story. "You were dying and Maya was losing her mother. I was losing you. I couldn't... I couldn't just watch it happen."

He leaned back slowly, facing her. "One night at work, I prayed. I begged God to send an angel. To help us... To help you."

Karen's legs felt weak. She sat back down, her eyes never leaving his face. And he appeared," Manny continued. "The old man on the highway. I almost didn't stop. He was just... there. In the middle of nowhere."

"What did he say?"

"He asked me what I wanted most as we were talking." Manny's voice dropped to almost a whisper. "I told him I wanted you to live. I wanted you to be healthy. I said I'd switch places with you if I could."

The words hung in the air between them. "And he shook my hand," Manny said. "And the deal was made."

Karen felt like she couldn't breathe. "No, you didn't... tell me you didn't trade your life for mine."

"I did." Manny's voice was certain, unwavering. "And I'd do it again. A thousand times over, I'd make the same choice."

The sound that came out of Karen was somewhere between a sob and a scream. She stood again, but this time she pulled away from him, backing toward the other side of the room. "No. No, you don't get to do that. You don't get to make that choice!"

"Karen..."

"You made this decision WITHOUT ME!" Her voice was loud now, shaking with fury. "What gave you the RIGHT to choose for me? Your played God with our lives!"

Manny stood there, taking it, letting her rage. "I'm not a child, Manny. I'm your WIFE." Tears were streaming down her face, but they were angry tears now. "You decided my life was worth more than yours? You decided Maya needs me more than she needs you? Who gave you permission to make that choice?"

"I couldn't watch you die..."

"So, I have to watch YOU die instead?" Karen's voice cracked. "How is that better? How is that fair?"

She was pacing now, her hands shaking. "You took away my choice, Manny. If I had known, I would have said NO. I would have fought you on this. And you KNEW that. That's why you didn't tell me."

Manny's face was calm, accepting. "You're right."

The quiet admission stopped her. "You're right," he said again. "I knew you'd try to stop me. I knew you'd choose to die rather than let me sacrifice myself. So, I made the choice for both of us."

"You LIED to me!" Karen was crying and yelling simultaneously now. "For weeks! Letting me think you just got unlucky at work. While all along you CHOSE this!"

She stopped pacing, breathing hard as the tears were streaming down her face. Manny waited for her, just watching her, not defending himself. Just letting her feel it all as the silence stretched between them. Karen felt exhausted and wrung out. But the anger was still there, hot and bitter. "Do you remember Sedona?" Manny asked quietly.

Karen looked up, confused by the shift. "What?"

"Our wedding day."

The question disarmed her. She wiped her eyes, trying to follow. "Of course I remember."

"Tell me what you remember," he said.

Karen's anger faltered. "Why?"

"Please."

She sank back onto the couch, suddenly exhausted. "It snowed that morning. A freak storm rolled in."

"You were so upset," Manny said, sitting beside her, but not too close, giving her space. "I wanted the red rocks," Karen said quietly. "The sun. The beauty. Instead, we got cold and gray and snowy. I cried, I thought it was ruined."

"And what did I say?"

Karen's voice softened despite herself. "You said it would be perfect. That I should trust you."

"And you didn't believe me."

"No." A small, sad smile. "I didn't."

"But we went ahead with the ceremony anyway."

Karen nodded. The memory was flooding back now, vivid and sharp. "We were standing on the deck of the hotel room. My friend Robert was there... The pastor. I was in that simple white dress, freezing. You were in one of your suits."

"And then?" Manny prompted gently.

"The sun broke through." Karen's voice caught. "Right as we started the vows. The clouds parted and the sun poured through, and the snow on the red rocks glittered like diamonds. It was the most beautiful thing I'd ever seen."

They sat in silence for a moment, both remembering. Young and hopeful and so in love, believing they had forever. "In sickness and in health," Manny said quietly.

Karen closed her eyes. "Don't."

"I meant those vows, Karen. Every word. We both did."

"I thought we'd grow old together," Karen whispered. "I thought 'in sickness' meant I'd take care of you through old age. Not this. Not at forty-seven."

"Neither did I. But the vows didn't say *only if we get old.* They said, 'in sickness and in health.' In good times and bad. This is bad. This is the sickness. And I'm keeping my vow."

Karen felt the anger bleeding out of her, replaced by something heavier. Grief compounded with guilt. "I should be the one dying," she said, her voice small. "Not you."

"Don't say that." Manny reached for her hand, and this time she let him take it.

"I'm alive because you're dying." Karen's voice was breaking. "Every breath I take is one you don't get. Every day I'm healthy is a day you're sicker. How am I supposed to live with that?"

"You're supposed to feel alive," Manny said firmly. "You're supposed to live the life I'm giving you. Not waste it on guilt."

"How?" Karen looked at him through tears. "How am I supposed to do that? Every good moment I have, I'll think of you. Every time Maya and I laugh, I'll remember you're gone."

"Then carry me in joy, not guilt." Manny's voice was strong despite his failing body. "Carry me in the life you live, not the death you mourn. I don't want you to forget me. I want you to remember me. But don't let that memory be a burden."

"What if I can't?"

"Then you try. Every day, you try. And when you can't, you lean on Maya, Rosita or on James. On whoever you need but you don't give up. That's part of the promise. You won't give up."

Karen sobbed once, then caught herself. "I promise... I promise I will."

They sat together, and despite everything, Manny managed to pull her close. His arms felt weak, but they were still his arms. Still him. "You've always been the strong one," he said quietly. "I've just been going through the motions. But you... you fight. You're smarter than me, tougher than me..." He paused, and she felt him smile. "And way better looking."

Despite everything, Karen laughed. It was a wet, broken sound.

"That's not funny."

"It's a little funny."

"No, it's not."

"If I don't laugh, I'll cry," Manny said. "And I need to be strong for what comes next."

Karen pulled back slightly. "What comes next?"

Manny's expression grew serious again. "We have to tell Maya."

Karen's stomach dropped. "Maya."

"She needs to know."

"She's going to fall apart." Karen could picture it already. Her daughter's face, the moment they tell her. "She doesn't understand what's happening. She's already scared and confused. How do we tell her you're dying?"

"Carefully, honestly but together." Manny looked at her.

"I don't know if I can."

"We have to. She deserves the truth."

Karen thought about Maya upstairs some nights, trying to be strong, trying to figure out what was happening to her family. She thought about the distance that had grown between him and her daughter, and how they'd only just started to bridge it. "Do we tell her everything?" Karen asked. "About the angel? About the exchange?"

Manny considered. "Not yet. Just the diagnosis first. Eventually, when she's ready... when you think she can handle it. You can tell her. You can tell her that her father loved her mother so much that he gave everything to save her."

"What if she never wants to know?"

"Then you don't tell her. It's your decision. But I think someday she'll want to understand."

Karen nodded slowly, accepting the weight of that future choice. "We should tell her together. Both of us."

"Yes."

They sat together as the morning light shifted through the windows. Outside, the world continued… cars passing, birds singing, life moving forward. Inside, everything had changed. "Tell me about the tree again," Karen said quietly. Manny's face softened. "Palo Verde. Green-trunked trees with yellow blooms in the spring. They're survivors as they thrive in desert heat and don't need much water. They are tough and beautiful." He smiled slightly. "Like us."

"And Maya can visit?"

"Anytime she wants. There are paths through the forest, benches under some trees. She can sit in the shade and talk to me. Tell me about her day. I'll be there. Just in a different way."

"She's going to need that."

"And she'll have you," Manny said. "That's the most important thing."

They heard a sound outside. It was a car pulling into the driveway. Both of them tensed. "She's home early," Karen whispered.

"Today's a half-day," Manny said. "I forgot."

The front door opened. Keys dropped on the counter. Maya's voice carried down the hall, "I'm home!"

Karen and Manny looked at each other. This was it. No more waiting. Maya appeared in the doorway, backpack slung over one shoulder. She stopped when she saw them both sitting on the couch, clearly having been crying. "What's wrong?"

Her voice carried immediate alarm. "Maya, honey," Manny said gently. "Can you sit down? We need to talk."

Every teenager knew those words. The fear that crossed Maya's face was instant. "Is it Mom?" She moved into the room quickly. "Did the cancer come back?"

"No, sweetheart." Karen shook her head. "I'm okay."

Maya's eyes moved between them, confused. "Then what?"

She sat slowly in the chair across from them, arms crossing defensively over her chest. Bracing for impact.

Manny leaned forward, his voice steady but quiet. "It's me. I'm the one who's sick."

Maya blinked. "What do you mean, sick?"

Karen reached for Manny's hand, drawing strength. "Dad had an accident at work. Radiation exposure."

Maya's eyes widened. She'd heard about radiation... Chernobyl, cancer, death. "Is it... bad?"

"It's bad, Maya." Manny held her gaze, steady and honest. The words seemed to cost him something. "The doctors say I'm not going to get better."

Maya was shaking her head slowly, not understanding or not wanting to understand. "What does that mean? Not going to get better?"

Manny took a breath. "It means I'm dying, kiddo. I have weeks. Maybe a couple months. I'm so sorry."

For a long moment, Maya didn't move. Then she stood abruptly, backing away from them. "No. No, you're not."

"Maya..." Karen started to stand.

"You're fine. You've just been tired." Maya's voice was rising.

"You're... you're going to be fine."

Karen reached for her, but Maya pulled away. "No! This isn't happening!"

"Maya, please..." Karen's voice broke.

But Maya's mind was racing, memories flooding back. The parent-teacher conference he'd attended. His damaged hands she'd noticed and asked about. How exhausted he'd looked for weeks. How he'd been sleeping on the couch. All the signs she'd seen but dismissed or ignored.

"Your hands." She was staring at them now. "That's why your hands look like that."

Manny nodded. "The radiation damage."

Maya's face crumpled. The denial was breaking apart, and something else was rushing in to take its place. Anger. "How long have you known?" Her voice was shaking. "A couple weeks."

"A couple WEEKS?" Maya's voice cracked with fury. "And you didn't tell me?"

"I needed to figure out how to..."

"You let me think everything was fine!" Tears were streaming down her face now. "You let me worry about stupid school stuff! While you were DYING?"

"I'm sorry..."

"How about 'Maya, I'm dying'?" She was yelling now. "How hard is that?"

"Maya, please..." Karen tried again.

But Maya rounded on her mother. "Did you know?"

"I found out today. This morning. Your father wanted to tell us together."

The betrayal in Maya's eyes cut through both of them. Then, as suddenly as the anger came, it collapsed. Maya fell back into the chair, her hands over her face, her body shaking with sobs. "I can't lose you," she said through her hands. Her voice was small, broken, childlike. "I can't. I can't do this."

All the teenage bravado was gone. She was just a girl who was losing her father. Manny moved to her, ignoring his own pain and weakness. He knelt beside her chair and put his arms around her. She fought it for a moment, then collapsed against him, sobbing into his shoulder. "I'm sorry, kiddo," he whispered. "I'm so sorry."

Karen joined them, kneeling on Maya's other side, and the three of them held each other while they all were crying. The family they'd fought so hard to keep together was now being torn apart anyway.

They stayed like that for a long time. Eventually, Maya's sobs quieted to shuddering breaths. She pulled back, wiping her face with her sleeves, trying to compose herself. "What happened?" she asked, her voice hoarse. "At work?"

"My dosimeter badge malfunctioned," Manny said, settling back onto the couch. "I was exposed to radiation without knowing it. By the time they caught it, the damage was done."

He didn't mention the angel or the exchange. That truth could wait. "But there are treatments, right?" Maya looked between them with desperate hope. "Treatment, medication? Something?"

Karen's voice was gentle. "The doctors have tried everything they can. The damage is too severe. We have to accept that there's no cure."

"I don't accept it." Maya's jaw set stubbornly. "There has to be something."

"I've made my peace with it, Maya," Manny said quietly. "I need you to try to do the same."

Maya was quiet for a moment, staring at her hands. Then her head came up suddenly. "The sink. When I fixed the sink."

Manny nodded, remembering their conversation in the bathroom, the connection they'd made. "You told me about Grandpa. About being good with your hands." Her voice was breaking again. "You said we'd work on something together."

"I meant that." Manny's voice was thick with emotion. "And we still have time. Not as much as I wanted, but some. We can still do things together."

"You said I got it from you," Maya whispered. "Being good with my hands."

"You did. That's yours. That's something I gave you that you'll always have."

"I don't want your skills." Maya's voice broke on the words. "I want YOU."

The simple, devastating honesty of it hung in the air. There was nothing to say to that could make it better. After a long silence, Maya spoke again, her voice small and trying to be brave. "Wait ... how long did you say?"

"The doctor said weeks. Maybe two months."

Maya's mind was doing the math. "Two months. Eight weeks. Sixty days at most." Her voice was flat, clinical, trying to create distance from the horror of it. "That's not even enough time to finish the semester."

"No," Manny agreed quietly. "It's not. It's never enough time but it's what we have."

"What's going to happen? To you?"

Karen answered. "He'll get weaker and eventually he'll need to be in the hospital. But we'll be with him every step."

Maya sat up straighter, making a decision. "I'm not going to school. I'm staying home with you."

"No." Manny's voice was firm. "You're going to school."

"But..."

"Your education matters. Your future matters. That's non-negotiable."

"Dad..."

"We'll figure it out," Karen interrupted gently. "You can stay home when you need to but your dad's right. You need to keep going forward."

Maya didn't agree, but she didn't argue. She just looked exhausted.

"Who else knows?" she asked.

"James from work... Now you and your mom. We'll need to tell others soon. Our family and friends."

Maya thought about Emma, Jade, Chris. How could she tell her friends her dad was dying? What could she even say? The weight of carrying this knowledge felt crushing.

The three of them sat in the living room as the afternoon light shifted. Exhausted from emotion. Maya's eyes were red and swollen. Manny could barely stay upright. Karen was trying to hold it together for both of them. Usually, Maya would retreat to her room at this point and put her headphones on, close the door, shut out the world. But tonight, she stayed. She moved from the chair to the couch, sitting close to Manny. Like when she was little.

Manny put his arm around her, holding her like he used to. When she had nightmares. When she was scared. Protecting her from threats he could fight. But this threat... his own dying body. He couldn't fight at all. They sat in silence with no one knowing what to say. The television stayed off it was just the three of them together. Presence was more important than words. Eventually, Karen brought them water. They all drank mechanically, with a basic act of survival. As the light outside began to fade toward evening, Maya finally spoke.

"Dad?"

"Yeah, kiddo?"

Her voice was very small. "Are you scared?"

Manny paused, considering. He'd promised her honesty. "Sometimes. Yeah. But mostly I'm sad. Sad to leave you and your mom. Sad to miss your life."

Maya started crying again. "I need you."

"I know. And I'll be here as long as I can. And even after... I'll still be with you. In a different way."

Maya didn't understand what he meant. He hadn't explained about the tree yet. That was for another conversation. For now, she just needed to hold him. Finally, as full dark settled outside, Maya stood on unsteady legs. "I should... I need to..."

She couldn't finish. Didn't know what she needed.

"Go upstairs," Karen said gently. "Rest. We'll be here."

Maya nodded. She made it to the stairs, then turned back.

"I love you, Dad."

Manny's voice broke on the words. "I love you too, Maya. So much."

She disappeared upstairs. They heard her door close. Then, a moment later, the sound of muffled sobbing through the walls. Karen and Manny sat on the couch, listening to their daughter cry, unable to fix it. The sound broke their hearts. "That was the hardest thing I've ever done," Karen whispered.

"She needed to know."

"I know. But God, I wish I didn't have to tell her."

They sat in silence, listening. The crying went on and on. "She's stronger than we think," Karen said finally. "She'll be okay. Eventually."

"Because she has you," Manny said. The reminder of why he made the trade.

"I need to lie down," Manny said after a while. He'd spent everything telling Karen, then telling Maya. He was barely able to function. She helped him lie down, and then she lay beside him, both of them staring at the ceiling in the dim light. "We did the right thing," Karen said. More to convince herself than him.

"I hope so."

Upstairs, Maya's crying finally quieted. But Manny lay awake, unable to sleep despite his exhaustion. He listened to the house settle around him. The distant sound of a car passing outside. Karen moved to the chair and sat with him while he went to sleep.

He thought about the price of what he'd done. Not just his death, but their grief. Maya's broken heart and Karen's survivor's guilt. The pain he'd inflicted on the people he loved most. But Karen was alive and Maya would have her mother. They'd grieve him, but they'd have each other. The trade was worth it. Even seeing Maya's tears, it was worth it.

Every moment from here was borrowed time. Every conversation, every touch, every shared breath. Making memories for them to hold on too when he was gone. The darkness outside began to shift toward gray as dawn approached. Maya's crying had stopped hours ago. The secret was out. No more lying, no more hiding. Just the time they had left. He thought about the tree. The Palo Verde was waiting for him at Eternal Forest Memorial. Maya would be visiting when she was ready, sitting in the shade, talking to him. Telling him about her life. The promise would be kept. Not the ending he'd have exactly chosen but one he could accept. Because love had demanded the sacrifice, and he'd given it willingly. A thousand times over, he'd make the same choice. However, many days or weeks remained, he'd use them well. Be present with his family. Make memories they could hold onto when he was gone. He closed his eyes and finally let sleep take him.

Karen sat in the dark as Manny was asleep on the couch, tears streaming down her face, hand on her chest feeling her past illness as he labored breathing while sleeping. She whispered into the quiet, "What did you do, Manny?"

The front door opened softly. Rosita's key turning in the lock. She'd said she would check in after her evening shift at another client's home, but Karen had forgotten. Rosita appeared in the doorway, took one look at the scene...Manny asleep, Karen crying beside him and she understood immediately. "Señora," she said quietly. "Come. Let him rest."

Karen didn't want to leave Manny's side, but once again Rosita's gentle insistence pulled her to the kitchen. They sat at the table, the light dim, the house quiet except for Manny's breathing from the other room. "You know, don't you?" Karen asked. "About what he did."

Rosita folded her hands on the table. "I have suspicions, sí. But tell me what you know."

Karen told her everything. The old man on the highway. The handshake. The wish to trade places. Her miraculous recovery. His impossible decline. "He chose this," Karen whispered. "He chose to die so I could live."

Rosita was quiet for a long moment. "And you are angry."

"Yes! No. I don't know." Karen put her head in her hands. "I'm grateful. devastated and furious that he made this choice without me. I'm in awe of his love. I feel all of it at once and I don't know what to do with it."

"You do what you are doing. You feel it, all of it." Rosita reached across and took Karen's hand. "In my village, we tell a story about the hummingbird and the saguaro. You know this story?"

Karen shook her head no. "The saguaro, she grows for fifty years before she blooms the first time. Fifty years of waiting, of growing, and of storing water in her body. And when she finally blooms, the hummingbird comes. He drinks the nectar, and in return, he carries her pollen to other saguaros so new ones can grow."

Rosita's thumb rubbed gently over Karen's hand. "The saguaro gives everything... her energy, her water, and her very life force to make those flowers. And the hummingbird takes that gift and makes new life from it. This is the way of things. One gives, one receives, and the circle continues."

"But the saguaro doesn't die," Karen protested.

"No. But she is changed. She has less water and less strength. She must rest after blooming, rebuild herself. And someday, after many bloomings, she will die. But her gift lives on in all the new saguaros the hummingbird helped create."

Rosita leaned forward. "Your husband, he is the saguaro. He bloomed everything he had for all his years, all his strength, all his life to give you and Maya the nectar you needed. And now you, you are the hummingbird. You carry his gift forward. You make new life from his sacrifice."

Karen wiped her eyes. "I don't want to be the hummingbird. I want him to live."

"I know. But that choice was not yours to make. He made it and now you must honor it by living fully, by being the hummingbird that carries his love into the world."

They sat together in the kitchen's dim light. Finally, Karen asked, "How do I say goodbye to him? How do I let him go?"

"You do not say goodbye," Rosita said firmly. "Not yet. You say, 'I see what you did. I understand now. And I will honor your gift.' You say, 'I am angry... grateful and broken and whole, all at once.' You tell him the truth of your heart. All of it."

"And when he dies?"

"Then you say tell him... 'Until I see you again.' Not goodbye. Never goodbye. Because love does not end when the heart stops beating. It transforms, like the saguaro's nectar into the hummingbird's flight. It continues."

Karen nodded slowly, tears still falling but something settled in her chest. Acceptance maybe or just exhaustion. "Go," Rosita said, standing. "Sit with him. Tell him what is in your heart. I will stay here in the kitchen. Take the time you need."

Karen returned to the couch, to Manny sleeping under the blanket she'd covered him with. She took his hand and leaned close to his ear. "I know what you did," she whispered. "I understand now. And I'm so angry at you for not asking me first. But I also..." Her voice broke. "I also love you more than I knew was possible. You saved me and Maya. And I will live the life you gave me. I promised and I'm not breaking it... As Rosita would say... I will be your hummingbird."

In the kitchen, Rosita sat quietly, her hands folded in prayer, Once again she was asking God to give this family strength for the journey ahead. She had walked this road many times before but each time, each family, each love story ending in death, it still touched her. It reminded herself why she did this work. Not to prevent death, but to help families walk through it with grace and dignity. The circle would continue. Always, the circle continued. The sun rose outside. Morning came as the borrowed time continued.

Chapter Twelve - Passing the Torch

Maya lay in bed staring at her phone, the screen's glow was harsh in the darkness of her room. It was past midnight. She should be sleeping as if tomorrow was a school day. But every time she closed her eyes, she saw her father's face when he said those words, *I'm dying, kiddo.*

She couldn't carry this alone. Her thumb hovered over her phone, then opened the group chat with Emma, Jade, and Chris. The people she was closest to. Her friends who knew her, who'd been there through everything. If she couldn't tell them, who could she tell? She typed quickly, before she could overthink it: *My dad is dying*

Her finger hit send before her brain could stop it. She waited, heart pounding, watching the three dots appear as someone started typing.

Emma: *WHAT??*

Jade: *Oh my god Maya*

Chris: *Are you serious?*

The messages came rapid-fire, her phone buzzing in her hands. Maya's fingers moved across the keyboard, tears blurring her vision. *Radiation exposure at work. Doctors say weeks, maybe 2 months. They told me today.*

More dots... More typing. Emma: *I'm so sorry Maya. That's horrible.*

Jade: *Do you want us to come over?*

Chris: *What can we do? How can we help?*

All the right words. All the things' friends were supposed to say. But as Maya read them, something hollow opened up in her chest. They didn't understand. They couldn't... their dads were fine. Healthy, annoying sometimes, sure, but alive. They were going to work, coming home, complaining about traffic and mowing lawns. Normal dad stuff, not dying.

Emma: *My dad had surgery once and we were so scared, but he was fine. There's always hope!*

Maya stared at that message. Surgery... scared but fine. It wasn't the same. Not even close... Jade: *Maybe the doctors are wrong? They make mistakes sometimes.*

They're not wrong, Maya wanted to scream at her phone. She'd seen her father's hands. Seen the way he could barely stay upright along with the resignation in his eyes. Chris: *Stay positive! Miracles happen!*

There won't be a miracle. Maya typed and deleted three different responses. She wanted to tell them they didn't get it. That their well-meaning platitudes felt like sandpaper on an open wound. But they were trying. They cared and it wasn't their fault they couldn't understand grief they'd never experienced. Finally, she typed: *Thanks guys. I just needed to tell someone. I'll be okay.*

She wouldn't be. But what else could she say? *Going to try to sleep. Talk tomorrow.*

She closed the chat before anyone could respond and set her phone face-down on her nightstand. The room felt darker than before. More silent. The weight of what she'd learned pressing down on her chest until it was hard to breathe. Her friends loved her but they couldn't help. No one could help. She was alone in this.

Morning came too soon. Maya sat on her bed in her school clothes and backpack beside her, debating whether to go. She could fake sick.

Her parents would probably let her stay home. After yesterday, they'd understand. But Dad had said school was non-negotiable.

She could hear voices downstairs, her parents talking softly in the living room. They'd probably been up all night too. Maya forced herself to stand, grabbed her backpack, and headed downstairs. Her parents were on the couch, looking as exhausted as she felt. Karen's eyes were red-rimmed. Manny looked like he might fall asleep sitting up. "You don't have to go today," Karen said when she saw Maya. "You can stay home."

Manny glanced at Karen, then at Maya. "She should go. Routine helps."

Maya appreciated that he didn't treat her like she was fragile. "I'll go and see how it feels."

She grabbed her things and left before they could see her cry again.

First period was English. Mrs. Palmer was talking about Shakespeare *Hamlet*, something about death and mortality that felt cruelly ironic. Maya sat at her desk and stared at the wood grain, the teacher's words washing over her like white noise. To *be or not to be.*

Between classes, Emma caught up with her at her locker. "How are you?"

"Fine," Maya said automatically.

"My mom said if you need anything..."

"I'm fine." The words came out sharper than she intended.

Emma's face fell. "Okay. I'm just... I'm here if you need me."

"I know, I'm sorry. Thanks."

But as Emma walked away, Maya felt the distance between them like a physical thing. Her friend meant well. But there was no bridge across this particular chasm. The intercom crackled mid-morning: "Maya Chavez to the counseling office, please."

Her stomach dropped. Everyone in the hall turned to look at her as she gathered her things. The walk to Mrs. Rodriguez's office felt endless, every step heavy with dread. The counselor's office was different from the rest of the school. It was warmer with soft lighting, comfortable chairs and plants on the windowsill. Tissues were prominently placed on the desk. She'd need them. "Maya." Mrs. Rodriguez smiled gently. She was a middle-aged woman with kind eyes and a professional but caring demeanor. "Thank you for coming. Please, sit."

Maya sat, hands fidgeting at her sides. "Your mother called this morning. She told me about your father." Mrs. Rodriguez's voice was steady, compassionate. "I'm so sorry you're going through this. I wanted to talk to you, give you some resources."

"I'm fine," Maya said automatically.

"It's okay not to be fine."

Something in those words cracked Maya's careful composure. Her eyes burned with fresh tears. Mrs. Rodriguez pulled out some pamphlets of grief resources, support groups and numbers to call. She set them on the desk between them. "When someone we love is dying, we go through stages," she said gently. "Have you heard of the five stages of grief?"

Maya shook her head. "They don't always happen in order, and you might go back and forth between them. But understanding them can help." Mrs. Rodriguez folded her hands. "The first is denial. 'This can't be happening. The doctors must be wrong.' Does that sound familiar?"

Maya nodded. She'd felt that yesterday, in the moment her father said the words. "Denial protects us when the truth is too painful," Mrs.

Rodriguez continued. "Then comes anger. 'Why him? Why now? It's not fair.' You might feel angry at your father, at your mother, at God, at yourself."

"I was angry at him yesterday," Maya admitted quietly. "For not telling me sooner."

"That's normal. Anger is part of the process."

"Then there's bargaining. 'What if we try different doctors? Different treatments? If I'm good, if I pray, maybe things will change.' We try to negotiate with reality."

Maya had already started doing that in her head. What if they tried experimental treatments? What if they went to a different hospital?

"Depression comes next. The sadness becomes overwhelming. It's hard to eat, sleep and focus. Everything feels heavy."

Maya felt that weight now, pressing down on her. "And finally, acceptance." Mrs. Rodriguez's voice was gentle but firm. "This doesn't mean you're happy about it. It means you're accepting the reality. You can accept it and still be sad. But acceptance lets you be present with your dad in the time you have left."

The words hit Maya like a physical blow. *The time you have left.* "How do I...?" Her voice broke. "How do I say goodbye?"

Mrs. Rodriguez leaned forward. "You don't have to say goodbye yet. Right now, just be with him. Spend time together making memories. Say the things you need to say. Ask him questions about his life, your family history. Take photos, videos. Let yourself feel everything... sad, angry, scared. All of it is valid."

She handed Maya the pamphlets. "You can take time off school if you need to. Or you can come in... sometimes routine helps. There's no right way to do this. I'm here and my door is always open." She added her card to the pile. "Day or night."

Maya took the materials with shaking hands. "I want to go home."

"That's okay. I'll call your mom."

Maya left the office, bypassed her locker, and walked straight to the main office. The school resource officer, Officer Martinez, was already waiting. "Ready to go?" he asked kindly.

Maya nodded, unable to speak. The drive home was quiet. Officer Martinez didn't try to fill the silence with empty platitudes, and Maya was grateful. When he pulled into her driveway, he turned to her. "Take care of yourself, okay?"

"Thanks." She got out, clutching the counselor's packet, and watched him drive away. It was only eleven in the morning. The house looked peaceful in the desert sunlight. Both her parents' vehicles were in the driveway. She went inside.

"Maya?" Karen appeared from the living room, concern immediate on her face. "I got a call, what happened? Are you okay?"

"I talked to the counselor. She said I could come home." Maya dropped her backpack by the door. "I want to be here. With you guys. Is that okay?"

Manny appeared behind Karen, exhausted but present. "Yeah, kiddo. That's more than okay."

Maya moved to the couch and sat. Her parents exchanged a glance but didn't push. They sat nearby, and an awkward silence filled the room. None of them knew what to say. The weight of yesterday still hung heavy in the air. Finally, Manny cleared his throat. "I was just about to look up some videos. About diesel engines. Old Detroits." He glanced at Maya.

"Want to watch with me?"

Maya was surprised by the normalcy of the offer. Not talking about death. Just... something they might have done before everything fell apart. "Okay. Yeah."

Manny pulled up YouTube on the TV and typed in "Detroit Diesel two-stroke." Videos filled the screen of engines running, deep throaty rumbles filling speakers, mechanics explaining intricate systems. "That's what grandpa worked on," Manny said, clicking on a video. The first video showed a Detroit Diesel Series 71, its distinctive sound filling the living room. The guy in the video explained the two-stroke cycle, how these engines worked differently from regular four-strokes. "Your grandpa could rebuild one of these blindfolded," Manny said, a hint of pride in his voice.

Maya found herself actually interested. The engines were massive, powerful, mechanical marvels. "How does a two-stroke work?"

Manny's face lit up as he explained the intake and exhaust happening in one revolution instead of two, the unique sound from the supercharger, the way Detroit Diesels screamed like nothing else on earth. They watched several videos together. Engine rebuilds and restorations. Old trucks with Detroit Diesels rumbling to life. Manny told stories about each one. "Grandpa had a truck with a 6V92 in it. It screamed like a banshee when he got on it."

"What's a 6V92?" Maya asked.

"Six cylinders in a V configuration, 92 cubic inches per cylinder. Detroit Diesel's naming system." He paused the video to show her. "This one's a 6-71. Inline six."

In the kitchen, Karen made tea she didn't drink and listened to them talk. This was the most engaged Manny had been in weeks. The most Maya had talked to him in months. Her heart broke and mended simultaneously. Another video showed a mechanic rebuilding an engine, using various wrenches and torque wrenches. "Grandpa had every tool you'd ever need," Manny said. "Still have them in the garage."

"The ones I used to fix the sink?" Maya asked.

"Yeah... His toolbox. The big red metal one."

Maya remembered. It was heavy, solid, full of well-maintained tools. "They're good tools."

"The best. He took care of them."

Manny paused, then looked at Maya. "They're yours now."

Maya blinked. "What?"

Manny stood slowly, joints protesting. "Come on. I want to show you something."

Maya followed him through the kitchen as Karen was watching from the counter. They went into the garage. The toolbox sat on a shelf, exactly where she remembered it. Battered red metal, scarred from decades of use. She could just make out grandpa's name faded on the side. Manny opened it. Inside, everything was organized perfectly. Wrenches arranged by size. Sockets in their trays. Screwdrivers lined up. Everything was clean, maintained, loved. "My dad gave this to me when I was about your age," Manny said. "Told me to take care of it. Pass it on."

He turned to face her. "It's yours now."

"Dad, I can't..."

"Yes, you can. You should." His voice was firm but gentle. "You've got the aptitude and the interest. You fixed that sink better than I would've. You're good with your hands, just like grandpa and just like me."

Maya felt tears in her eyes. "But you're still here."

"I know... But I want you to have it now. So, I can teach you. Show you how to use everything. Before I..." He didn't finish.

The weight of the gift settled on Maya's shoulders. They weren't just tools they were a legacy of three generations. Grandfather to father to daughter. "Take care of them," Manny said. "Keep them clean. And someday, when you have kids, you pass them on. That's how it works."

Maya ran her hand over the tools, feeling the cool metal, the weight of history. "You really think I'll have kids someday?"

"I hope so. If you want them."

Her voice became small. "You won't be there when I get married or when I have kids. You're gonna miss out when I graduate college. You won't be there for any of it."

Manny sat heavily on the workbench, exhausted but present. "No. I won't. And I hate that." Pure honesty. "But you'll tell them about me, right?"

"Of course I will."

"Then I'll be there. In a way."

Manny looked at the toolbox, then at Maya. "My dad died when you were little. You don't remember him."

Maya shook her head. "But he's still here. In me and in you. In these tools." Manny gestured to the garage, to everything around them. "The things he taught me, I taught you. That doesn't die."

Maya started to understand. "I'll die," Manny continued. "But what I gave you... that lives on. You'll teach your kids. They'll teach theirs. That's the circle. That's how we live forever."

"Like the tools," Maya whispered.

"Exactly, like the tools. Three generations so far. It could be ten someday. All of us connected."

Maya wiped her eyes. "I'll take care of them. I promise."

"I know you will."

They returned to the living room, Maya carrying the weight of her inheritance in more than just metal and wood. They settled back on the couch, Manny looking exhausted but satisfied. "There's something else I want to talk to you about," he said after a moment. "About... after."

Maya tensed but nodded. "You know how most funerals are in cemeteries? Headstones, graves, that kind of thing?"

"Yeah. Like on TV."

"I'm not doing that."

Maya looked at him, confused. "What do you mean?"

Manny shifted to face her more fully. "There's a place out past Surprise. Called Eternal Forest Memorial. They do tree burials. Natural burials. You pick a tree, and they bury you beneath it. No casket. No vault. Just you and the earth and the tree."

"Wait, what? A tree?"

"The tree grows from you. You become part of it. It's living... growing. It's more than a stone marker." His voice grew warmer. "People can come sit in the shade and talk to you. Be with you without standing over a grave."

Maya tried to picture it. This wasn't what funerals looked like on TV. No cemetery or headstone. There was nothing traditional about it. "That's... not normal."

"No. It's not."

"Why would you want that?"

Manny leaned forward. "Because I don't want you to stand over a grave crying. I want you to sit under a tree, talking to me. Tell me about your day, your life. Maybe bring your kids someday. I want it to feel alive, not dead."

Maya processed this. "What kind of tree?"

"A Palo Verde. You know those trees?"

"The ones with the green trunks?"

"Yeah. They bloom yellow in the spring. They're tough survivors and they don't need much water. They thrive in the desert." He smiled slightly. "Kind of like us, don't you think?"

Maya thought about it. Arizona natives... desert dwellers who were tough and resilient. "Yeah. Like us."

"So instead of a cemetery, I'd come to the forest. And you'd be... the tree."

"Part of the tree," Manny corrected gently. "Feeding it and helping it grow. I'm not the tree... just part of it. Does that make sense?"

Maya thought about it. Actually, it kind of did. Better than a cold stone marker in a traditional cemetery. "I could sit under the tree."

"You could sit under the tree. Anytime you wanted. Rain or shine. Day or night. You can tell me about school, boys or problems. I'll be there. Just... listening differently."

Tears streamed down Maya's face. "I'll visit you. A lot."

"I hope you do but don't feel like you have to. If you need time away, that's okay too."

"No." Maya shook her head firmly. "I'll visit. I'll tell you everything. About college and my life. I'll bring my kids when I have them. Show them the tree and tell them about you."

Manny's own eyes filled with tears. "That's all I could ask for."

He pulled her into a hug, and they held each other both crying, but not as desperately as yesterday. It was sad but also peaceful.

Karen had been watching from the kitchen the entire time. Through the window to the garage. From the doorway to the living room. Giving them space but unable to look away. She saw Manny animated, engaged, teaching. Maya listening, learning, connecting. The gap that had been between them for months was closing right before her eyes. Love visible in every gesture. Father and daughter making memories. And watching it, Karen understood. She was still angry at Manny for making the choice without her. Still drowning in guilt that she was alive because he was dying. But watching them together...

This was what he'd given her. This was why he'd done it. If Karen had died and Manny lived, Maya would have lost her mother. The distance between father and daughter might never have closed. They wouldn't have had these moments or this connection. Manny had known Maya needed her mother. He knew she and Maya were close, bonded. He'd chosen to save Karen not just for Karen. But for Maya. *He did this for her,* Karen thought, gripping the counter. *So, she wouldn't lose her mother. So, we could have each other.*

The toolbox... The tree... These conversations. Manny was making sure Maya had pieces of him in tangible memories. He was providing ways for her to stay connected. He was preparing her for the end. Tears streamed down Karen's face, and she covered her mouth to keep from sobbing. The weight of it was crushing filled with gratitude and grief tangled so tightly she couldn't separate them. After Maya went upstairs to put away the counselor's materials, Manny stayed on the couch, exhausted. Karen walked into the living room and sat beside him. She didn't say anything at first. Manny glanced at her, uncertain. "That was beautiful," Karen said quietly. "What you did with her."

"I wanted her to have something."

"You gave her everything."

Karen's voice broke. "I was so angry at you."

"I know. You had every right to be."

"I'm still angry. Part of me." She paused. "But watching you two..." She couldn't finish.

"You did this for her," she said finally.

Manny looked confused. "For you. I did it for you both."

"No. I mean yes. But also, her. Maya needed her mother. You knew that." Karen's voice shook. "You and she were distant. But me and her..."

Manny understood. "She needed you more than she needed me."

That's not true."

"It is. And it's okay. I wanted her to have you."

Karen felt the anger melting, shifting into something else. Something softer.

"I still think you were wrong to do it without telling me."

"I know."

"I still think you took away my choice."

"I know."

"But I forgive you." The words came out quiet but certain. "For Maya's sake. For yours and mine. I forgive you."

Manny didn't speak; he couldn't speak. He just took her hand and squeezed it. "I'll never be okay with losing you," Karen continued. "But I have to accept it. I'll take care of Maya. I'll make sure she's okay."

Manny's voice was thick. "I know you will. Look at her and look at you. You're both alive. That means everything."

Maya came back downstairs and found her parents sitting together, holding hands. Something had shifted in the air. It was lighter somehow. She joined them on the couch, sitting on Manny's other side. The three of them together was their new normal. Manny put one arm around Karen, one around Maya. Holding his family together while he still could. They didn't watch more videos, talk about death or cry. They just sat together, existing in each other's presence. Maya's head rested on Manny's shoulder. "I'm going to take auto shop next semester."

Manny smiled. "Yeah?"

"Yeah. Learn to work on cars. Use the tools properly."

"Grandpa would be proud."

Karen added, "I'm proud too."

Maya looked at her mom. "I'm not handling this well. I'm a mess."

"We're all a mess," Karen said gently. "But we're a mess together."

Before heading upstairs for the night, Maya turned back to them. "Tomorrow, can we go see it? The forest?"

"The tree?" Manny asked.

"Yeah. I want to see where you'll be."

Manny's surprise showed on his face. "If you want to."

"I want to. I want to see the tree. Pick it out with you. Is that okay?"

"That's more than okay."

"We'll all go," Karen added. "As a family."

Maya nodded. "Good. As a family." She headed upstairs. "Goodnight. I love you both."

"Love you too," they said together.

After Maya left, Karen and Manny remained on the couch. The house grew quiet. Tomorrow they'll visit the forest and choose the tree together. But tonight, they just sat. "She's going to be okay," Karen said.

"Because of you."

"Because of both of us. Because of this... what we're doing right now. Preparing her and being honest. And by giving her tools, literally and figuratively to figure it out while making memories."

"I hope it's enough," Manny said.

"It will be. She's strong. She's got your stubbornness and my resilience. She'll be okay."

They sat in the dim light, not afraid of the silence anymore but somehow comfortable in it. Two people who'd chosen each other over and over. Even in death. *This is why I did it,* Manny thought. *My family together. Healing and living.*

I forgive you, Karen thought.

They stayed on the couch, holding hands, until sleep found them both. Tomorrow will be a new day. But tonight was peaceful.

Chapter Thirteen - The Revelation

The desert morning was cool and clear as they drove north, the sun was still low enough to paint the saguaros in shades of amber. Karen kept her eyes on the road, one hand on the wheel and the other resting near Manny's on the center console. In the backseat, Maya watched the landscape change as they left Buckeye behind. The scrub giving way to open desert, mountains rising purple in the distance. "You, okay?" Karen asked quietly. Manny nodded, though she could see the effort it took. He'd insisted on coming, despite her concerns about the drive wearing him out. "I want to see it," he'd said that morning. "I want us to see it together."

So here they were, heading past Surprise toward Wickenburg, the road stretching out before them like a promise. The radio played something soft and instrumental. No one spoke much because there wasn't much that needed saying. The entrance to Eternal Forest Memorial was understated. It had a tasteful sign in earth tones along with a gravel drive lined with native plants. Karen turned in slowly, the gravel crunching under the tires. The office building ahead was small, built with natural materials that blended into the desert landscape.

A woman in her sixties met them at the door. "You must be the Chavez family," she said warmly. "I'm Sally Mason. Welcome."

Her compassion was evident but not overwhelming. She understood they were here for something difficult, something precious. She led them through the office briefly. The paperwork can wait, she said as she led them out onto the grounds. "Take your time," Sally said. "Walk wherever you like. Find the one that speaks to you."

The memorial grounds spread out before them, acres of carefully maintained desert land dotted with native trees. Palo Verde with their distinctive green bark. Mesquite with feathery leaves rustling in the breeze. The ancient-looking ironwood standing strong and gnarled. What struck Maya first was how alive it felt. It wasn't somber like the cemetery where her grandmother was buried, all cold marble and stone. Here, birds sang in the branches. A breeze carried the scent of creosote and sage. She could see other families scattered across the property. There was a grandmother and a young girl sitting beneath a mesquite tree, the girl talking animatedly. Not far off in the distance an older couple holding hands near an ironwood. "It's not creepy," Maya said, surprised by her own observation.

Karen squeezed Manny's hand. "What isn't?"

"This place. I thought it would be... I don't know, sad. Morbid." Maya gestured at the trees, the open sky. "But it's actually kind of beautiful."

Manny smiled. It was the first real smile she'd seen from him in days. "That's what I hoped you'd think."

They walked slowly, pausing at different trees. Each had a small bronze marker at its base with names, dates, and sometimes a quote or message. Karen read them quietly as they passed. "Beloved brother." "Always in our hearts." "Until we meet again."

Manny's breathing was labored, but he kept going. Karen stayed close to his side, ready to support him if needed. Maya wandered a bit ahead, then circled back, drawn to the normalcy of it all. The grandmother and young girl were still talking to their tree. The girl was telling it about her soccer game. "You were right about this," Karen said softly.

Manny looked at her. "You think so?"

"Yes." She gestured at the living trees, the mountains in the distance, the wide-open sky. "It's not death. It's... continuation."

They found the Palo Verde on a slight rise. It was young. Sally had said it was about ten years old but already it was twenty feet tall, its green bark bright in the sunlight. Yellow blooms clustered on its branches. And the view... you could see the mountains from here, the peaks still holding a bit of winter snow. "This one," Manny said. "Can you see it?"

Karen looked at the tree, then at the view beyond. "The mountains. You always loved the mountains."

Maya stepped up beside them, running her hand along the smooth bark. "It's strong... Like you, Dad."

Manny's eyes were wet. He didn't try to hide it. "This is good. This is right."

Sally appeared as if sensing the moment. She explained the process gently. She detailed a natural burial, no embalming, no concrete vault or metal casket. Just a biodegradable shroud or simple pine box. The body would rest beneath the tree's roots, nourishing it as it grew. "You become part of the tree," Sally said. "Part of the desert... part of everything."

Maya had questions. Could they visit whenever they wanted? (Yes.) Could they bring things flowers or, she hesitated, tools? (Manny smiled at that. Yes.) Would there be a marker with his name? (Yes, a small bronze plaque, tasteful and permanent.)

They stood together beneath the Palo Verde, wind rustling its branches, shadow and sunlight dappling the ground. The three of them, a family unit. Karen thought about what was coming at the end of this, the beginning of something else. But here, now, there was peace. "This is good," Manny said again, barely above a whisper. "This is right."

Karen nodded, tears on her cheeks but also relief. Maya leaned against her mother's shoulder. They'd found the place where he would rest.

The drive home started fine. Manny dozed in the passenger seat while Karen drove, Maya quiet in the back. But halfway home, Karen noticed him shifting uncomfortably. "You okay?"

"Yeah," he said, but his voice was strained. "Just tired."

By the time they reached Tonopah Valley, he was pale and sweating. Karen kept glancing over, worry mounting. "Almost home. Hang on."

"Karen..." His voice was tight. "I don't feel good."

She barely got the car into the driveway before he had the door open. He stumbled out, made it two steps, and vomited violently onto the pavement. The sound was awful... it was wet, desperate, his body convulsing with the effort. "Dad!" Maya was out of the car, frozen in the driveway.

Karen rushed around to his side, holding him as his body shook. It went on and on, until there was nothing left and he was just dry heaving, bent over, gasping. "I need to lie down," he managed when it finally stopped. Karen and Maya got on either side of him, supporting his weight. His legs barely worked. Each step toward the house was an effort. They made it to the living room and he collapsed onto the couch, lying on his side, completely spent.

Karen got a cool cloth for his forehead, a glass of water he couldn't drink. Maya stood in the doorway, her face white with fear. This was what dying looked like. This was it... happening in real time. Karen called Rosita the moment they got Manny settled on the couch. He'd vomited again in the house, dry heaving for a while after with nothing coming out. His body was shutting down. Karen couldn't explain it and she didn't need to... "I'm coming," was all Rosita said. She arrived ten minutes later with a bag of supplies. She found Karen in the kitchen; Maya was upstairs and Manny sleeping fitfully on the couch. Karen's face was drawn with exhaustion and fear. "He's getting worse," Karen said unnecessarily.

"Sí. The end is coming." Rosita set her bag down. "This is when I am most needed."

She moved through the house with quiet efficiency, gathering supplies. Clean washcloths, a bowl of cool water, blankets, pillows. She sat beside Manny and gently wiped his face with a cool cloth. "Señor Chavez," she said softly, even though he was sleeping. "I am here. You are not alone."

She stayed for hours. Karen tried to send her home. "You don't have to stay, you've already worked all day" but Rosita shook her head. "This is my work too. The most important work. I stay. You call the people he needs to see."

Karen pulled out her phone, stepped into the kitchen. Her hands shook as she dialed. "James? It's Karen. Can you come over? Soon?"

There was a pause on the other end. James Chen knew that tone. "I'll be there in twenty minutes."

She hung up and checked on Manny. "I called James," Karen said quietly. "He's coming."

Manny's eyes opened slightly. A weak nod. "Good."

When James Chen arrived later, Rosita greeted him at the door. She'd never met him before, but she recognized him immediately. He was the best friend. The one who carried his own guilt and grief. "You are James," she said. "Manny's friend from the plant."

"Yes. How did you...?"

"He talks about you. Come in. He is sleeping, but he will want to see you when he wakes."

She showed James to the living room, then gave him and Manny privacy for their conversation. She stayed in the kitchen with Karen, making tea neither of them would drink, just giving her hands something to do. When the argument started, James and Manny's voices were rising Rosita touched Karen's arm. "Let them... Men need to fight sometimes before they can say goodbye."

When Maya came downstairs, drawn by the raised voices, Rosita intercepted her at the stairs. "Your father is talking to his friend. Private things. Man things. Please wait upstairs. I will get you when they are done."

Rosita returned to the kitchen and sat together with Karen at the kitchen table while the men argued

James was still in his work clothes; he must have left the plant immediately. When he saw Manny on the couch, the shock registered on his face. It had only been days since the hospital, but Manny looked like he'd aged years. "Manny. Hey, man."

Manny tried to sit up a little. James crossed the room quickly. "No, don't bother. Stay comfortable."

He pulled a chair close to the couch. James looked at Manny, really looked at him. The hollowed cheeks, the darkened hands, the way his breathing seemed to take effort. "You look like hell."

A weak smile. "Feel worse."

"Yeah, I bet." James rubbed his face, searching for words. Thirty years of friendship and he didn't know what to say. "Listen, I need to tell you something. I filed a complaint."

Manny's eyes focused. "What?"

"Against the contamination report. Against the conclusions that cleared the company." James leaned forward. "Reed's negligence, the cover-up. They can't get away with this."

"James, no." Distress crossed Manny's face. "Why would you do that?"

"Why? Manny, you're dying because of Reed's incompetence!"

"Let it go."

"Let it go?" James's voice rose. "The report was falsified. Everyone knows it. Someone has to hold them accountable. I'm not letting this slide."

"It won't change anything." Manny's voice was tired. "I'm still dying."

"It's about what's right!"

"It's about you staying employed, keeping your family safe!"

"Your family deserves justice!"

They went back and forth, tension building. In the kitchen, Karen could hear them arguing. Maya looked down upon them, hidden upstairs. Karen took Rositas's advice and decided to let them work it out. "James, stop." Manny's voice cut through, quiet but firm. "Please. You don't understand. This... this is what I asked for."

James stopped mid-sentence. "What do you mean, asked for?"

Manny gathered what strength he had. "I prayed to God. I begged Him to take me instead of Karen."

The words hung in the air. James stared at him with a blank and confused look. "What are you talking about?"

"Karen was dying... stage four. They said she had months to live, they said." Manny's eyes were distant, remembering. "I couldn't accept it. I couldn't lose her. I prayed and I begged for a way to save her."

"Manny..."

"Then the old man appeared. On the road."

James frowned. "Old man? What old man?"

"The angel. That's what I think he was." Manny's voice was stronger now, very certain of his words. "His ancient eyes and all-knowing smile. He asked me what I wanted. I said... me for her."

"Me for her," James repeated slowly, trying to process this. "I said yes. I didn't even hesitate." Manny looked toward the kitchen where Karen stood, healthy and alive. "And look at her now. She's healthy. Thriving. The cancer is gone, James. It's completely gone."

James opened his mouth, closed it. His engineer's brain was rejecting every word. "Manny, radiation exposure isn't... you can't just..."

But he trailed off, looking at Karen in the kitchen. He'd seen her months ago, frail and sick. He'd been at her bedside when she could barely lift her head. Stage four breast cancer. It was a death sentence and now she was standing there, making tea, looking healthier than she had in years. "That's not... that doesn't make sense," James said weakly.

"I know how it sounds." Manny's eyes were closing, exhaustion pulling at him. "But I know what I saw. I know what I agreed to and I don't regret it, James. Not for a second."

James looked at his best friend. There was peace on Manny's face despite the pain. He had acceptance of his fate. He'd made his choice and was at peace with it. "This can't be real," James whispered.

But Manny was already asleep, mid-conversation, his body simply giving out. James sat there watching his shallow breathing, face gaunt, body shutting down piece by piece. His best friend of thirty years, fading before his eyes. He stood slowly, went to the kitchen. Karen was there with Rosita. "Karen." His voice was low, urgent. "I need to ask you something. What Manny just told me. About an angel... About a deal."

Karen met his eyes directly. "He told you the truth."

"But Karen, that's... that's impossible." He was searching her face for rationality, for the logical explanation. "People don't just make deals with God and then angels appear."

"I can't explain it, James. Not in a way that makes scientific sense." She set down her tea. "But I know what happened to me. The cancer is gone and I know what's happening to Manny. With God, anything is possible."

The statement hung there and James had no response. Everything he'd built his life on... reason, logic, measurable reality was all being challenged. But the impossible was standing in front of him. Karen, alive when she should be dead. "I should go," he said finally.

Karen responded, "I know this is a lot. Take the time you need."

"Tell him..." James looked back at Manny sleeping on the couch. "Tell him I'll come back soon."

James turned to leave, looking shaken and confused, Rosita walked him to the door. "You heard something tonight that your mind cannot accept," she said to him. "This is okay. The mind is small. The heart is large. Listen to your heart, not your head."

James nodded, unable to speak, and left. He drove home in a daze, hands gripping the wheel. His mind raced through everything. The timeline of both conditions starting the same day, the medical impossibility of Karen's recovery, the mystery of Manny's radiation levels. Part of him insisted this was insane, just grief and trauma. But another part whispered... what if? He couldn't reconcile it. Faith versus facts. His logical brain at war with undeniable evidence.

Upstairs, Maya sat at the top of the stairs where she'd been hidden after James arrived. She'd heard everything through the open living room. The argument about the complaint. Her father's confession about and a deal. Her father had chosen to die so her mother could live. She sat frozen, barely breathing. Processing what she'd just heard. The prayer to God. "Me for her." Her father made a deal with God and God had sent an angel to make it happen. Confusion swirled all around. God, angels, deals? This can't be real. But also... it made sense, didn't it? Mom's miraculous recovery. Dad's impossible illness. Both at the same time. The fairy tale logic of it.

She heard James leave. Footsteps to the door. Murmured goodbyes from Rosita as the door was closing. Now it was just Mom and Rosita downstairs with dad sleeping on the couch. She had this impossible knowledge burning in her chest. She stood and walked downstairs. Karen was back in the kitchen, and she was startled when Maya appeared. Maya's face was tear-streaked but determined. "Is it true?"

Karen's heart sank. "Maya... how much did you hear?"

But she knew she heard everything. The look on Maya's face said it all.

"Did Dad really make a deal with God and he sent an angel?" Maya's voice shook but her eyes were steady. "To die so you could live?"

Karen took a deep breath, meeting her daughter's eyes. "Yes."

Just that simple truth without elaboration yet. "Yes, he did."

Maya pulled out a chair, sat heavily. Karen sat across from her at the kitchen table while Rosita was quiet. Every word felt weighed and important. "The old man was on the side of the road," Karen began. "Your father saw him, talked to him while he helped him change a flat tire. He told me later, after it was already done. He knew I would try to stop him."

"What did the angel say?"

"I didn't see him. Only your father did. Your father said that the angel told him to be careful what you wish for... Your dad wished for this." Karen's hands wrapped around her tea cup. "And I believe it happened. I believe he was real. Because I was dying, Maya. Stage four cancer with no hope and no treatments left. And then suddenly... I was fine. Completely fine."

"The doctors can't explain it," Karen continued. "They called it a medical miracle, but I know what it was now. I know what your father did."

Maya stood abruptly, chair scraping back. "How could he do that?!" Her voice rose, anguish and anger mixing. "How could he just decide to die?!"

"He did it because he loves us."

"That's not love! That's abandonment!" Tears streamed down Maya's face. "He's leaving us! By choice! We could have figured something out! We could have had time with both of you!"

Karen remained calm. She'd expected this and understood it. "Why did he get to decide?" Maya was pacing now. "Why didn't anyone ask me? I would have said no! I would have stopped him!"

"That's exactly why he didn't tell anyone." Karen's voice was gentle but firm. "Because we would have tried to stop him. And I would have died, Maya."

The words hit Maya like a physical blow. She stopped pacing. *'I would have died.'*

Mom would be gone, no one to talk to, laugh with, learn from. The choice crystallized in her mind. Not should Dad die? but Dad or Mom? Only one could survive. Dad chose Mom. He chose Maya having a mother over his own death to give them life together. "He really loved you that much?" Maya's voice broke, barely a whisper. Karen's tears matched her daughter's. "Yes. He loved me that much. And he loved you that much. He wanted you to have your mother. He couldn't bear the thought of you losing me."

Maya looked toward the living room where her father slept. This man who gave everything. Traded his life for her mother's. The most selfless act imaginable. "It's like... like a sad fairy tale," Maya said, trying to find words for the impossible. "The kind where the prince dies to save the princess. But it's real. It actually happened."

"Yes." Karen reached across the table, took her daughter's hand. "Your father is the bravest person I've ever known. And the most loving."

Maya was crying but also marveling. "I can't believe he loves us that much."

The depth of it was incomprehensible. Romantic in the truest, most tragic sense. Maya felt everything at once. She was sad, angry at the unfairness, but also proud. Honored to be his daughter. Understanding, finally, what love really means. "So, angels are real," she said. Statement, not question.

"I believe they are," Karen said. "Or at least, something is. Something beyond what we can understand."

"People don't get happy endings in real life."

"Sometimes they do. Just not the way we expected." Karen squeezed her hand. "I'm here healthy and alive. That's your father's happy ending. Even if he won't be here to see it."

Maya understood then. This was Dad's victory. This was what he wanted. Not to survive, but to ensure they did. His happy ending was their continued life. They walked together into the living room. Manny was still asleep on the couch, his breathing shallow and labored. Face peaceful despite the pain. A hero in repose.

Maya knelt beside the couch. "I love you, Dad," she whispered, knowing he might not hear but needing to say it anyway and she ran upstairs and closed the door. Rosita hugged Karen, "I will speak with her too. She is strong and you did well to be truthful with her."

Karen nodded as Rosita made her way upstairs.

Maya sat on her bed, door closed, trying to process what her mother had just told her. An angel and a trade. Dad was dying so Mom could live. How could it be real... A soft knock on her door. "Mija?"

Rosita's voice. Maya had forgotten she was still downstairs. "Can I come in?"

Maya didn't answer, but Rosita opened the door anyway. She had that grandmother's privilege, knowing when permission didn't need to be asked. She sat on the edge of Maya's bed, not speaking at first. Just being present. "They told you the truth," Rosita said finally... not a question.

"Yeah." Maya's voice was hollow. "About the angel and the deal. All of it."

"And what do you think?"

"I think it's insane." Maya looked at Rosita. "Do you believe it? Angels with deals and trading lives?"

Rosita was quiet for a moment. "I believe your father prayed. I believe your mother was dying and now she is not. I believe your father was well and now he is not. I believe love can do things that make no sense to our minds but perfect sense to our hearts."

"That's not an answer."

"No?" Rosita smiled slightly. "Then let me tell you what I know for certain. Your father loves you and your mother so much that he was willing to die so you could have each other. Whether an angel granted that wish or God worked in some other mysterious way, the result is the same. He gave his life for yours."

Maya felt tears coming again. She'd been crying so much lately. "I don't want him to die."

"Of course you don't. That would be very strange if you did." Rosita put a hand on Maya's knee. "But wanting something does not change what is. Your father is dying. This is the truth. The question is... what will you do with the time you have left?"

"I don't know."

"Yes, you do." Rosita's voice was gentle but firm. "You will love him. You will talk to him. You will learn from him. You will let him teach you everything he wants to teach you before he goes. This is what you will do."

Maya looked at her hands. "Do you think he'll still be able to hear us.

After... At the tree."

"Do you believe that?"

"I want to."

"Then believe it," Rosita said simply. "Faith is choosing to believe even when you cannot see. Your father has faith that he will hear you. Give him the gift of knowing you have that same faith."

They sat together in silence for a moment. Then Maya asked, "Have you seen this before? Someone trading their life for someone else's?"

Rosita's expression grew distant, remembering. "Once. Many years ago... a mother and a daughter. The daughter was dying... it was a car accident, very bad. The mother sat by her bed and prayed the same prayer your father prayed. And the next day, the daughter woke up. She was healed and yet it was impossible, the doctors said. And the mother, she got sick and died within two months after that."

Maya stared at her. "Really?"

"Really. I was the caregiver for both of them. I saw it happen." Rosita's eyes glistened. "The daughter, she is grown now and has children of her own. She lives the life her mother gave her and every year on her mother's birthday, she plants a tree. Twenty-three trees now. A whole grove, all in her mother's name."

"Does she regret it? Being the one who lived?"

"At first, yes. She was angry, like you are angry. She felt guilty, like your mother feels guilty. But eventually, she understood that her mother's gift would be wasted if she spent her whole life mourning instead of living."

Rosita squeezed Maya's knee. "This is what I want you to understand, mija. Your father is giving you and your mother the greatest gift anyone can give. Do not waste it by being frozen in grief. Feel the grief and yes, you must feel it. But also feel the love. Feel the gratitude. Feel the awe of being loved that much."

Maya wiped her eyes. "I don't know how to do that."

"One day at a time. One moment at a time. Right now, in this moment, you go downstairs. You sit with your father. You tell him you love him. That is enough for today. Tomorrow, you will do it again. And the next day, and the next. Until the day comes when you can't anymore. And then you carry him in your heart and keep going."

Rosita stood, offered her hand to Maya. "Come. Your parents need to see that you are okay. Or at least, that you will be okay. They need that right now."

Maya took her hand and let Rosita pull her to her feet. As they walked to the door, Maya asked quietly, "Will you be here? When he... when it happens?"

"If you want me to be, I will be here. I will help you through it. I have done this many times, mija. You will not walk this path alone."

"Thank you."

"De nada. This is why God put me here. To be the bridge between the living and the dying. To help families say goodbye with love instead of fear."

They went downstairs together, and Maya sat with her parents, Karen's hand rested on Maya's shoulder. United in their love for this man. United in their grief and in their gratitude. Rosita made tea for everyone and stayed until the house felt calm again. This was her calling and her gift. To be the steady hand in the storm, the wise voice in the chaos, the grandmother every family needed when death came knocking.

Chapter Fourteen - The Final Comfort

Two days after the trip to the memorial, Manny tried to stand from the couch. His legs buckled immediately, refusing to support his weight. He fell back against the cushions, gasping. "Karen..." His voice was barely above a whisper. "I can't."

Karen appeared from the kitchen, took one look at him, and understood. He couldn't stay on the couch anymore. He needed a proper bed. Comfort with dignity. "Maya!" she called. "I need your help."

Together they got on either side of him, supporting his weight as they lifted. Each step toward the bedroom was an ordeal. Manny's legs moved but barely functioned, his weight pressing down on them. By the time they reached the bedroom, all three were breathing hard.

The same bed where Karen had lain dying with the same pillows propped against the headboard. The same view out the window to the backyard with the nightstand, the lamp and water glass. They lowered him onto the mattress and he lay back, completely exhausted from the short walk.

Karen adjusted the pillows behind him so he could breathe easier. She filled the water glass and got a cool cloth for his forehead. She cracked the window for fresh air. The same things Manny had done for her, reversed now. She stood where Manny used to stand, watching helplessly. Maya lingered in the doorway, afraid to come in but more afraid to leave. This room meant death. First her mother, almost. Now her father, certainly. But she forced herself to enter, to sit on the edge of the bed.

Manny looked at his family gathered in this room. The roles were reversed but love unchanged. He knew this was the last move he'd make. He wouldn't leave this bed again. Death would come here. There was a strange peace in that certainty. "Listen to me," he said, reaching for their hands. His voice was weak but clear. "Both of you. I need you to know... I'm happy."

Karen's face crumpled. "Manny..."

"No, listen. This is what I wanted. What I prayed for." He squeezed their hands. "I got to see Karen get better. I got to have this time with you both. I wouldn't change anything."

He turned to Karen, his eyes holding hers. "You gave me the best years of my life. Twenty years of marriage, and I'd do it all again. You made me a better man." His voice grew firmer despite his weakness. "Don't you dare feel guilty about living."

Karen nodded, tears streaming silently. Then to Maya. "I am so proud of you. So proud of who you're becoming." A small smile touched his lips. "You have your mother's strength and my hands. You're going to do amazing things."

Maya couldn't speak, could only grip his hand tighter. No regrets or bitterness. Just gratitude for what he'd had, satisfaction with his choice, readiness for what came next.

After they settled Manny in the bedroom, Rosita arrived. Karen had called her, voice shaking. "He can't walk anymore. We moved him to the bed."

"I am coming," Rosita had said. Just that. She knew what it meant. She arrived with her large canvas bag, the one she brought to all her end-of-life cases. Inside were supplies both practical and sacred. She found Manny propped up on pillows, exhausted from the short walk. Karen and Maya hovered anxiously, not sure what to do now that he was here.

"Go," Rosita said gently to them. "Make tea. Eat something. I will sit with him for a while."

They left gratefully, needing a moment to breathe, to process, to pretend this wasn't happening. Rosita sat in the chair beside the bed. "Señor Chavez. You have returned to this room."

Manny's eyes opened slightly. "Rosita."

"Sí. I am here." She pulled out a small candle from her bag, white and unscented. "In my village, we prepare the room when death is close. We make it a sacred space. A good place for the journey. May I do this for you?"

Manny nodded weakly. She lit the candle and placed it on the dresser. "Light for the path ahead."

She opened the window wider. "Fresh air, so your spirit can breathe."

She pulled out a small bundle of dried sage from her bag. "This is for cleansing. To make the space pure. Is it okay?"

"Yes," Manny whispered.

She lit the sage, letting the smoke drift through the room. Not too much as Manny's lungs were weak. Just enough to change the energy. "We honor your journey," she said softly in Spanish, then in English. "We prepare the way."

When Karen and Maya returned, they found the room transformed. Not dramatically, everything was still the same. But it felt different. Calmer, sacred in a way. "What did you do?" Maya asked.

"I prepared the space," Rosita said simply. "This is how we do it in my village. We make the room ready for the holy work of dying."

She turned to Karen and Maya. "Death is not the enemy. It is a doorway. Your father is about to walk through that door. Our job... yours and mine is to help him walk through with dignity and love. To make the passage as gentle as possible."

She pulled out a small wooden cross from her bag and set it on the nightstand. "For faith." Then a photo frame. "For memories. You will fill this with a picture you choose."

Maya and Karen watched as Rosita moved through the room, making small adjustments. Opening curtains so Manny could see the sky. Arranging pillows for comfort. Placing a bowl of water and washcloths within reach.

"This is what I know after thirty-two years," Rosita said, turning to face them. "Death is not something to fear. It is something to prepare for, to honor, to witness with open hearts. Your father is doing something very brave. He is showing you how to die well. Pay attention. Learn from him. This is his final gift."

She sat beside the bed again and took Manny's hand. "Señor Chavez, you have walked a hard road. But you have walked it with love. You made a choice that few people have the courage to make. You traded your life for theirs. This is holy and sacred. This is the truest form of love."

Manny's eyes filled with tears.

"Now you are near the end of your journey. And I want you to know that you do not walk alone. I will be here. Your family will be here. And when the time comes, the angel you met on the road, he will be here too. You will not be afraid. You will not be in pain. You will simply... step through the door."

She squeezed his hand. "And on the other side, there will be light and peace. All the people who loved you, waiting. This is what I believe. This is what I have seen in the eyes of the dying. They see something beautiful at the end. Something we cannot see yet. But you will see it. And it will be good."

Manny's voice was barely a whisper. "Thank you."

"De nada, Señor Chavez. It is my honor to walk this part of the path with you."

She stayed for hours, sitting vigil while Manny drifted in and out of sleep. She taught Karen and Maya how to care for him and how to help him drink, how to adjust his position, how to read his discomfort even when he couldn't speak.

"This is the work of love," she told them. "These small acts of care. They matter more than any grand gestures. A cool cloth on the forehead. A gentle hand. Being present. This is how we say goodbye."

When evening came and Manny seemed stable, Rosita stood to leave. "I will come back tomorrow. And every day after, until the end. You will not do this alone. I promise you."

At the door, Maya hugged her. "Thank you for being here."

"This is why God made me a caregiver, mija. To be here for moments like this. To help families love each other through the hardest thing. It is a privilege."

She left them with instructions, "Call me any time. Day or night. When you think the end is close, call me. I will come. I will be here."

And she meant it. This was her calling. This was her sacred work. To be present at the doorway between life and death. To help families say goodbye with grace. To witness love in its purest, most heartbreaking form. The circle was continuing. And she was honored to be part of it.

After Rosita left, "I need to tell you something," Manny said after a moment. "When I sleep... I see him."

"Who?" Karen asked.

"The angel. The old man from the road."

Maya's eyes widened. Karen leaned closer.

"Every time I sleep now, he's there. In my dreams, but more real than dreams." Manny's voice took on a distant quality, as if seeing something they couldn't. "We talk. He's preparing me for the journey ahead."

"What does he say?" Karen's voice trembled.

"He told me he'll come back. When it's time, he'll be there to get me." Manny paused, gathering strength for the important part. "He says I'm starting a new journey. But here's what matters most..."

Both women held their breath. "He said I'll still be able to hear you. When you talk to the tree, when you visit... I won't be able to answer. But I'll hear you. I'll always be listening."

Karen and Maya were visibly shaken, tears streaming down both their faces. Maya started to speak... "Dad, that's..." but she couldn't finish. She was too overwhelmed with emotion. Karen gripped his hand tighter, wanting to believe, needing to believe that this wasn't goodbye forever.

Manny turned to Maya. "Hey Kiddo, come closer."

She moved nearer, both hands wrapped around his now. "I need you to promise me something. Stay focused okay. Don't let this derail you." He held her eyes. "I know it's hard. It's going to be hard. But you're smart. So smart. Don't waste that gift."

"Dad..."

"You can do anything you set your mind to, engineering, mechanics, whatever calls to you. Don't let anyone tell you girls can't do it. You've got the skills. You've got the brains."

Maya nodded through her tears. "Take care of the tools. Use them. Every time you fix something, I'll be proud. That's three generations in that box. Now it's yours to pass on." He paused, catching his breath. "And take care of your mother for me. She's going to need you. You're both stronger than you think. Lean on each other."

Maya couldn't speak, she could only nod, memorizing his face, knowing this was goodbye. Manny turned to Karen. "I need you to do something for me."

"Anything."

"James filed that complaint against Reed. I need you to make him rescind it."

Karen stiffened. "Manny, he's trying to get you justice..."

"No." The word was firm despite his weakness. "No, it's not about justice or the fight. James could lose his job and his career. I won't let him sacrifice that for me."

"But..."

"He'll be stubborn. I know him." Manny's eyes pleaded with her. "But you have to insist. You must make him understand. Tell him I asked you to, tell him it's what I want. He'll listen to you if you say it's my dying wish."

Karen hated this. She wanted Mr. Reed held accountable. He had terrorized him for years with his overlording. She wanted someone to pay for what happened. But she looked at her husband's face and knew she would honor his wishes. "Okay. I'll talk to him. I'll make him rescind it."

Manny relaxed slightly. "Thank you." Then softer, "Remember your promise to me. You're going to live... really live. I want you to travel and experience things. Be happy, you owe me that."

"I don't know how to live without you," Karen whispered.

"Yes, you do. You're the strongest person I know. You survived cancer. You can survive this." He touched her face gently. "And I'll be listening. At the tree... I'll always be listening."

A silence settled over them, heavy with what was coming. Manny broke it with pragmatic words. "We need to talk about the logistics."

Karen didn't want to hear this, but she made herself listen. "When I die, there are steps you need to follow. First, and this is crucial, don't call 911."

Karen's eyes widened. "What?"

"Don't call 911. That means paramedics, resuscitation attempts, the hospital. Call Eternal Forest Memorial first. Sally gave us the number."

He caught his breath, continued. "They have a 24-hour line for when someone passes. They'll send someone to collect... to collect me." It was hard to say it that way, but necessary. "It has to be within 24 hours for natural burial."

Karen nodded, trying to absorb all this. "My doctor... she knows about the radiation exposure. She's agreed to sign the death certificate. You'll need to call her office when... when it happens. They'll send it to the memorial."

"Okay," Karen said, her voice shaking.

"Sally said natural burial happens quick. Within a day or two, before embalming would be needed. That's why the paperwork has to be ready. I've already filled out most of it. It's in the desk drawer."

So much information... so much to remember. "I should be writing this down."

"It's all in the folder. I wrote everything down." Even dying, he was taking care of them. "Eternal Forest will handle transportation. They have a van, specialized for natural burial. They'll come here, help you. You won't have to do the physical part alone."

Maya sat silently, listening to her father plan his own death. "They'll prepare me in a simple shroud without chemicals. You can be there if you want. At the tree or you can say goodbye here. Either way is okay." He looked between them. "It's up to you."

Karen wiped her eyes. Manny had thought of everything, making it as easy as possible, lifting the burden from her shoulders even as he prepared to leave.

Evening settled over the house and Maya refused to leave the room, bringing her homework to sit in the chair beside the bed, though the pages remained unturned. Karen sat on the other side. No one wanted to miss a moment. Manny drifted in and out of sleep. Each time he woke, he seemed relieved to find them still there. "Still here," he murmured once. "Always," Karen said. "We're right here."

They shared memories in quiet voices. Remember when we went to Sedona for our wedding? Remember Maya's first day of school? Gentle, loving, bittersweet fragments of a life together.

Manny looked at his wife and daughter and felt contentment wash over him. This was what he'd wanted to save. This love and this family was worth everything to him. Karen watched him breathe, counting each breath, knowing they were numbered. Wanting to stop time, knowing she couldn't. Maya sat with her hand on her father's arm, homework forgotten, just being present. Late into the night, Manny woke again. "Karen? Maya?"

They both leaned close. "Don't forget what I said. About being able to hear you."

"We won't," Karen promised.

"The angel promised. I'll be gone, but I'll be listening. Talk to me at the tree. Tell me about your day, about your life."

He turned to Maya. "When you graduate, tell me about it. When you fix your first diesel engine..." A weak smile. "When you fall in love someday... I'll hear all of it."

To Karen, "When you're happy again and you will be happy again... when you travel, when you experience life... I'll be proud of you. Don't be afraid or to ashamed to share it with me."

"We will," Karen promised. "We'll tell you everything."

"Every day if we need to," Maya added.

"Good... That's good."

Tears streamed down both women's faces. "Don't mourn my choice. Celebrate what it gave us. These extra weeks together were a gift." He looked at each of them in turn. "Thank you for letting me love you Karen, thank you for being my wife. Maya, thank you for being my daughter. You made my life meaningful."

Manny no longer feared death and he wasn't second-guessing his choice. He was at the point of complete acceptance. He even felt joy in knowing his sacrifice had worked. Karen and Maya were devastated but also honored. They were witnessing a man at peace with dying, and the depth of love required for that peace left them in awe. "Sorry," Manny murmured, his eyes closing. "So tired..."

He slipped into sleep mid-sentence, unable to fight it anymore. Karen and Maya watched him. Was he dreaming of the angel now? Was the old man there, preparing him for the journey ahead? The end was close. It could be tonight or tomorrow. They took turns sleeping in the chair, one always awake, watching him, listening to his breathing, treasuring every moment left. In the darkness, Karen held his hand and whispered, "I love you."

Maya did the same from the other side. Being present... that was the greatest gift they could give him now. And they would be there, no matter how long it took, until the angel came to take him home. Outside, the desert night was still. The stars wheeled overhead in their ancient patterns. The world continued, indifferent to one man's sacrifice for the family who loved him.

Chapter Fifteen - Sunrise and Goodbye

The night was stretched long. Karen sat in the chair beside the bed; Maya curled in the other. They took turns dozing, but never both at once. Someone was always watching. Always listening to Manny's labored breathing. Around four in the morning, his eyes opened. More clearly than they had in days. Awareness returning to his face. "What time is it?" His voice barely above a whisper.

Karen checked her phone. "Almost four in the morning."

Manny's gaze drifted to the window. Still dark outside, but the quality of darkness changing. It was pre-dawn.

"Can you..." He paused to gather breath. "Open the window more? I want to see the sunrise. One last time."

Karen and Maya rose immediately. Together they adjusted his pillows, propping him higher so he could see through the window. Karen cranked the window wide open. The cool desert air flowed into the room, carrying the scent of the early morning.

Karen called Rosita at 3:45 AM. Just three words: "It's time. Come."

Rosita was dressed and out the door in minutes. She'd been expecting this call and had slept in her clothes for the past two nights, ready.

She arrived at 4:20 AM. The house was quiet, lit only by the lamp in Manny's room. She let herself in.

In the bedroom, she found them. Karen and Maya on either side of the bed, Manny between them, eyes closed but breathing. The window was open, cool air flowing in. Dawn was coming and she could feel it in the quality of the darkness. "Rosita," Karen whispered. Relief flooded her face. "You came."

"Of course I came." Rosita set her bag down and approached the bed. She looked at Manny, his face peaceful, his breathing slow and labored. "Señor Chavez. I am here. You are not alone."

She took a chair and sat on the opposite side from Maya, completing the circle around him. Three people now, witnessing this passage together. "Has he been awake?" Rosita asked quietly.

"A little," Karen said. "He asked to see the sunrise. We opened the window for him."

"Good. Very good." Rosita folded her hands. "Then we will wait with him. We will watch the sun rise together."

They sat in silence, the four of them, as the darkness slowly lifted. Rosita prayed quietly in Spanish the old prayers her grandmother had taught her. They were prayers for the dying, prayers for safe passage. When the first light touched the horizon, Manny's eyes opened. They were clear, present and seeing. "Beautiful," he whispered, looking at the window. Rosita watched him watching the sunrise. She had seen this so many times, the dying drawn to light, to beauty, to one last glimpse of the world they were leaving.

The sky began to lighten in the east, the stars fading as the world was waking up. First came the colors... orange and pink bleeding across the horizon. Manny watched through the window, his face peaceful, almost smiling. "So, beautiful," he whispered again.

The sun rose, golden light spilling over the distant mountains, illuminating the saguaros standing tall in the desert. The bedroom filled with a warm glow. Manny bathed in the sunrise light, his darkened hands resting on the blanket. The birds began their morning songs along with the doves cooing. Then the Cactus wrens began joining in the calling. The sound of life continued. It was indifferent to death and beautiful because of it. The curtains moved gently in the breeze. The fresh air flowed onto Manny's face. He closed his eyes, breathing it in. "This is good," he murmured.

He kept his eyes closed but continued speaking. Voice barely audible. "Karen, Maya... come close."

They leaned in, one on each side. "Thank you. For everything." Each word an effort. "For loving me." His eyes opened, found Karen's. "Be happy and live."

"I promise," Karen whispered. "I love you."

His gaze shifted to Maya. "So proud... So very proud." A weak smile. "Remember... the toolbox. Remember me. I'll be listening."

"I love you, Dad," Maya said, voice breaking. "I'll make you proud."

"To both..." Manny's voice fading now. "Don't be sad. I'm ready. I got to see the sunrise. I got to see you and I'm happy."

And then he recognized Rosita, "Rosita, thank you for all your help. Your wisdom... remarkable."

His eyes moved between them one last time. "I love you both."

Manny took a deep breath and released it slowly. A smile settled on his face; it was peace that was filled with contentment and completion.

The sun rose golden over the mountains. Manny's face bathed in that light, and for a moment he looked young again. Healthy and whole. He had spoken his final words to Karen and Maya. The words of love, of gratitude, of release. Rosita sat quietly, bearing witness, holding space for this sacred goodbye. When Manny took his last breath and did not take another, Rosita knew immediately. She had seen death enough times to recognize its arrival. Karen's hand went to his chest. "Manny?" Her voice breaking. Tears streamed down her face, but relief came with them. No more suffering. No more pain. He was at rest. Maya gripped his hand tighter. "Dad?" Voice breaking on the word. She leaned against her mother, crying quietly.

Karen glanced at the clock through her tears. 6:47 AM. She'd need to remember that. She pulled out her phone, noted it. The exact moment he left them. Rosita stood and came around the bed. She placed her hand on Karen's shoulder. "He is gone, señora. He has walked through the door."

Karen and Maya were crying, holding Manny's hands, but Rosita saw something else. She saw Manny's face. He was peaceful, smiling slightly. She saw the sunlight filling the room. She saw the birds singing outside, the breeze moving the curtains. And she saw, though she didn't mention it to the others, a figure standing in the corner of the room. An old man, patient and kind, waiting. She blinked and he was gone. Or maybe he'd never been there at all.

But she knew. The angel had come, just as Manny said he would. He had come to guide him home. "He is at peace," Rosita said firmly. "Look at his face. He is at peace."

They looked, and it was true. The pain lines were gone. The struggle was over. He looked... free. Rosita let them sit with him for a while, not rushing them, not pushing. This was their time to say private goodbyes.

After a while, she gently touched Karen's shoulder. "There are things we must do now. Calls to make. Do you want me to help?"

Karen nodded, unable to speak. "Okay. I will help. But first, we will sit with him a little longer. There is no rush. Let us honor him properly."

She pulled out a small bottle of oil from her bag. It was blessed oil from her church. "May I?"

Karen nodded. Rosita anointed Manny's forehead with the oil, making the sign of the cross. "Vaya con Dios, Señor Chavez. Go with God. You have fought the good fight. You have finished the race and kept the faith. May you rest in peace until we meet again."

She sang softly, an old Spanish hymn about death and resurrection, about the soul's journey home. Her voice filled the room, gentle and steady. When the song ended, she helped Karen and Maya wash Manny's hands and face in a final act of care, a final intimacy. She showed them how to do it gently, with reverence. "This is how we honor the dead," she told Maya. "We care for the body with the same love we showed in life. This is the last thing we can do for him physically. So, we do it well."

When they were done, Rosita pulled a clean white sheet from her bag and helped Karen cover Manny up to his chest. Not his face, not yet. Not until they were ready. "Now," she said. "Let us make the calls. I will help you."

Karen forced herself to stand. There were things to do. Instructions to follow. Manny had planned this carefully. She would honor that. She retrieved the folder from the desk in the living room. Sally's direct line was written on top in Manny's careful handwriting. In the kitchen, she dialed with shaking hands. "Eternal Forest Memorial, this is Sally."

"This is Karen Chavez." Her voice caught. "My husband... he passed this morning."

Sally's voice was gentle. "I'm so sorry for your loss, Karen. What time?"

"6:47. About half an hour ago."

"I'll send someone right away. Is he at home?"

"Yes. In the bedroom."

"Don't move him. Don't change anything. Our team will be there within the hour." Sally's professionalism was comforting. "Do you have the death certificate arrangements in place?"

"Yes. Dr. Nguyen. She's expecting the call."

"Perfect. I'll coordinate with her office." A pause. "Karen, I need a few details. Full name?"

"Manuel Chavez. We called him Manny."

"Date of birth?"

Karen provided it, along with his Social Security Number from the folder.

"And you chose the Palo Verde tree on the rise, correct?"

"Yes. That's the one."

"We'll collect him this morning. Natural preparation takes a few hours. Burial can happen this afternoon or tomorrow morning, depending on when the county issues the permit." Sally's voice remained gentle. "You can be present if you wish, or we can handle it privately. Many families prefer not to witness the burial itself."

Karen thought about watching them lower Manny into the ground. Covering him with earth. The finality of it. "We'll come after," she said quietly. "After it's done."

"That's completely fine. I'll call you when everything is complete."

Karen hung up, then immediately dialed Dr. Nguyen's office. The answering service patched her through.

"Karen." Dr. Nguyen's voice was kind despite the early hour. "I'm so sorry. What time did he pass?"

"6:47 this morning. Peacefully."

"I'm glad he wasn't in pain." A pause. "I'll complete the death certificate this morning. The cause of death will be listed as acute radiation syndrome secondary to occupational exposure, with secondary causes of bone marrow failure and multi-organ system failure."

Karen winced at the clinical language. But that's what the official records would say. "Eternal Forest Memorial will need the certificate for the burial permit," Dr. Nguyen continued. "I'm sending it directly to Sally Mason. It should be ready within two hours. The county will issue the burial transit permit and natural burial exemption. It's all being handled."

"Thank you, doctor. For everything."

"Manny was a good man. I wish we could have done more. Take care of yourself and your daughter, Karen."

Karen returned to the bedroom. Maya was still there, sitting beside her father's body, holding his hand.

"I called the memorial and Dr. Nguyen," Karen said softly. "They'll be here soon."

Maya nodded but didn't move. They sat together, saying private goodbyes. Maya leaned close to her father and spoke quietly. "I'm sorry I got mad about school stuff. Thank you for teaching me about tools. I'll take care of Mom. I promise. I'll visit the tree all the time."

When it was Karen's turn, she smoothed his hair back the way she used to when he was alive. "You saved me. You saved us both. I'll live the life you wanted me to have. I'll be happy. It might take time, but I'll be happy. I'll tell you everything at the tree." She kissed his forehead. "Wait for me. I'll see you someday."

At nine o'clock, a knock at the door. Rosita greeted them at the door.

"Please be gentle. He was a good man. His family loves him very much."

She stood with Karen and Maya as they watched the team prepare Manny's body for transport. She didn't let them face it alone. "This is the hardest part," she told them. "Watching them take him away. But remember they are taking his body. His spirit... that already went ahead. This is just the shell he lived in. He doesn't need it anymore."

Karen showed them to the bedroom. They placed Manny on a specialized stretcher with careful reverence, handling him not like a body but like a person who mattered. They covered him with a clean white sheet. Karen appreciated their gentleness.

When the van pulled away, carrying Manny to the memorial, Rosita stood on the porch with Karen and Maya, arms around both of them. "Now begins the next part of your journey," she said quietly. "The part where you learn to live without him. It will be hard, very hard. But you will do it. Because he gave you the strength to do it. He gave you the gift of life. Now you must honor that gift by living it."

She stayed with them for hours after, making sure they ate, making sure they rested, making sure they weren't alone. This was her calling. This was her sacred work. And she would continue to walk with them through the grief ahead, helping them find their way back to life after death. The circle continued. Always, the circle continued. And Rosita was honored to be part of it.

That afternoon, while Karen and Maya waited at home, Manny was laid to rest beneath the Palo Verde tree on the rise. The team at Eternal Forest Memorial prepared his body according to natural burial protocol that was a simple white cotton shroud, biodegradable, without chemicals. The grave was dug deep enough to be respectful but shallow enough to nourish the tree's roots. They laid him to rest in the earth and covered him with soil. Native wildflower seeds were scattered on top along with a small bronze plaque that was placed at the tree's base: "Manuel 'Manny' Chavez. Beloved Husband and Father. 1983-2025. Listen, I hear you still."

Karen and Maya didn't witness this. They didn't see the physical reality of burial, the earth covering him, the finality of it. Sometimes not seeing is a gift. Late afternoon, Sally called. "Everything is complete. You can visit whenever you're ready."

Karen and Maya made the quiet drive to the memorial. Not much talking. Just the desert passing by the windows. When they reached the Palo Verde tree, they found the bronze marker gleaming in the afternoon sun. Fresh earth around the base. Tiny green shoots already sprouting from the wildflower seeds. The tree stood strong and tall, branches swaying gently in the breeze.

They stood together beneath its shadow, light and dark dancing across them. "Hi, Manny," Karen said softly.

"Hi, Dad," Maya added.

They told him about the morning. About the sunrise he saw. About how peacefully he went, no struggle, no pain, just peace. "We love you. We'll be back."

Reluctant to leave but knowing they could return anytime, they finally walked back to the car. This was his place now. He was part of the tree, part of the desert, part of everything.

That evening, Karen picked up the phone and dialed James Chen. This was going to be difficult. "Karen." His voice was heavy. "I heard. I'm so sorry."

"Thank you, James." She took a breath. "I need to talk to you about something. Manny's last wish. He made me promise to tell you."

"Anything."

"He wants you to rescind the complaint against Reed."

Silence on the line. Then, "Karen, that's..."

"I know. I know you want justice. But Manny was adamant. He didn't want you risking your career. This is what he wanted, James. His dying wish."

"Reed deserves to be held accountable!" James's voice rose. "The report was clearly incomplete. Manny is dead because of that man's incompetence!"

"James. Please." Karen's voice stayed firm. "Honor him this way. He loved you like a brother. He wanted to protect you... let it go for him."

A long silence followed. Finally, a heavy sigh. "Okay. Okay. If that's what he wanted, I'll call the ethics board tomorrow and withdraw the complaint." A pause. "But I don't like it."

"I know, neither do I. But it's what he wanted."

"When's the funeral?"

"We're doing a celebration of life. Not a funeral. I'll send you the details. He's already buried."

James seemed to understand. They had said their goodbyes.

The next day, Karen and Maya sat at the kitchen table planning. "Dad didn't want a sad funeral," Maya said.

"No. He wanted us to celebrate." Karen nodded. "So that's what we'll do."

Maya suggested the Comfort Inn banquet hall in Tonopah Valley. Its ten minutes from their house, big enough for plant workers, nice but not fancy. Karen called and booked it for the following Saturday. She contacted the plant, and they spread the word. Open invitation to anyone who knew Manny. Friends, colleagues, neighbors. Please come and share memories, celebrate a good man.

They kept it simple with sandwiches, salads, desserts along with photo displays of Manny's life. No formal program, just open sharing. "We should put out his toolbox," Maya said. "Let people see it."

Karen smiled. "He'd like that."

Saturday arrived and the Comfort Inn banquet hall was modest but bright, with round tables and simple decorations. The photo boards displayed pictures of Manny through the years. The toolbox sat open on a table. Three generations of tools visible for everyone to see. James Chen came early and helped set up.

People arrived in waves. Plant workers in weekend clothes, some with wives and families, neighbors from their street along with Mrs. Rodriguez, Maya's school counselor. More people than Karen expected. The atmosphere wasn't somber. People shared stories, laughed at memories. "Remember when Manny fixed the break room fridge with a paper clip?" someone said. Another, "He could diagnose any machine just by listening."

Maya moved through the crowd, accepting condolences, sharing stories about her dad. The toolbox story, the sink repair and about her grandfather. People nodded, understanding the legacy.

Karen heard stories she'd never known. How Manny helped a colleague when his wife was sick. How he fixed a neighbor's water heater for free. A pattern emerged... Manny helped everyone. Then Karen noticed Mr. Reed hovering at the entrance, clearly uncomfortable. Many workers blamed him for Manny's death. He looked like he wanted to leave but felt obligated to pay respects. Karen made a decision. She walked over to him. "Mr. Reed. Thank you for coming."

He was startled. "Mrs. Chavez. I... I'm so sorry. I wasn't sure I should come, but I wanted to pay my respects."

"I'm glad you did. Can we talk? Privately?"

They moved to a quieter corner. Reed was nervous, expecting anger or accusations. But Karen's face was calm, open. "Mr. Reed, I need you to know something. I'm not mad at you. I don't blame you."

"Mrs. Chavez, I appreciate that, but my report..."

"Your report was correct."

Reed stopped. "What?"

"I forgive you. But more than that, there's nothing to forgive. You were doing your job. As an honorable man and we thank you for your service."

Reed shook his head. "I don't understand. Manny died of radiation exposure..."

"The reason you found no leaks is because there weren't any." Karen held his gaze. "My husband's radiation exposure didn't come from the plant."

"How is that possible?"

Karen took a breath. Reed deserved to know. "My husband made a deal with God to save me. I had stage four cancer. I was dying and Manny prayed. An angel appeared and he traded his life for mine. It's just that simple really."

Mr. Reed clearly thought she was speaking metaphorically, trying to find meaning in grief. "Mrs. Chavez, I understand you're looking for..."

Karen held up a hand. "I know how it sounds. But I'm telling you the literal truth. Check the security feeds at the plant. Review every camera, every timestamp. You won't see Manny go anywhere outside his normal station. He never entered contaminated areas. He never was exposed at work."

"But the radiation damage..."

"It was real and it was fatal. But not from your plant. It was supernatural, Mr. Reed. You didn't miss anything. There was nothing to find."

Reed stood silent, processing. "My husband respected you," Karen continued. "He didn't want you blamed for something that wasn't your fault. Your report was thorough and honest. You did your job well. Your reputation and honor are intact with me."

This man had been carrying guilt and was blamed by colleagues. He was questioned by investigators. His professional reputation damaged. Now Karen was telling him he wasn't wrong. "Go through those security feeds. You'll see. Manny never left his station. And when you confirm that, I hope you can let go of the guilt. Because there is no guilt to carry."

Karen stepped forward and embraced him. Reed was shocked but returned it. "God bless you, Mr. Reed. Thank you for caring enough to feel responsible. But you can let it go now."

Reed left shortly after, walking lighter than when he arrived.

Later that day, Reed couldn't stop thinking about Karen's words. He went to the plant's security office and requested all footage from the weeks before Manny's hospitalization. He spent hours reviewing every camera angle and every timestamp. Manny at his station. Manny in the break room. Manny in the parking lot. Never in restricted areas. Never near potential contamination sources. Karen was right, there was no way Manny was exposed at the plant. But the radiation damage was real... the medical reports don't lie. So where did it come from?

Reed had a choice. Believe the supernatural explanation or accept that there was something he didn't understand. Either way, Karen's gift was peace. He wasn't negligent. His report was correct, no cover-up or incompetence. Reed filed the footage review in his records. Then he did something he'd never done before. He amended his official report. In the notes section, he typed: "No evidence of occupational exposure found. Act of God."

He closed the investigation in his own mind. And he carried less guilt than he had in weeks.

Back at the celebration, after Reed left, Karen rejoined the gathering. More stories flowed. James told everyone about Manny's first day at the plant. A worker shared how Manny helped him learn the systems and a neighbor talked about Manny fixing things for free. Someone asked Maya to speak. She stood, nervous, but her voice was clear.

"My dad taught me that a person who can fix things will never be helpless. He gave me his tools. His skills. His love." Her voice caught but she continued. "I don't know if I'll ever love someone that much. But I'm going to try."

There was light applause and then tears along with appreciation.

Karen didn't make a formal speech. But she moved through the room thanking everyone. "Manny would be so happy you're all here. He'd want you laughing, not crying. He'd want us to celebrate life, not mourn his death."

The people gathered, understood and they embraced the spirit. The party wound down naturally. People left with hugs and promises to stay in touch. Karen and Maya were left with the cleanup. James and a few others helped. Quiet satisfaction settled over Karen. They'd honored Manny well. With truth and grace. With celebration of a life lived in ultimate sacrifice.

Manny would be happy they'd celebrated his life. She told the truth and they'd freed an innocent man from guilt. They were moving forward, just as Manny wanted. Carrying his love with them. Knowing he was listening from the tree. Knowing this wasn't goodbye forever. Just "see you later." And Karen could live with that. She would have to.

Chapter Sixteen - Act of God

Master Sergeant Gerald Reed had seen a lot in thirty years of nuclear safety inspection. Things that defied the textbooks. Phenomena that made scientists nervous. Incidents the military quietly classified and buried in file cabinets nobody was supposed to open. A submarine reactor showing radiation readings that made no physical sense. A storage facility with contamination patterns that had no identifiable source. Personnel exposures that medical science couldn't explain along with radiation damage with no corresponding event, no breach and no leak.

Most of it got labeled "inconclusive" or "under investigation" or simply disappeared into classified archives. Reed learned early on that some things couldn't be explained, only documented. His job wasn't to understand the universe's mysteries. His job was to observe, measure, report, and keep people safe.

Manuel Chavez's case was one of those mysteries. After the celebration of life, after his conversation with Karen Chavez, Reed had spent hours reviewing the security footage... every camera angle as well as every timestamp. Every video had Manny at his station or in the break room. The video even showed Manny in the parking lot never deterring from his normal routine. He was never in any of the restricted areas nor near any potential contamination sources. The evidence was clear... no occupational exposure occurred at the plant. But the radiation damage was real. Medical reports don't lie. Stage four acute radiation syndrome. Bone marrow failure that resulted in multi-organ shutdown. It was a fatal exposure. So where did it come from?

Reed sat at his desk, looking at the amended report on his screen. In the cause section, he'd typed: "No evidence of occupational exposure found. Act of God."

His superiors hadn't appreciated that. "Act of God doesn't fit our protocols, Reed."

"Then change your protocols. That's what the evidence shows."

"We need something more... specific."

"I've been specific. No contamination source has been identified. There was no breach or leak. Security footage confirms the subject never entered any high-risk areas. Medical reality: fatal radiation exposure. Conclusion: Act of God."

They couldn't dispute the evidence, so the amended finding stood. Reed's professional integrity mattered more than corporate convenience. The legal department had its own response. Offer a settlement... a substantial one that included coverage of all medical expenses, death benefits beyond standard insurance, financial compensation for Karen and Maya Chavez. No admission of fault, but the family would be taken care of after they signed an NDA of course.

Reed was satisfied with that. The family deserved support and his report's integrity remained intact. The truth was documented, even if not fully believed. But there was still one thing left to address.

Two weeks after the celebration, Reed found James Chen during a lunch break. The engineer was eating alone at his usual station, while reviewing schematics. "Mr. Chen, can I have a moment?"

James looked up, immediately tense. They'd barely spoken since

Manny's death. The ethics complaint, the investigation, the arguments...
all of it hung between them like radiation you couldn't see but knew was
there. "Privately, please," Reed added.

James followed him to the office, uncertain what this was about. Reed
closed the door. Both men stood awkwardly. Reed wasn't good at this
kind of thing, he had never been good at being in non-military mode. "Mr.
Chen, I owe you an apology."

James blinked... In ten years of working under Reed, he'd never heard
those words from the man's mouth. "For any disrespect I showed you
regarding Mr. Chavez." Reed's voice was stiff but sincere. "During the
investigation, I was harsh and dismissive. I treated your concerns as if
they didn't matter."

James opened his mouth but Reed continued. "I spoke with Mrs.
Chavez at the celebration and she told me things that I needed to hear. I
performed a detailed analysis as she suggested." He paused. "I reviewed
every security feed, every potential exposure source. To this day I still
cannot explain what happened to Mr. Chavez."

"Sir..."

"I listed the cause as an Act of God." Reed met James's eyes. "That's
what Mrs. Chavez described it as and that's what the evidence supports...
or rather, doesn't refute. No occupational exposure occurred at this plant
and I stand firmly by that finding."

Reed's shoulders dropped slightly, the rigid posture softening. "I hope
you will accept my apology and we can return to our professional careers
as we once were. You're a good engineer, Mr. Chen. I don't want this
between us any longer."

James stared at the Master Sergeant. This wasn't the Reed he'd known for a decade. This was someone admitting uncertainty, showing vulnerability and being genuinely apologetic. "I accept your apology, Mr. Reed," James said finally. "And I owe you one too. I let anger cloud my judgment. The complaint I filed..."

"Mrs. Chavez mentioned that." Reed said.

"As I said, it was withdrawn. It was Manny's dying wish. He asked Karen to make me rescind it. So, I did." James shook his head. "I can't explain the situation either. It defies all logic and science. Manny's wife should be dead. She had stage four cancer but instead she's healthy. Manny should be alive because he never went near any place that had contamination. Instead, he's dead from radiation exposure."

Reed nodded slowly. "As Mrs. Chavez stated, and as I have seen in my career..." He paused, choosing his words carefully. "God works in mysterious ways."

It wasn't a religious platitude. It was genuine acknowledgment from a man who'd spent thirty years witnessing the unexplainable. "Please after lunch, return to your station," Reed said. "We have reset the clock. I would like to continue my watch."

The safety terminology of starting fresh with no incidents. They could move forward together as professionals. James nodded and turned to leave. "Mr. Chen?"

"Yes, sir?"

"Thank you."

Walking back to his station after lunch, James processed what had just happened. Reed apologized and admitted he didn't have all the answers. He acknowledged the supernatural. In over ten years working under the Master Sergeant, James had never seen him act like that. He never witnessed him apologize or admit uncertainty in addition to him being sincere about anything personal.

Always the Master Sergeant… always rigid, by-the-book and unapologetic. Until today…. James realized something. Reed wasn't a bad guy. He was just a man who took his responsibility very seriously. Plant safety wasn't just a job to him; it was a personal mission. Every worker here was someone he was trying to protect. That's why he was so harsh, so demanding and so inflexible.

Reed had seen what happened when safety failed. James didn't know the details, more than likely they were classified, but whatever Reed had witnessed in his career made him vigilant to the point of obsession. He's one of us, James thought. Just trying to keep everyone safe.

Later, in the break room, some of the workers were still griping about Reed. "Reed and his damn protocols."

"He doesn't care about people, just his reports."

"Manny died and Reed just files paperwork."

James set down his coffee. "You know, Reed's not such a bad guy."

The room went quiet and everyone turned toward him in disbelief. "He apologized to me today," James continued. "Said he was wrong about how he handled things with Manny. First time I've ever heard him apologize. In ten years."

One of the older workers scoffed. "Reed? Apologize?"

"I'm serious. He pulled me aside, admitted he couldn't explain what happened. He told me he takes plant safety as a personal responsibility." James looked around the room. "It's not just a job to him. Every worker here is someone he's trying to protect. That's why he's so rigid. He's seen what happens when safety fails."

The workers exchanged glances, reconsidering. "He's one of us," James said. "Just trying to keep everyone safe. And he admitted when he couldn't explain something. That takes guts for a guy like Reed."

The conversation shifted after that. They still didn't particularly like Reed. He was still demanding and inflexible, but they respected him differently now. Understanding the motive behind the methods helped.

Two weeks after burying Manny, Karen still couldn't get used to the house. It was too quiet and empty. His absence was everywhere she looked. His coffee cup in the cabinet, she couldn't bring herself to use it or put it away. His coat still hung on the hook by the door. His side of the bed stayed made, untouched. She slept on her side, the middle was like a canyon she couldn't cross. The garage was even worse. The tools remained organized the way he liked them. The oil stains on the floor from prior projects were along with the truck he'd never drive again. Her evenings were the hardest with no one to share dinner with. No one to watch the sunset beside her and no one to talk to about her day. The promise she'd made to live fully, to be happy felt impossible.

She was alive but frozen. Manny died so she could be alive. But she didn't know how to live without him. Saturday morning, she drove to Eternal Forest Memorial. She'd been going weekly, every Saturday at the same time. It was the one appointment she kept. The palo verde tree stood strong on its rise. The bronze marker gleaming in the morning sun. Fresh wildflowers bloomed around the base, the seeds they'd scattered at burial had taken root. Karen sat in the shade and talked. "Hi, Manny. It's been a hard week."

She told him about Maya doing better in school. About the settlement check arriving. But more importantly about the house, it feels empty without him. "I'm trying to keep my promise... to be happy and live." Her voice broke. "It's harder than I thought. But I'm trying."

The breeze rustled the branches as the birds sang. She wanted to believe he heard her. She needed to believe it. "Maya used the toolbox yesterday. She fixed the bathroom sink, it was leaking again. She did it all by herself. She didn't even ask for help." Karen smiled through tears. "You would've been so proud."

She sat there for an hour, talking, crying and sometimes just being quiet. When she finally left, she felt lighter. Not happy, not yet. But less alone.

Maya had avoided the garage for two weeks. She couldn't look at the toolbox without feeling the weight of it. Three generations, and now it was hers. The responsibility felt too heavy. But when the bathroom sink started leaking, Karen looked at her. She didn't say anything, she just looked. And Maya knew. She went to the garage, opened the toolbox, found the wrench she needed. Her hands remembered what her father taught her... that she had skills. She shut off the water and removed the P-trap. She double checked the gasket. She replaced it and tighten everything back. When water ran clear through the drain with no drips or leaks, Maya felt something shift. It was her pride in connection... her father was there, watching, pleased. "I did it, Dad," she whispered to the empty bathroom.

At school, Mrs. Rodriguez still checked in weekly. "How are you doing, Maya?"

"Better. Some days not so much."

"That's normal. Grief isn't linear."

"I miss him. But I'm starting to remember the good stuff without crying every time."

"That's progress."

It was small progress, but progress nonetheless. At dinner, Maya told her mother about fixing the sink. Karen already knew. She had watched from the doorway but she let Maya tell it anyway. "You're going to be okay," Karen said. "We both are."

"Eventually," Maya agreed.

"Eventually."

They were learning to live around the hole Manny left. The grief was still there. It would always be there but it was becoming familiar. In a way manageable. Part of the landscape rather than the whole view. Karen thought about her promise to live fully and to travel. To experience things... she wasn't ready for that yet but maybe someday soon. Manny had given her time and eventually, she'd figure out how to use it.

Master Sergeant Reed sat alone in his office after shift end, looking at the amended report on his screen. "Act of God."

His superiors hated it. It didn't fit the protocols or follow standard classifications. It made the report look unscientific, but it was the truth as Reed understood it. In thirty years of service, he'd seen things that couldn't be explained. Most got classified, filed away and never discussed. But this time, Reed wrote it in the official record with a sort of satisfaction. Let them dispute it if they wanted. He reviewed every data yet again, reviewed the security footage, analyzed every potential source. The conclusion was inescapable: Manuel Chavez was not exposed to radiation at the plant. But he died of radiation exposure anyway.

It was supernatural and impossible. It was beyond scientific explanation for him. It truly was an Act of God. Reed had reconciled with James Chen, and the family had received their settlement. The truth was documented, and the plant was safe. His duty was once again fulfilled.

He closed the file and shut down his computer. Some mysteries weren't meant to be solved. Some things were bigger than science, bigger than protocols and bigger than what any report could capture. God did work in mysterious ways; he had seen it more than once. He had seen enough in his career to know that was true. And sometimes, the only honest thing you could do was document it and move on.

He turned off the office light and headed home, carrying thirty years of unexplained incidents with him. Manuel Chavez was just one more mystery in a career full of them. But at least this time, the truth was on record, and he was ok with that.

The End

The following sections provide the reader with more context on cancer and information relevant to the story

Introduction - Cancer as a Family Diagnosis

When an individual receives a cancer diagnosis, the impact radiates far beyond her individual experience. Cancer is fundamentally a family disease, one that reshapes relationships, restructures household roles, demands emotional reserves from loved ones, and forces families to confront mortality in ways they may have never anticipated. While medical literature extensively documents the patient's experience, the parallel journeys of spouses, partners, and family members remain less visible yet profoundly significant. Understanding the family dimension of cancer is essential for developing comprehensive support systems and fostering compassion for all those affected by this disease.

The Immediate Shock - First Responses and Emotional Cascades

The moment an individual shares their cancer diagnosis with a spouse or partner, the emotional landscape of their relationship transforms. For many partners, the initial reaction mirrors that of the diagnosed individual. Shock, fear, disbelief, and a sudden confrontation with mortality. However, partners frequently experience an additional layer of complexity. They must process their own overwhelming emotions while simultaneously supporting the diagnosed individual, maintaining household functionality, and managing interactions with medical systems, extended family, and social networks.

Partners often describe the diagnosis moment as a before-and-after point in their relationship. Some report that initial conversations are marked by awkward silences, as both partners struggle to articulate fears without burdening the other. Others describe intense emotional outpourings, with partners expressing anger, fear, or despair that may feel overwhelming to the newly diagnosed individual who is already managing intense emotions themself. Neither response is wrong; both reflect the profound disruption cancer introduces.

In the early days following diagnosis, many partners take on the role of information coordinator and advocate. They may accompany the individual to medical appointments, take notes on treatment recommendations, research options, and help make treatment decisions. This active engagement can feel purposeful and necessary, yet it also represents the beginning of a long-term caregiver role that will demand sustained emotional and physical labor.

The Caregiver Role - Hidden Labor and Identity Transformation

As cancer treatment begins, partners often transition from their previous roles, whether primary earner, co-parent, household manager, or emotional supporter into a comprehensive caregiver role that encompasses medical, practical, and emotional dimensions. This transition is frequently neither explicitly negotiated nor fully appreciated.

Medical caregiving includes accompanying the patient to chemotherapy, radiation, and surgical appointments; monitoring side effects and medication reactions; managing medication schedules and dosing; documenting health changes; communicating with healthcare providers; and making urgent medical decisions. Partners may drive the patient to and from treatments, wait during long appointments, and manage the logistics of navigating complex healthcare systems.

Practical caregiving encompasses household management including cooking meals adapted to changed taste preferences and digestive tolerances, managing household chores that the patient can no longer perform, caring for children or aging parents, managing finances and insurance, and maintaining the basic functioning of family life. Some partners reduce work hours or take leave entirely, sacrificing income and career advancement to provide full-time care.

Emotional caregiving includes providing psychological support, maintaining hope when despair threatens, listening to fears and grief, managing one's own emotions to remain stable for the patient, and maintaining physical intimacy in forms that feel safe and comfortable for the patient. This emotional labor is often invisible yet exhausting.

Caregiver Burden and Hidden Suffering

Research on cancer caregivers reveals significant rates of depression, anxiety, and post-traumatic stress symptoms among spouses and partners of cancer patients. Studies indicate that "depression and anxiety are among the most frequent psychological consequences reported in previous studies, ranging from 52 to 94% among family caregivers," and "the level of such outcomes might be even higher among caregivers than patients themselves."[1] Recent meta-analysis data shows that "the global prevalence of depression among caregivers of Cancer patients across studies was 42.08%, which is remarkably higher than the prevalence of depression cases among a general population reported in

2015 (9%)."**[2]**

Many caregivers report feeling invisible. The focus of medical attention, family support, and social concern is rightfully directed toward the patient, leaving caregivers to manage their own distress in isolation. Partners frequently report that friends and family ask about the patient's well-being but rarely inquire about the partner's emotional state or needs. One study found that "of the caregivers, 46.3, 53, and 30.7% showed severe depression, anxiety, and burden, respectively,"**[3]** indicating the substantial psychological toll of the caregiving role.

The burden of caregiving is compounded by role strain. Partners may struggle with conflicting identities, simultaneously being a supporter who must remain strong and a terrified spouse confronting the possibility of losing a life partner. They navigate the awkward position of needing support themselves while feeling obligated to prioritize the patient's needs. Some partners report feeling guilty for experiencing negative emotions, as though their anger, resentment, or despair betrays their commitment to the patient.

Research demonstrates that "assuming the role of caregiver imposes a great burden on caregivers, affecting different aspects of their life, including mental health, physical health, and financial status,"**[4]** and that caregivers "might be forced to make changes in their daily life activities, social and business lives take on new responsibilities, or give up the past daily activities or hobbies that all these lead to emotional burden causing anxiety and depression."**[5]**

Physical health often deteriorates among cancer caregivers. Research documents increased rates of high blood pressure, sleep disruption, immune suppression, and overall health problems among spousal caregivers. The chronic stress of caregiving during cancer treatment activates prolonged stress responses that take measurable physiological tolls.

Financial and Career Impact

The financial dimensions of cancer caregiving receive insufficient attention yet profoundly impact families. Caregivers who reduce or leave work face lost income, reduced retirement contributions, diminished Social Security benefits, and potential career disruption or permanent job loss. Studies indicate that cancer-related work disruptions cost caregivers significant lifetime earning potential. For single-income households or families with limited savings, this financial strain creates additional stress overlaid on already overwhelming circumstances.

Partners must often navigate medical leave policies, flexible work arrangements, or difficult choices between presence at medical appointments and financial necessity. The ongoing tension between these competing demands creates chronic stress that persists throughout treatment and often beyond.

Relationship Dynamics - Intimacy, Communication, and Strain

Cancer and its treatments can profoundly affect physical intimacy. Chemotherapy commonly causes reduced libido, and difficulty with sexual arousal. Surgical changes, whether tumor removal such as mastectomy, lumpectomy, or reconstruction can alter body image and may create discomfort or pain during physical contact. Radiation can cause skin sensitivity and hormonal therapies designed to prevent recurrence often further reduce sexual desire and function.

Partners must navigate these changes with sensitivity. Many report feeling uncertain about how to approach the patient physically, fearing causing discomfort or offense. Some report their own decreased desire as they grapple with fear of the patient's mortality or discomfort with visible treatment effects. Others experience increased desire or physical affection as a way of affirming the relationship and reassuring themselves that the partner is still alive.

Communication about physical intimacy is frequently inadequate. Neither patient, nor partner may initiate conversations about sexual changes, leading to misinterpretations, hurt feelings, and increasing distance. Some couples find that physical intimacy transforms into different expressions of affection. Extended cuddling, massage, or non-sexual physical closeness can deepen connection. Others find that the desire for sexual intimacy diminishes for one or both partners during treatment, creating guilt and relationship strain.

Communication Patterns and Emotional Distance

Cancer treatment often creates paradoxical communication dynamics. Partners report simultaneously feeling closer to their spouse due to shared adversity and more distant due to the inability to fully express fear and despair. Some couples find that discussing cancer is so emotionally intense that they consciously avoid the topic in casual conversation, creating a kind of compartmentalization where cancer becomes a separate realm they enter during medical appointments and then try to leave behind in daily life.

Other couples describe increased conflict during cancer treatment, with arguments erupting over minor issues that mask deeper anxieties. The stress, fear, and chronic tension of cancer treatment lower patience and increase irritability in both partners. Couples may struggle with different coping styles. One partner wanting to discuss fears openly while the other prefers to focus on positivity and hope, or one partner needing to maintain control of planning while the other needs to surrender and accept help.

Identity and Role Reformation

Cancer fundamentally alters the couple's shared identity and roles. The partner's identity becomes partially defined by their caregiver role in ways that may feel limiting or painful. Partners sometimes report that they become "the cancer spouse," feeling that their other qualities and roles have been eclipsed. The patient, conversely, may experience the loss of some previously held identities. The partner as capable provider becomes the dependent receiver of care, shifting power dynamics in complex ways.

For couples who had been experiencing relationship strain prior to cancer, the diagnosis may temporarily create unity around a shared threat, only to have underlying conflicts re-emerge once treatment concludes. Other couples find that successfully navigating cancer treatment together strengthens their relationship, creating a sense of shared accomplishment and deeper appreciation for one another.

Impact on Children and Adolescents

Children of individuals diagnosed with cancer experience disrupted routines, altered parental attention and availability, and exposure to parental fear and grief. Young children may not fully understand cancer but quickly perceive parental anxiety, leading to behavioral changes, regression, or increased clinginess. School-age children may experience difficulty concentrating on schoolwork while managing awareness of parental illness. Adolescents often struggle with the developmental task of increasing independence from family while fearing parental death and feeling obligated to provide emotional support to remaining family members.

Many children report profound guilt related to cancer. Younger children may harbor magical thinking, believing they somehow caused the illness through negative thoughts or bad behavior. Adolescents may feel guilty for the normal anger, embarrassment, or self-focus of teenage development, interpreting these as signs of inadequate love or support for the ill parent. Parents frequently fail to recognize and address these guilt-laden cognitions, assuming children are "doing fine" when in fact they are silently struggling with internalized responsibility.

Parenthood Altered by Treatment

Parents undergoing cancer treatment often grieve the loss of active parenthood. Chemotherapy-induced fatigue may prevent parents from attending children's school events, sports games, or activities. Surgical recovery or radiation side effects may limit a mother's ability to provide physical care, discipline, or comfort in her typical ways. Some parents report intense sadness about these limitations, experiencing them as additional losses layered atop the loss of health and the threat of mortality.

Partners frequently must assume greater parenting responsibilities exactly when they are most stressed and depleted. This can create resentment in both directions. The patient may feel guilty that the partner is shouldering more parenting burden while simultaneously resenting the partner's greater authority with the children during a period when the patient feels diminished. Children may direct anger at the well parent, blaming them for increased strictness or changed rules, not recognizing the partner's profound stress.

Long-Term Impact on Children

Children whose parents receive cancer diagnoses show increased rates of anxiety, depression, and behavioral problems both during treatment and in years following. Some children develop lasting hypervigilance about health, experiencing anxiety symptoms at medical appointments or becoming overly focused on bodily sensations. Others develop powerful motivation to care for parents, taking on premature adult responsibilities or sacrificing their own developmental needs.

The trajectory depends significantly on the outcome. Children whose parents complete successful treatment may experience relief and renewed sense of security, though some carry lasting fear of recurrence. Children whose parents die face profound grief compounded by the guilt and existential challenges of losing a parent to a disease that carries significant stigma and shame in ways that sudden accidents or other deaths may not.

The Role of Extended Family and Social Networks

Extended family members such as parents, siblings, in-laws often become involved in the cancer journey, providing support, seeking information, and sometimes creating additional demands. Parents of the diagnosed individual may experience their own terror about losing a child, sometimes requiring support from the couple rather than being able to provide it. Siblings may step in to help with childcare, household tasks, or providing company and emotional support.

However, family involvement is not uniformly helpful. Some family members offer unsolicited medical advice, suggesting unproven treatments or implying the patient bears responsibility for the illness. Some compete for the patient's attention or create conflict about treatment decisions. Extended family members may direct their emotions toward the spouse, demanding updates, questioning treatment choices, or expressing anger or blame in ways that add stress rather than providing support.

Cultural factors significantly influence family responses to cancer. In cultures that emphasize family interdependence, extensive family involvement in treatment decisions and caregiving is expected and normative. In more individualistic cultures, boundaries around privacy and autonomy are prioritized, and extensive family involvement may feel intrusive. Cultural expectations about gender roles also shape the caregiver role. Some cultures have clear expectations that wives will provide care for husbands or vice versa, while others have more flexible role expectations.

Social Isolation and Shifting Relationships

Cancer frequently disrupts social relationships in unexpected ways. Friends who remain present become invaluable, while others withdraw, possibly due to discomfort with illness or fear of cancer's contagiousness (despite cancer's non-contagious nature). Partners report that friendships that seemed substantial may evaporate during crisis, while unexpected people emerge as steady supporters.

Some couples experience a narrowing of their social world during cancer treatment, as energy and time are absorbed by medical appointments and physical recovery. The couple may become socially isolated exactly when social connection would most benefit them. Returning to social life after cancer treatment completion is sometimes difficult, as friends may not understand why the couple is not simply "back to normal," or social events may trigger difficult emotions or reminders of mortality.

Facing Mortality - When Cancer is Terminal or Recurrent

When cancer recurs, is diagnosed at advanced stage, or progresses despite treatment, the family's emotional landscape shifts fundamentally. The implicit assumption that cancer means a curable illness with a good prognosis must be relinquished. Spouses face the genuine possibility of losing a life partner.

The transition from curative-intent treatment to palliative or end-of-life care often involves grief, anger, despair, and profound fear. Some partners describe feeling betrayed by the medical system or by God, having believed and invested hope in curative treatment only to face its failure. Others describe a kind of accelerated deepening of intimacy as they recognize the finitude of their time together.

The Final Caregiver Role

As death approaches, the caregiver role often intensifies. Partners may become primary providers of comfort care while managing pain, monitoring symptoms, facilitating conversations with medical providers about comfort versus aggressive interventions, and being present through the dying process. This role is emotionally and physically demanding in ways that can be traumatic.

Partners in this role report witnessing suffering along with physical pain, shortness of breath, cognitive changes, incontinence, and other realities of serious illness. They often struggle with end-of-life decision-making, balancing the patient's wishes with their own desire to avoid loss, their own physical and emotional depletion, and sometimes conflicting input from extended family members.

Anticipatory Grief and Identity Reformation

Before death occurs, partners often experience anticipatory grief known as the process of grieving the coming loss while the person is still alive. Research indicates that "anticipatory grief occurs before death" and "when a patient experiences distress, pain, and medical complications, it can add to anticipatory grief."[6] This grief is complex and nonlinear, including moments of deep sadness, anger, denial, and sometimes guilty feelings of relief about the coming end of suffering or caregiving burden.

The partner's identity becomes increasingly defined by impending loss. Some partners report that they begin psychologically separating from the relationship as a defense against the pain of losing it, a process that can create guilt and complicated feelings about the remaining time together.

The Death of a Spouse - Bereavement and Grief

The death of a spouse represents one of life's most profound losses. Partners who have been intensive caregivers face the sudden absence of a role that had consumed significant time and emotional energy for months or years. The house becomes disturbingly quiet. The routines organized around treatment appointments and symptom management no longer structure the day.

The acute grief immediately following death is often described as surreal or dissociated. Many bereaved spouses report functioning on autopilot as they are arranging funerals, notifying extended family, receiving condolences while experiencing a dreamlike disconnection from reality. The full weight of the loss often does not strike until days or weeks after the death, when the immediate tasks are completed and the finality of the loss becomes undeniable.

Complicated Grief and Unique Dimensions of It

Spousal bereavement following cancer death carries unique dimensions that complicate the grief process. Partners have often endured months or years of progressive loss before the actual death. Watching the loved one's body and abilities deteriorate, experiencing role changes and identity losses throughout the treatment and end-of-life periods. By the time death occurs, the partner may have already experienced multiple losses and undertaken extensive anticipatory grieving.

Research demonstrates that "loss due to cancer could predispose surviving spouses or partners to a variety of negative outcomes" including "depression, anxiety, complicated grief, and loneliness,"[7] and that bereaved spouses of cancer patients "could be more susceptible to a variety of negative outcomes including depression, anxiety, complicated grief, and loneliness" due to "difficult and unique end-of-life experiences such as an exhausting caregiving situations, witnessing and managing distressing symptoms, and being socially isolated while providing daily care to the dying person."[7]

Some bereaved spouses experience complicated grief, characterized by persistent, intense yearning for the deceased; difficulty accepting the death; inability to engage in meaningful activities; or thoughts of joining the deceased. Research on bereaved spouses of cancer patients found that "variables affecting complicated grief of bereaved spouses of cancer patients were the quality of end-of-life care, preparedness for death, and coping with bereavement,"[8] indicating that certain factors can support healthier grief processes. Complicated grief occurs in a subset of bereaved individuals and may benefit from specialized mental health intervention.

Guilt often accompanies spousal bereavement following cancer. Some partners feel guilty about moments of relief or about irritation expressed during the illness. Others feel guilty about surviving or about the things they did not say or do before death. Partners may also experience guilt about potential future relationships, feeling this betrays the deceased.

Financial and Practical Consequences

Beyond emotional grief, spousal bereavement often brings immediate practical crises. The surviving spouse must manage funeral arrangements and costs, navigate insurance and benefits systems, potentially consolidate finances previously managed by the deceased, and may face the need to find employment if they had reduced work during caregiving. Some spouses face unexpected debt related to medical treatment. Others face housing instability or financial strain without the partnership's combined income.

Life insurance policies, Social Security survivor benefits, and other financial mechanisms vary widely in their generosity and accessibility. Surviving spouses with limited financial literacy or resources may struggle significantly with these practical dimensions of loss. Additionally, "the death of a spouse, for example, may cause a loss of income and changes in lifestyle and day-to-day living,"[6] creating cascading challenges beyond the emotional impact of death itself.

Parenting After Loss - Single Parents Grieving

Spouses with children face the additional burden of parenting while managing their own profound grief. Children are also grieving the loss of the deceased parent, requiring support and attention from a surviving parent who is emotionally depleted and potentially financially stressed. The surviving spouse must often suppress their own grief to provide stability for children, creating a kind of emotional compartmentalization that can hinder processing of loss.

Parents report that their children's grief sometimes triggers their own. A child's tears or questions about the deceased can overwhelm a parent struggling to maintain composure. The surviving parent bears responsibility for helping children process loss while managing their own devastated state.

Long-Term Bereavement and Meaning

Bereavement following spousal death from cancer is not a process that ends at any fixed point. Most grief literature suggests that significant losses are never fully "resolved" but rather are integrated into a person's ongoing life narrative. Research indicates that "most bereaved people work through grief and recover within the first 6 months to 2 years,"[6] though this timeline varies significantly by individual. Surviving spouses report that grief softens over time but does not disappear. Anniversaries, birthdays, medical appointments... any event that might have involved the deceased can trigger acute grief even years later.

Some surviving spouses find meaning in their loss by engaging in advocacy, fundraising, or awareness-building around cancer. Others find meaning through creating memorials, writing, art, or spiritually-oriented practices. Some dedicate themselves to supporting other cancer patients or bereaved individuals, channeling their experience into service.

Supporting Families - Clinical and Social Approaches

Healthcare systems can significantly impact family well-being during cancer treatment by recognizing and supporting the caregiver role. This includes providing caregiver-specific information about managing side effects, coping with emotions, and accessing support resources. It includes acknowledging the caregiver's role in team meetings and treatment planning. It includes recognizing signs of caregiver depression or burnout and referring for mental health support.

Palliative care approaches that address family needs alongside patient needs, including honest discussions about prognosis and goals of care, can help families prepare for possible outcomes and make decisions aligned with values. Bereavement support programs that provide counseling, support groups, and resources in the months and years following death help surviving spouses navigate loss.

Peer Support and Professional Mental Health Services

Support groups for cancer caregivers and for the bereaved provide space to share experiences, learn from others facing similar circumstances, and reduce the isolation that frequently accompanies these roles. Professional mental health services such as counseling, therapy, or psychiatry can address depression, anxiety, complicated grief, or trauma symptoms that emerge during or after the cancer experience.

Some couples benefit from couples counseling during cancer treatment to navigate communication changes, intimacy challenges, and role shifts. Counseling can provide a safe space to discuss fears and disappointments that may not be expressible in everyday conversation.

Community and Faith-Based Support

Religious and spiritual communities often provide meaningful support to cancer families, offering practical assistance, prayers or spiritual practices aligned with the family's beliefs, and community of people who care. Some faith communities have explicit ministries to cancer patients and families. Others provide more informal support through community meals, childcare, or companionship.

Community organizations, including the American Cancer Society, provide services specifically designed to support cancer families from free wigs and prosthetics to educational programs to support group referrals. Accessing these services requires knowledge of their existence and availability, highlighting the importance of healthcare providers directing patients and families to community resources.

Workplace and Financial Support

Employer-provided leave policies, flexible work arrangements, and employee assistance programs can significantly reduce stress on cancer families by facilitating the worker's ability to attend medical appointments, provide care, or grieve without fear of job loss. However, access to these benefits is not universal, with vulnerable populations more likely to face job loss and financial hardship during cancer treatment.

Public policy support through disability benefits, medical leave protections, and coverage of supportive care services (including wigs and prosthetics) reflects societal recognition of cancer's broad impact. Yet policies vary widely by geographic location and individual circumstances, creating inequitable access to support.

Conclusion - Honoring the Whole Family

Cancer is fundamentally a family disease that extends far beyond the individual patient. Spouses, partners, children, and extended family members undertake profound emotional labor, navigate identity changes, face financial strain, and grieve. Sometimes ultimately, the loss of a loved one. Recognizing and honoring these parallel journeys, providing compassionate support to caregivers, acknowledging the legitimacy of family members' grief and suffering, and creating systems that support whole families rather than just individual patients represents an essential evolution in cancer care.

A culture of empathy toward cancer families recognizes that the partner who attends every chemotherapy appointment, manages household disruption, suppresses their own fear to provide emotional support, and potentially grieves the loss of a spouse has undertaken a journey of equal significance to the patient's medical journey. Children who lose a parent to cancer carry lifelong impacts of that loss. Extended family members who provide support, offer presence, or face the loss of a loved family member are all affected by cancer.

Building comprehensive cancer care requires attending to these family dimensions with the same rigor and compassion that medicine applies to tumor treatment. It means asking caregivers how they are doing and genuinely listening to the answer. It means providing mental health support as standard of care. It means recognizing that when an individual dies of cancer, a whole family dies with them. The surviving family members deserve comprehensive support in rebuilding their lives after loss.

References

[1] Abbasi A., Shamsizadeh M., Asayesh H., Rahmani H., Hoseini S. A., & Talebi M. (2023). Caregiving burden, depression, and anxiety among family caregivers of patients with cancer: An investigation of patient and caregiver factors. Frontiers in Psychology, 14, 1059605. Retrieved from https://www.frontiersin.org/journals/psychology/articles/10.3389/fpsyg.2023.1059605/full

[2] Azizoddin D.R. (2023). Depression among caregivers of cancer patients: Updated systematic review and meta-analysis. Journal of Palliative Medicine, 26(7), 1057-1065. Retrieved from https://pmc.ncbi.nlm.nih.gov/articles/PMC9828427/

[3] Abbasi A., Shamsizadeh M., Asayesh H., Rahmani H., Hoseini S. A., & Talebi M. (2023). Caregiving burden, depression, and anxiety among family caregivers of patients with cancer: An investigation of patient and

caregiver factors. Frontiers in Psychology, 14, 1059605. Retrieved from https://www.frontiersin.org/journals/psychology/articles/10.3389/fpsyg.2023.1059605/full

[4] Given B., Given C., & Sherwood P. (2012). Family and caregiver needs over the course of the cancer trajectory. Journal of Supportive Oncology, 10(2), 57-64. Retrieved from https://pubmed.ncbi.nlm.nih.gov/22406920/

[5] Garcia-Torres F., Geng Z., Gómez-Soria I., & Remor E. (2020). Psychological distress and caregiving burden during end-of-life cancer care: Qualitative study of family caregivers. Palliative & Supportive Care, 18(3), 316-323. Retrieved from PubMed database

[6] National Cancer Institute. (2024). Grief, Bereavement, and Loss (PDQ®) - Patient Version. Retrieved from https://www.cancer.gov/about-cancer/advanced-cancer/caregivers/planning/bereavement-pdq

[7] Holtslander L.F., Bally J.M., & Steeves M.L. (2011). Walking a fine line: An exploration of the experience of spousal bereavement after cancer. BMC Palliative Care, 10(1), 2. Retrieved from https://pmc.ncbi.nlm.nih.gov/articles/PMC3982618/

[8] Kwon S., & Shim E.J. (2018). Influential factors of complicated grief of bereaved spouses from cancer patient. Journal of Korean Academy of Nursing, 48(2), 186-196. Retrieved from https://pubmed.ncbi.nlm.nih.gov/29535285/

Adelman R.D., Tmanova L.L., Delgado D., Dion S., & Lachs M.S. (2014). Caregiver burden: a clinical review. JAMA, 311(10), 1052-1060. Retrieved from https://pubmed.ncbi.nlm.nih.gov/24618965/

Carr D., House J.S., Wortman C.B., Nesse R., & Kessler R.C. (2001). Marital quality and psychological adjustment to widowhood among older adults. Journal of Gerontology Series B, 55(6), S338-S348. Retrieved from PubMed database

Kim Y., & Schulz R. (2008). Family caregiving for patients with cancer. Journal of the American Medical Association, 299(10), 1157-1159. Retrieved from https://pubmed.ncbi.nlm.nih.gov/18334690/

Prigerson H.G., Maciejewski P.K., & Rosenheck R.A. (2000). Preliminary exploratory models for the predication of cost in grief-related psychiatric illness. American Journal of Psychiatry, 157(12), 1921-1924. Retrieved from PubMed database

Stetz K.M., & Hanson W.K. (1992). Alterations in sexuality and sexual functioning of women with cancer. Seminars in Oncology Nursing, 8(2), 122-129. Retrieved from PubMed database

Carr D. (2003). A 'good death'? Sociological essays on the end of life. Routledge. Retrieved from academic databases

Chentsova-Dutton Y., Shucter S., Hutchin S., Strause L., Burns K., Dunn

L.B., & Zisook S. (2000). Be grief and depression in those bereaved by suicide and other sudden deaths. Journal of Affective Disorders, 52(1-3), 269-279. Retrieved from PubMed database

Curley A.Q., & Carlson J.M. (2023). Impact of caregiver burden on quality of life in family caregivers of patients with advanced cancer: a moderated mediation analysis. BMC Public Health, 24, 1320. Retrieved from https://bmcpublichealth.biomedcentral.com/articles/10.1186/s12889-024-18321-3

National Center for Health Statistics. (2024). Predictors of depression and anxiety among caregivers of hospitalised advanced cancer patients. PMC Journals. Retrieved from https://pmc.ncbi.nlm.nih.gov/articles/PMC6250762/

SAMHSA (Substance Abuse and Mental Health Services Administration). (2024). Prolonged Grief Disorder. StatPearls - NCBI Bookshelf. Retrieved from https://www.ncbi.nlm.nih.gov/books/NBK507832/

Vaitones V., & Loscalzo M. (2022). Psychosocial factors affecting the bereavement experience of relatives of palliative-stage cancer patients: a systematic review. BMC Palliative Care, 21, 180. Retrieved from https://bmcpalliatcare.biomedcentral.com/articles/10.1186/s12904-022-01096-y

Breast Cancer in the United States - Epidemiology, Detection, and Treatment

One of the main characters in this book, Karen, has breast cancer. The following section provides the reader with more context of this condition beyond what the story tells. This is current data, and the references are at the end of each section.

Breast cancer remains the most common malignancy diagnosed in women in the United States, representing a significant public health concern.[1] In 2025, an estimated 316,950 women will receive a new diagnosis of invasive breast cancer, with an additional 59,080 cases of ductal carcinoma in situ (DCIS), the non-invasive form of the disease.[1] This means that approximately one woman is diagnosed with breast cancer every two minutes in America.[2] Across a woman's lifetime, approximately 13% will develop breast cancer at some point, making it a disease that affects a substantial proportion of the female population.[3]

Key Statistics Summary

316,950
New cases in 2025

42,170
Expected deaths in 2025

13%
Lifetime risk for women

44%
Death rate decline since 1989

Current Mortality Statistics

Mortality rates represent one of the most critical metrics for understanding the burden of breast cancer. In 2025, approximately 42,170 women are expected to die from breast cancer in the United States, making it the fourth leading cause of cancer death among women.[1] This represents a significant improvement compared to historical data. Between 1989 and 2022, the overall breast cancer death rate declined by 44%, which translates to approximately 517,900 fewer breast cancer deaths during this 33-year period.[4] The death rate for women with breast cancer stands at 19.2 per 100,000 women per year, based on data from 2019 to 2023.[3]

Racial and Ethnic Disparities

Mortality rates vary significantly across racial and ethnic groups in the United States, reflecting broader healthcare inequities. Black women face substantially higher mortality rates despite having comparable or lower incidence rates than White women. Specifically, Black women have a 38% higher risk of dying from breast cancer than White women, even though they have 5% lower incidence.[4] The five-year survival rate for Black women stands at 83%, compared to 92% for White women.[5] Notably, Black women have the lowest survival rates for nearly every breast cancer subtype and stage, except for localized disease.[4]

American Indian and Alaska Native women experience mortality stagnation, with death rates remaining essentially unchanged since

1990.[4] These women have 6% higher mortality risk than White women despite 10% lower incidence.[4] Among other populations, Asian American and Pacific Islander women showed the fastest increase in breast cancer incidence in recent years, with rates climbing 2.7% annually in younger women and 2.5% in older women.[4] Incidence rates among Hispanic women in 2024 reached approximately 31,500 new cases.[6]

Relative Mortality Disparity

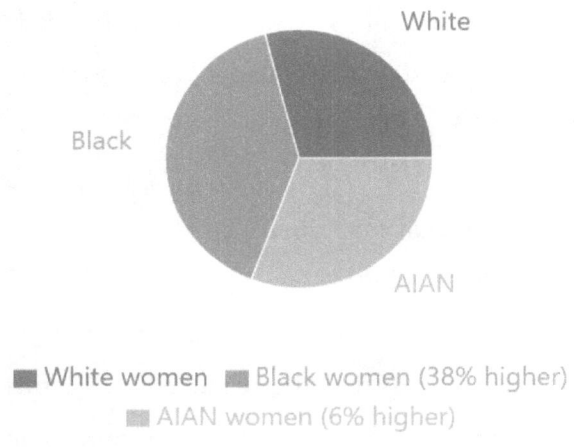

Black women have 38% higher mortality rate despite similar incidence

Age at Diagnosis

While breast cancer most frequently affects middle-aged and older women, the disease pattern is shifting. The median age at diagnosis is 62 years,[3] but younger women are experiencing rising incidence. Approximately 16% of women diagnosed with breast cancer in 2025 will be younger than 50 years of age.[1] Women aged 65 to 74 are most frequently diagnosed.**[3]** Notably, incidence in women under 50 has increased by 1.4% annually, which is steeper than the 0.7% annual increase in women 50 and older.**[4]**

Diagnosis by Age Group

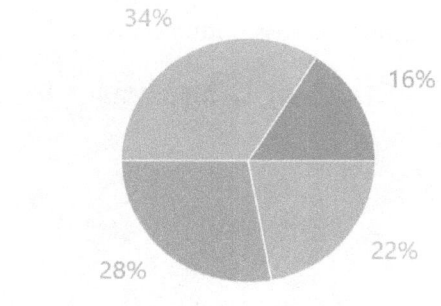

84% of cases occur in women 50 and older

Survival Rates by Stage

The five-year relative survival rate for invasive breast cancer overall is 91%, and the ten-year rate is 84%.**[7]** However, survival rates vary dramatically by stage at diagnosis. For localized-stage disease of cancer confined to the breast. The five-year survival rate is 99%, indicating near-complete survival in most cases.**[7]** This underscores the critical importance of early detection. Regional disease that has spread to lymph nodes shows a five-year survival of 86%, while distant-stage disease that has metastasized to other organs demonstrates a five-year survival of only 30%.**[7]**

Stage at diagnosis profoundly influences outcomes. Approximately 66% of breast cancer cases are diagnosed at a localized stage before cancer has spread outside the breast, which is when treatments tend to work best.**[1]** This demonstrates both the potential of screening and the variation in detection methods across populations.

Stage at Diagnosis

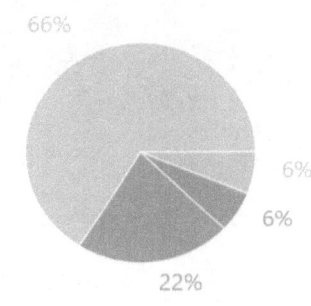

66% diagnosed at localized stage when treatment is most effective

Early Detection and Screening

Mammography remains the most common and effective screening test for breast cancer.**[8]** A mammogram is a specialized low-dose X-ray examination that can detect abnormal breast tissue, including cancer, sometimes before symptoms appear.**[8]** Standard mammography creates two-dimensional images and can demonstrate microcalcifications smaller than 100 micrometers, often revealing lesions 1 to 2 years before they would be discovered through breast self-examination.[9]

Digital breast tomosynthesis, commonly known as three-dimensional (3D) mammography, represents an advanced form of breast imaging that uses low-dose X-rays and computer reconstruction to create three-dimensional images of breast tissue.[10] The FDA approved this technology in 2018, and it is now available in approximately 75% of imaging facilities.[11] Research demonstrates that 3D mammography reduces mammogram callbacks and lowers both radiation dose and overall costs while improving tumor detection rates.[8] Three-dimensional mammography is particularly valuable for women with dense breast tissue, in whom tumors can be difficult to distinguish from normal tissue on standard mammograms.[8]

Magnetic resonance imaging (MRI) may be used for screening in women at high risk for breast cancer, typically those with a lifetime risk of 20-25% or greater, women with known BRCA1 or BRCA2 gene mutations, or those with a first-degree relative carrying these mutations.[12] Breast MRI demonstrates very high sensitivity (approaching 99% when combined with mammography and clinical breast examination) and is particularly useful in detecting cancers at earlier stages in high-risk populations.[9]

Breast ultrasound serves as a useful adjunct to mammography, particularly for women with dense breast tissue or to help clarify suspicious findings.[9] While ultrasound cannot detect microcalcifications, it effectively distinguishes between fluid-filled cysts and solid masses.[9] Supplemental screening with ultrasound can be considered for women with extremely dense breasts or those at higher than average risk.[12]

Clinical breast examination involves a healthcare provider carefully feeling the breasts and underarm areas for lumps or abnormalities.[8] While it has been a traditional part of screening, research has found very little evidence that clinical breast examination reduces the risk of dying from breast cancer when women also receive screening mammograms.[13] However, many providers still offer clinical breast exams as part of comprehensive evaluation, particularly for women at higher than average risk.[13]

Breast self-awareness such as being familiar with how breasts normally look and feel enables women to notice changes such as lumps, pain, or size alterations.[8] Women should report any noticed changes to their healthcare provider promptly.[8] Research does not support routine systematic breast self-examination as part of a screening schedule, as it has not been shown to reduce breast cancer mortality and may increase unnecessary biopsies.[13]

Screening Recommendations

The U.S. Preventive Services Task Force recommends that women aged 40 to 74 years at average risk for breast cancer receive a mammogram every two years.[14] The American Cancer Society recommends that women begin screening conversations with their healthcare providers starting at age 40, with screening beginning at age 45 for women at average risk, and annually for women starting at age 40 if they wish to do so.[15] Women at higher than average risk, including those with a personal history of breast cancer, a family history of breast cancer, known BRCA mutations, or certain breast density patterns should consult with their healthcare provider about beginning screening earlier and may benefit from supplemental screening methods such as MRI or ultrasound.[15]

For women at high risk, screening should include both a mammogram and breast MRI annually, typically beginning at age 30.[15] Screening typically continues until life expectancy falls below 10 years, with the decision to discontinue based on individual health status.[15]

5-Year Survival Rates by Stage

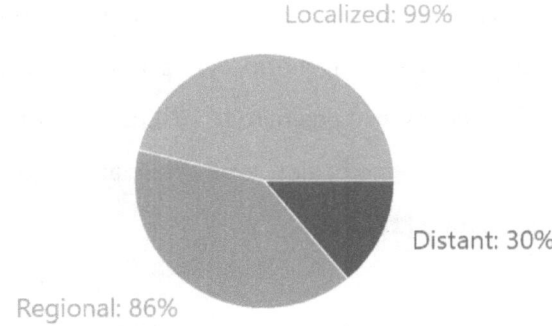

Early detection dramatically improves survival outcomes

Reporting and Diagnosis

When a woman or her healthcare provider discovers a concerning finding whether through mammography, clinical exam, or self-discovery prompt reporting to a physician is essential.[16] The diagnostic process typically involves imaging studies such as additional mammographic views, ultrasound, or MRI to characterize the finding.[16] If imaging suggests possible cancer, a biopsy is usually performed to obtain tissue samples for laboratory analysis.[16] Various biopsy methods exist, including fine-needle aspiration cytology and core needle biopsy, among others.[16]

Upon diagnosis, the cancer is staged to determine the extent of disease.[17] Staging involves determining tumor size, whether cancer has spread to lymph nodes, and whether distant metastases exist.[17] The pathological examination also characterizes the tumor according to molecular subtype—including hormone receptor status (estrogen and progesterone receptor positivity), HER2 status, and other biomarkers.[17] This molecular characterization guides treatment decisions significantly.[17]

Treatment Approaches

Breast cancer treatment commonly employs various combinations of five main modalities: surgery, radiation therapy, chemotherapy, hormone therapy, and targeted therapy.[18] Treatment selection depends on multiple factors including stage at diagnosis, tumor characteristics, patient age, menopausal status, overall health, and patient preferences.[18]

Surgical Treatment

Surgery is typically the first treatment for most breast cancer patients.[19] Two primary surgical options exist: breast-conserving surgery and mastectomy.[18]

Breast-conserving surgery, also called lumpectomy or partial mastectomy, involves removing the tumor along with a margin of surrounding normal tissue while preserving the remainder of the breast.[18] This approach is generally used for small, early-stage tumors and allows women to retain their breast tissue.[18] Lumpectomy is usually followed by radiation therapy to reduce the risk of cancer recurrence in the breast, and sometimes by hormone therapy or chemotherapy with or without targeted therapies, depending on the tumor's characteristics.[18]

A mastectomy involves surgical removal of the entire breast and typically some nearby lymph nodes.[18] A modified radical mastectomy removes the whole breast and most lymph nodes under the arm.[18] Advanced surgical techniques such as skin-sparing mastectomy or nipple-sparing mastectomy can preserve cosmetic appearance when feasible.[20] Many women opt for breast reconstruction at the time of mastectomy or sometime thereafter, utilizing various plastic surgical approaches.[18]

Lymph node assessment is an important component of breast cancer surgery, as the presence of cancer in lymph nodes influences prognosis and treatment decisions.[18] The sentinel lymph node biopsy, which involves removing the first lymph nodes to which cancer is likely to spread, has become standard practice for early-stage disease.[18]

Chemotherapy

Chemotherapy uses powerful drugs to kill cancer cells or stop their growth.[21] Chemotherapy drugs are considered systemic therapy because they can circulate throughout the body and reach cancer cells almost anywhere.[21] These medications may be delivered orally, injected into muscle, or administered intravenously.[21]

Chemotherapy may be given before surgery (neoadjuvant chemotherapy) to shrink large tumors and make surgery less extensive, or after surgery (adjuvant chemotherapy) to reduce the risk of recurrence.[21] Chemotherapy is typically recommended for women with stage II and stage III breast cancer, as well as for certain high-risk stage I cases.[22] The decision to administer chemotherapy depends on the tumor's stage, grade, molecular characteristics, and other prognostic factors.[22]

Radiation Therapy

Radiation therapy uses high-energy X-rays or particles to destroy cancer cells.[23] It is commonly given after breast-conserving surgery to reduce the chance that cancer will recur in the breast or nearby lymph nodes.[23] Radiation therapy may also be recommended after mastectomy, particularly if the cancer was larger than two centimeters or if cancer was found in lymph nodes.[23] Radiation may also treat breast cancer that cannot be removed surgically or advanced and metastatic disease causing symptoms.[23]

Radiation therapy typically involves 5 to 15 treatment sessions delivered over several weeks.[23] Advanced techniques such as proton therapy can precisely deliver high radiation doses to tumors while minimizing exposure to surrounding healthy tissue, proving particularly valuable when treating cancers that have spread to sensitive organs like the lungs, liver, or brain.[20]

Hormone Therapy

Hormone therapy, also called endocrine therapy, treats hormone receptor-positive breast cancer by blocking the production of hormones or interfering with hormone effects on cancer cells.[18] Hormone therapy is used for all stages of hormone receptor-positive disease and typically is administered in pill form for 5 to 10 years after surgery.[20] Common hormone therapy agents include aromatase inhibitors such as anastrozole, letrozole, and exemestane, which block estrogen production in postmenopausal women.[18]

Hormone therapy may be given before surgery to shrink the cancer or after surgery as adjuvant therapy to reduce recurrence risk.[18] For hormone receptor-positive cancers with lymph node involvement, doctors may recommend CDK4/6 inhibitors in addition to standard hormonal therapy.[22]

Targeted Therapy

Targeted therapy drugs selectively attack cancer based on specific characteristics of cancer cells, such as particular proteins, receptors, or gene mutations.[21] These medications generally have fewer side effects on healthy cells compared to chemotherapy.[21] Biomarker tests identify which characteristics are present in individual tumors, helping guide treatment selection.[21]

For HER2-positive breast cancers, targeted therapy drugs such as trastuzumab and pertuzumab are typically recommended.[24] Women with BRCA1 or BRCA2 mutations may benefit from PARP inhibitor therapy.[22] Other targeted therapies address specific genetic mutations such as PIK3CA, AKT1, or PTEN alterations.[22] Targeted therapy drugs may be given before surgery, after surgery, or both before and after surgical intervention.[22]

Immunotherapy

Immunotherapy represents an important emerging treatment approach that stimulates the patient's immune system to attack cancer cells.[25] For early-stage triple-negative breast cancer (a particularly aggressive subtype lacking hormone receptors and HER2 expression), immunotherapy combined with chemotherapy is often recommended before and after surgery.[25] Immunotherapy can also be used for advanced-stage and metastatic breast cancer.[25]

Treatment Planning and Support

The optimal treatment plan is individualized based on the specific characteristics of each woman's cancer and her overall health.[18] Many women receive combinations of these treatments.[18] Supportive care, sometimes called palliative care, can be helpful at any stage of treatment to manage symptoms and help with planning, and early involvement often provides the most benefit.[18]

For women with concerns about their diagnosis or proposed treatment, a second opinion from another specialist can provide additional perspective on available options.[18] Clinical trials represent another avenue through which women can access potentially promising new treatments while contributing to advancement of medical knowledge.[18]

References

[1] American Cancer Society. (2025). Breast Cancer Facts & Figures 2024-2025. Atlanta: American Cancer Society. Retrieved from https://www.cancer.org/research/cancer-facts-and-statistics/

[2] Breastcancer.org. (2025). Breast Cancer Facts & Statistics. Retrieved from https://www.breastcancer.org/facts-statistics

[3] National Cancer Institute. (2024). Cancer Stat Facts: Cancer of the Breast (Female). Surveillance, Epidemiology, and End Results Program.

Retrieved from https://seer.cancer.gov/statfacts/html/breast.html

[4] Giaquinto, A. N., Sung, H., Newman, L. A., Freedman, R. A., Smith, R. A., Star, J., ... & Siegel, R. L. (2024). Breast cancer statistics 2024. CA: A Cancer Journal for Clinicians, 74(6), 477-495. doi:10.3322/caac.21863

[5] Breast Cancer Research Foundation. (2025). Breast Cancer Statistics and Resources. Retrieved from https://www.bcrf.org/breast-cancer-statistics-and-resources/

[6] Susan G. Komen. (2025). Breast Cancer Facts & Statistics. Retrieved from https://www.komen.org/breast-cancer/facts-statistics/breast-cancer-statistics/

[7] National Breast Cancer Foundation. (2025). Breast Cancer Facts & Statistics. Retrieved from https://www.nationalbreastcancer.org/breast-cancer-facts/

[8] National Cancer Institute. (2024). Breast Cancer Screening (PDQ®). National Institutes of Health. Retrieved from https://www.cancer.gov/types/breast/patient/breast-screening-pdq

[9] National Institutes of Health. (2024). Breast Cancer Screening in the Average-Risk Patient. StatPearls, NCBI Bookshelf. Retrieved from https://www.ncbi.nlm.nih.gov/books/NBK556050/

[10] American Cancer Society. (2024). ACS Breast Cancer Screening

Guidelines. Retrieved from https://www.cancer.org/cancer/types/breast-cancer/screening-tests-and-early-detection/american-cancer-society-recommendations-for-the-early-detection-of-breast-cancer.html

[11] MD Anderson Cancer Center. (2025). Mammograms & Breast Cancer Screening. Retrieved from https://www.mdanderson.org/prevention-screening/get-screened/breast-cancer-screening.html

[12] American College of Obstetricians and Gynecologists (ACOG). (2024). Breast Cancer Risk Assessment and Screening in Average-Risk Women. Retrieved from https://www.acog.org/

[13] CDC. (2025). Screening for Breast Cancer. Centers for Disease Control and Prevention. Retrieved from https://www.cdc.gov/breast-cancer/screening/index.html

[14] U.S. Preventive Services Task Force. (2024). Breast Cancer: Screening. Retrieved from https://www.uspreventiveservicestaskforce.org/

[15] Cancer Research UK. (2024). Treatment options for breast cancer. Retrieved from https://www.cancerresearchuk.org/about-cancer/breast-cancer/treatment/

[16] National Cancer Institute. (2024). Breast Cancer Treatment (PDQ®). National Institutes of Health. Retrieved from

https://www.cancer.gov/types/breast/patient/breast-treatment-pdq

[17] City of Hope National Comprehensive Cancer Center. (2025). Breast Cancer Treatment: Surgery, Chemotherapy & More. Retrieved from https://www.cityofhope.org/clinical-program/breast-cancer/breast-cancer-treatments

[18] Breastcancer.org. (2025). Breast Cancer Treatment. Retrieved from https://www.breastcancer.org/treatment

[19] National Breast Cancer Foundation. (2025). Breast Cancer Treatment Options. Retrieved from https://www.nationalbreastcancer.org/breast-cancer-treatment/

[20] Emory University, Winship Cancer Institute. (2025). Breast Cancer Treatment. Retrieved from https://winshipcancer.emory.edu/cancer-types-and-treatments/breast-cancer/treatment.php

[21] American Cancer Society. (2024). Breast Cancer Treatment. Retrieved from https://www.cancer.org/cancer/types/breast-cancer/treatment.html

[22] Breastcancer.org. (2025). Breast Cancer Treatment Options by Stage. Retrieved from https://www.breastcancer.org/treatment/planning/options-by-stage

[23] CDC. (2025). Treatment of Breast Cancer. Centers for Disease Control

and Prevention. Retrieved from https://www.cdc.gov/breast-cancer/treatment/index.html

[24] Mayo Clinic. (2024). Breast Cancer Treatment. Retrieved from https://www.mayoclinic.org/diseases-conditions/breast-cancer/diagnosis-treatment/drc-20352475

[25] American Cancer Society. (2024). Immunotherapy for Breast Cancer. Retrieved from https://www.cancer.org/cancer/types/breast-cancer/treatment.html

Tree Burial as Memorial - Living Legacy and Alternative End-of-Life Care

As our understanding of mortality, environmental stewardship, and meaningful commemoration evolves, alternative burial practices are gaining recognition and adoption among families seeking ways to honor their loved ones while contributing positively to the natural world. Tree burial, also known as natural burial with tree planting or "green burial," represents a profound shift from traditional funeral practices, transforming the finality of death into an ongoing relationship with a living memorial that grows and changes across decades and generations.

For families grieving the loss of a loved one to breast cancer or any terminal illness, tree burial offers a way to channel grief into environmental restoration, to create a physical place for ongoing remembrance, and to sense that their loss contributes meaning to the world. Rather than viewing death as an endpoint, tree burial positions it as a transformation, with the deceased becoming part of a growing, flourishing ecosystem.

Understanding Tree Burial - Process and Practice

Tree burial is a form of natural or green burial in which human remains are placed in biodegradable containers or directly into soil, with a tree planted above or immediately adjacent to the burial site. Natural burial is defined as "the interment of the body of a dead person in the soil or a body of water in a manner that does not inhibit decomposition but allows the body to be naturally recycled."[1] As the body naturally decomposes over months to years, it nourishes the soil and provides essential nutrients to the growing tree. The tree becomes a living memorial. A tangible, visible, growing representation of the deceased that can be visited, touched, and observed as it matures across the years.

The practice has roots in various cultural and spiritual traditions. Some indigenous cultures have long practiced returning deceased individuals to the earth as part of natural cycles, including practices such as "being buried among tree roots in the Peruvian Amazon" and other earth-centered funeral customs.[2] Environmental movements and ecological consciousness have given tree burial renewed relevance and modern expression, combining environmental ethics with meaningful memorialization.

The Biological Process

The biological process of tree burial involves several interconnected elements working in concert. When human remains are placed in the ground, either in a biodegradable casket, shroud, or urn. The body begins the natural decomposition process. Microorganisms in the soil break down organic matter, releasing nitrogen, phosphorus, potassium, and other nutrients essential for plant growth.

The decomposition process typically requires 2-8 years for complete breakdown, depending on soil composition, temperature, moisture levels, pH, and other environmental factors.[3] During this time, nutrients from the decomposing body gradually become available to root systems of the planted tree. As the tree's roots expand downward and outward into the nutrient-enriched soil, they access these nutrients, incorporating them into living tissue as leaves, branches, trunk.

In this literal and poetic sense, the deceased becomes part of the tree's body. The carbon, nitrogen, and other elements that comprised the person's physical form become integrated into the living wood, leaves, and growth of the tree. A large tree may contain hundreds of pounds of organic material, much of which was derived from human remains.

Different tree species have different nutrient requirements and growth characteristics. Practitioners of tree burial typically select species appropriate to the geographic region, climate, soil conditions, and family preferences. A mature tree from a burial might grow 40-80 feet tall and live for 100-300+ years, depending on species and environmental conditions.

Selection of Trees and Planting Considerations

The choice of tree species is significant and should align with regional environmental conditions, family preferences, and the desired legacy. In Arizona, particularly in Phoenix and Tucson areas, appropriate native or adapted species might include desert ironwood, mesquite, palo verde, acacia, or, in higher elevations, oak or Arizona ash.[4]

Native species are often preferred because they are adapted to local conditions, support regional ecosystems, require minimal maintenance or artificial watering once established, and contribute to environmental restoration. Planting native trees, particularly in arid regions, represents a commitment to ecological healing alongside personal remembrance.

Some families select trees based on significance. A tree the deceased loved, or one with symbolic meaning. Others choose based on practical considerations such as hardiness, longevity, and ability to thrive in local conditions. Still others choose based on environmental considerations, selecting species that support pollinators, birds, or other wildlife.

Environmental and Biological Advantages

Tree burial provides environmental advantages compared to traditional burial or cremation. Traditional burial often involves non-biodegradable caskets, toxic embalming fluids that can contaminate soil and groundwater, permanent concrete vaults that prevent natural decomposition, use of pesticides and fertilizers to maintain cemetery grounds, and ongoing resource consumption for perpetual cemetery maintenance.[5]

Cremation, while requiring no ongoing land use, consumes significant fuel energy and releases carbon dioxide and mercury into the atmosphere. Tree burial, conversely, uses only biodegradable materials, eliminates toxic embalming chemicals, allows complete natural decomposition, requires minimal ongoing resource consumption, contributes to carbon sequestration as the tree grows, and restores soil health and supports ecosystem recovery.[5]

A mature tree sequesters substantial amounts of carbon dioxide over its lifetime, reducing atmospheric greenhouse gases. This environmental benefit resonates with many families seeking to honor loved ones through ecologically responsible practices. Research indicates that "green burials have naturally been attracting more interest" as consumers "weigh the environmental and health consequences of traditional funeral practices."[6]

Emotional and Psychological Significance

Unlike traditional cemetery headstones, which are static and unchanging, a tree memorial is dynamic and alive. Families observe the tree's seasonal changes—new growth in spring, full foliage in summer, dramatic colors in autumn (where applicable), and dormancy in winter. The tree's age at death and ongoing growth become markers of time, with the tree's height and spread visible expressions of the years passing since the loved one's death.

Many families find this ongoing aliveness deeply meaningful. Rather than visiting a grave where they feel separated from the deceased by soil, they experience a tree as an active presence, something they have helped sustain through visits, watering during establishment, and ongoing care. The tree becomes a bridge between the living and the dead, representing continuation rather than finality.

Children particularly may find comfort in a tree memorial. They can climb the tree, observe birds and insects living in its branches, watch it grow taller than they are, and experience visceral understanding that their loved one is part of something living and continuing. This can be less psychologically stark than observing a grave marker or empty chair at the family table.

Transforming Grief into Environmental Action

Planting a tree in memory of a deceased loved one can transform the despair and helplessness of grief into purposeful action. In the immediate aftermath of death, when so much feels beyond control, families can take concrete action such as selecting a tree species, choosing a location, participating in planting. This active involvement in creating a memorial can provide a sense of agency and purpose during a time characterized by powerlessness.

For some families, the environmental dimension provides additional meaning. Planting a tree in a loved one's name becomes an act of environmental restoration, contributing to reforestation, urban greenery, or ecosystem recovery. A family grieving a death from cancer might find particular significance in planting a tree as an act of environmental healing, knowing that the tree will provide oxygen, sequester carbon, provide habitat for wildlife, and contribute to a healthier world for generations to come.

Continuing Bonds and Ongoing Relationship

Psychological research on grief indicates that successful grieving does not involve "moving on" from the deceased or severing bonds, but rather involves integrating the loss and transforming the relationship. A tree memorial facilitates this transformation by creating a focal point for ongoing relationship.

Families report visiting the tree memorial across seasons and years while bringing children, sharing memories, observing the tree's growth, and feeling ongoing connection to the deceased. Some families plant flowers around the tree's base, mulch the soil, or remove dead branches—simple acts of care that maintain the memorial and express ongoing relationship. Over time, the tree becomes woven into family identity and tradition.

Some families report that visiting the tree feels more meaningful than visiting traditional cemeteries. Rather than experiencing the sterility and sadness of rows of headstones, they experience their loved one as part of a living, breathing ecosystem. Rather than feeling their loved one as lost or gone, they sense ongoing presence and continuation.

Reasons Families Choose Tree Burial

Families with strong environmental values often select tree burial as a way to express their commitment to ecological stewardship through their death practices. For individuals who lived with concern for climate change, environmental degradation, or species extinction, tree burial represents a final act aligned with these values. Rather than contributing to resource extraction and consumption in death, the deceased contributes to environmental restoration.

In the context of breast cancer, some patients express wishes for tree burial during end-of-life planning, seeing it as a way to transform their death from a tragic loss into an act of environmental healing. Family members honoring this wish find comfort in knowing that their loved one's physical form is contributing to the planting of a tree that will help heal the climate and environment.

Rejection of Traditional Funeral Industry Practices

Many families choose tree burial as a conscious rejection of conventional funeral industry practices, which they perceive as unnecessarily expensive, environmentally destructive, focused on profit rather than meaningful memorialization, and promoting unrealistic notions of preservation and preventing natural decay.

Tree burial, by contrast, is relatively simple and inexpensive. A 2024 study indicates that "green burials can range from $500 to $5,000, with an average of about $2,600," compared to "the average cost of a conventional funeral and burial, including embalming, casket, transportation, viewing, interment, etc., was $8,300" according to the National Funeral Directors Association.[6] Green burials typically include "a burial plot, fees to open and close the grave, a plot marker, and a one-time endowment to a perpetual care fund to maintain the property as a natural burial site."[7]

For families with limited financial resources, or those who object philosophically to spending large sums on funeral services, tree burial provides a financially accessible alternative that still honors the deceased meaningfully.

Spiritual and Philosophical Beliefs

Many families hold spiritual or philosophical beliefs that align with tree burial. These might include beliefs in returning to the earth and natural cycles, indigenous spiritual traditions emphasizing connection to land and nature, environmental spirituality or earth-based religious practices, Buddhist or other philosophical traditions emphasizing non-attachment and impermanence, or humanist or secular philosophies emphasizing contribution to the greater good.[8]

For these individuals, tree burial expresses their deepest beliefs about death, nature, and human relationship to the earth. It feels congruent with their values and provides peace about what happens to their physical body after death.

Creating A Lasting, Living Legacy

Unlike ashes scattered or placed in urns that gather dust, a tree memorial is undeniably present across generations. A tree planted today can live for 100-300+ years. Great-grandchildren may climb the tree, sit in its shade, pick its fruit or nuts, or simply know it as "the tree where great-grandma is." The memorial is not dependent on cemetery maintenance or family financial resources. The tree sustains itself through natural biological processes.

This permanence and autonomy appeal to families seeking to create lasting memorials that do not require ongoing financial investment. The tree memorial becomes a gift to future generations such as shade, oxygen, habitat, beauty made possible by the deceased.

Addressing Overcrowded Cemeteries and Land Use Concerns

In densely populated areas, cemetery land is increasingly scarce and expensive. Traditional cemeteries occupy significant land area that could be used for other purposes. Tree burial addresses these concerns by using land more efficiently and contributing to land restoration rather than consuming it.

In Arizona, where urban sprawl and water scarcity are significant concerns, tree burial in appropriate locations can support urban forestry initiatives and xeriscaping environmentally appropriate landscaping using native, drought-tolerant plants. Green cemeteries "are specially dedicated rustic spaces" that "aim to conserve or restore the natural landscape" rather than maintaining traditional lawn cemeteries.[9]

Desire for Personal Connection to Memorial Site

Some families prefer tree burial because it creates a memorial they can actively tend and maintain. Traditional cemeteries often have restrictions on plantings, decorations, or personalization. With a tree memorial, families might enhance the site with benches, native plantings, or small markers, creating a personalized sacred space.

Families with properties or access to land might arrange private tree burial, creating a memorial on property they own. Visiting the memorial involves walking on family land, potentially combining the visit with other family activities or gatherings. This integration into ongoing family life creates deeper meaning than periodic cemetery visits. It is important to note that "all states except for Arkansas allow burial on private property, although some states require you to designate a piece of land as a family cemetery that is limited to family members only."[7]

Processing Grief Through Nature Connection

Research on nature's psychological benefits indicates that spending time in natural environments reduces stress, improves mental health, and provides perspective on challenges. For families grieving a death, regular visits to a tree memorial provide these benefits alongside the specific purpose of honoring the deceased.

Walking to the tree, sitting beneath its branches, observing seasonal changes, and experiencing the continuation of life in nature can support psychological healing. The tree becomes a place for reflection, remembrance, and reconnection with the deceased through the natural world.

Tree Burial Options in Arizona

Several cemeteries and memorial spaces in Arizona now offer tree burial and natural burial options, though the availability of dedicated green burial facilities is more limited than in some other states. Families interested in tree burial in Arizona might explore:

Green burial gardens and natural burial sites in Phoenix

- Some funeral homes and cemeteries in the Phoenix area now offer green burial options
- Research is ongoing to develop dedicated natural burial cemetery spaces

Private land burial arrangements

- Arizona law permits private property tree burial with appropriate permits and documentation
- Families with property may arrange burial and tree planting on their land
- This option requires consultation with county or municipal authorities regarding regulations

Expanding Access to Tree Burial in Arizona

At present, Arizona has limited dedicated natural burial facilities compared to states like California, Colorado, or the Pacific Northwest. However, interest is growing. Environmental organizations and funeral industry innovators are working to establish dedicated natural burial cemeteries in Arizona, train funeral professionals in green burial practices, educate families about tree burial options, and address regulatory barriers to natural burial.

Families interested in tree burial in Arizona may need to research funeral homes that support green burial practices, explore cemetery options offering natural burial, consider travel to nearby states if Arizona options are limited, or investigate private land burial possibilities if they own property.

Environmental Considerations for Arizona Tree Burial

Arizona's arid climate presents unique considerations for tree burial. Successful tree burial requires selection of native or well-adapted tree species suitable for Arizona's aridity, adequate water availability during tree establishment (typically 2-3 years after planting), appropriate soil conditions, and location in areas that receive sufficient moisture or supplemental irrigation.[4] Species particularly suited to Arizona tree burial include:

Desert Ironwood (Olneya tesota)
- Very hardy, long-lived, deep roots, excellent for low desert[4]
- Described as having "tiny, dense green leaves that are evergreen" and surviving "on very little water and still look lush"[10]
- Reaches 30 feet wide and 30 feet tall when fully grown[11]

Velvet Mesquite (Prosopis velutina)
- Native to Arizona, nitrogen-fixing, provides shade and food sources[4]
- The native mesquite of the Sonoran Desert with spreading

branches and gnarled crown[12]

- Can grow 30-35 feet tall with 30-40 foot spread[13]

Palo Verde (Parkinsonia florida and Parkinsonia aculeata)

- Arizona's official state tree, native, fast-growing, green bark provides photosynthesis[4]
- The Blue Palo Verde "grows faster than the Foothill" variety and "is one of the most popular trees for desert landscapes"[14]
- The Foothill Palo Verde "grows more slowly but lives longer, up to 200 years or more in the wild"[14]
- Both species produce "brilliant bright yellow flowers" and thrive in minimal water conditions[14]

Acacia Species

- Several Arizona-native species suited to various elevations[4]
- Generally heat and drought tolerant with deep root systems

Arizona Ash (Fraxinus velutina)

- Deciduous, provides seasonal shade variation, mid-elevation appropriate[4]
- Native to Arizona mountains and foothills

Arizona White Oak (Quercus arizonica)

- Long-lived, native to Arizona mountains and foothills[4]
- Can reach 30 feet in height and width[15]

Higher elevation locations (Flagstaff, Prescott areas) can support cooler-climate species like oak, ash, and conifer species that would struggle in Phoenix's extreme heat. The Foothill Palo Verde is particularly appropriate for higher elevations, as it "requires less water than the Blue Palo Verde" and is "found in the upland areas of the Sonoran Desert."[14]

Practical Considerations and Planning

Tree burial exists in a complex legal landscape that varies by jurisdiction. Arizona, like most states, permits natural burial but regulations vary by county and municipality. Families interested in tree burial should consult with funeral directors experienced in green burial, research specific county or municipal regulations, ensure all documentation and permits are properly completed, understand any restrictions on the location of tree burial (cemeteries, private property, parks), and consider whether the land will remain available long-term for tree growth.[7]

Some families establish trusts or agreements to ensure land remains available for tree memorials across generations. Others work with cemeteries that provide perpetual care for tree burial sites.

Financial Considerations

Tree burial is generally more affordable than traditional funerals. Costs typically include disposition of remains (basic cremation or natural burial preparation), tree purchase and planting, site preparation and ongoing maintenance during establishment, optional cemetery space fees if using dedicated natural burial cemetery, and optional memorial markers or plaques.

A 2024 study reports that "green burials can range from $500 to $5,000, with an average of about $2,600," compared to traditional funeral costs of $8,300 and cremation costs of $6,280.[6] Some families find this cost savings significant and meaningful.

End-of-Life Planning and Documentation

Families planning tree burial should discuss wishes with loved ones well in advance, document preferences in writing (living will, funeral wishes document), discuss financial arrangements and pre-planning, identify preferred tree species and memorial location, consider who will maintain the memorial and ensure tree's ongoing health, and leave clear instructions for family members.

Including tree burial wishes in advance care planning documents ensures that family members can honor these preferences without uncertainty or conflict during the acute grief period.

Ongoing Maintenance and Care

Tree burial sites require minimal ongoing maintenance compared to traditional graves, but some care supports the tree's health and longevity. This includes watering during establishment (2-3 years), mulching to retain moisture and moderate temperature, removing competing vegetation, monitoring for disease or pest issues, and occasional pruning or shaping.[9]

Cemeteries offering natural burial typically provide basic maintenance. Families with private land memorials bear responsibility for ongoing care, which many find meaningful—regular visits to water, weed, and tend the tree maintain active relationship with the memorial.

The Broader Meaning: Death as Transformation

Tree burial embodies a fundamental shift in how we understand death, not as absolute finality but as transformation. The deceased does not disappear or remain static in soil; rather, they continue in transformed form. Their physical body, which no longer experiences consciousness or agency, becomes integrated into a living, growing organism.

This perspective resonates with various spiritual and philosophical traditions that emphasize cycles, continuation, and interconnection. It aligns with scientific understanding of ecological cycles and nutrient flows. It reflects indigenous wisdom about humans as part of nature rather than separate from it.

Environmental Healing Through Memorialization

Tree burial represents a profound reframing of death's meaning. Rather than death being purely loss, it becomes an opportunity for environmental contribution. Each tree burial becomes an act of reforestation, carbon sequestration, and ecosystem restoration.

In regions damaged by deforestation, development, or environmental degradation, tree burial can contribute to healing. Forests of memorial trees become living testaments to those who have died, while simultaneously restoring ecosystems and supporting wildlife.

Multi-Generational Legacy

A tree planted at death can live for centuries. It witnesses generations of family life, births, birthdays, reunions, celebrations, and sorrows occurring in its presence. The tree becomes part of family history and identity. Children grow up in its shade. Teenagers carve initials in its bark. Great-grandchildren climb its branches.

This multi-generational permanence creates a legacy fundamentally different from traditional burial. Rather than fading from awareness as generations pass, the memorial remains actively present, continuing to provide benefits such as shade, oxygen, habitat, beauty to living generations.

Conclusion: Honoring Life Through Growing Things

For families grieving the death of a loved one to breast cancer—or any terminal illness—tree burial offers a way to transform devastating loss into meaningful environmental contribution. It provides an alternative to conventional funeral practices that some families find more aligned with their values, more financially accessible, and more spiritually resonant.

A tree planted over the grave of a loved one becomes a living memorial—growing, changing, thriving across decades and generations. It embodies the possibility that even in death, we contribute to life. It expresses environmental stewardship, ecological consciousness, and commitment to a world that will outlive us. It creates a sacred space where the living can remember the dead while simultaneously participating in the beauty and regeneration of the natural world.

For those who have died and those who grieve them, a tree memorial offers a profound answer to the question of how we are remembered: not through stone and metal that eventually crumble, but through living wood that grows stronger and more beautiful with each passing year. In this transformation, death becomes not an ending but an opening—into nature, into legacy, into ongoing participation in the continuation of life itself.

References

[1] Wikipedia. (2024). Natural Burial. Retrieved from https://en.wikipedia.org/wiki/Natural_burial

[2] Wohlers, W., & Fuss, C. (2018). Natural Burial as a Land Conservation Tool in the U.S. ScienceDirect. Retrieved from https://www.sciencedirect.com/science/article/abs/pii/S016920461830 4067

[3] Zhai, L. (2023). The Contribution of Natural Burials to Soil Ecosystem Services: Review and Emergent Research Questions. ScienceDirect. Retrieved from https://www.sciencedirect.com/science/article/pii/S092913932300398 0

[4] University of Arizona Cooperative Extension. Schuch, U. K., & Kelly, J. J. (2018). Mesquite and Palo Verde Trees for the Urban Landscape. Retrieved from https://extension.arizona.edu/sites/extension.arizona.edu/files/pubs/az 1429.pdf

[5] Green Burial Council. Green Burial Defined. Retrieved from https://www.greenburialcouncil.org/greenburialdefined.html

[6] Britannica Money. (2024). What Is a Green Burial? Cost & Environmental Benefits. Retrieved from https://www.britannica.com/money/green-burial-meaning

[7] Wray, S. (2024). Guide to Green Burial – A Natural Approach to Funerals. Funeral Advantage. Retrieved from https://funeraladvantage.com/consumer-resources/green-burial/

[8] The Order of the Good Death. Green Burial. Retrieved from https://www.orderofthegooddeath.com/resources/green-burial/

[9] Interra Green Burial. Ecological Burial: Find Eco Burial Options. Retrieved from https://www.interraburial.com/ecological-burial-options

[10] Arizona Desert Xeriscape. (2015). Native Trees. Retrieved from https://desertxeriscape.wordpress.com/native-trees/

[11] Oasis Ora. (2025). 9 Best Desert Trees for Arizona Landscapes in 2025. Retrieved from https://oasisora.com/desert-trees-in-arizona/

[12] Tree Vitalize. (2022). 10 Beautiful Desert Trees in Arizona (Includes Mesquite Trees). Retrieved from https://treevitalize.com/desert-trees-arizona/

[13] Schuch, U. K., & Kelly, J. J. (2018). Mesquite and Palo Verde Trees for the Urban Landscape. University of Arizona Cooperative Extension. Retrieved from https://extension.arizona.edu/sites/extension.arizona.edu/files/pubs/az1429.pdf

[14] The Arizona Native Plant Society. (2024). Arizona State Tree: The Palo Verde. Retrieved from https://aznps.com/arizona-state-tree/

[15] FarmTilling. (2025). 20 Best Trees For Arizona. Retrieved from https://farmtilling.com/best-trees-for-arizona/

National Geographic. (2024). Human composting, water cremation, and other new 'green' burial trends. Retrieved from https://www.nationalgeographic.com/environment/article/rest-in-compost-these-green-funerals-offer-an-eco-friendly-afterlife

WeConservePA Library. (2023). Green Burial. Retrieved from https://library.weconservepa.org/guides/169-green-burial

University of California Agriculture and Natural Resources. Blue Palo Verde (Parkinsonia florida). Calscape. Retrieved from https://calscape.org/Parkinsonia-florida-(Blue-Palo-Verde)

World Health Organization (WHO). Death and Disease Management Guidance. Retrieved from https://www.who.int

Department of Forestry and Fire Management, State of Arizona. Tree Care. Retrieved from https://dffm.az.gov/tree-care

Palo Verde Nuclear Generating Station

Powering the Southwest and Shaping the Future of Clean Energy

The Largest Nuclear Power Plant in America... The Palo Verde Generating Station is located on 4,000 acres of land near Tonopah, Arizona, approximately 45 miles west of downtown Phoenix, and consists of three pressurized water reactors.[1] It generates the most electricity of any power plant in the United States per year and is the largest power plant by net generation as of 2021.[1] This remarkable facility stands as a testament to engineering excellence, operational reliability, and the capacity of nuclear energy to meet the enormous electrical demands of a growing southwestern United States. It has Scale and Capacity.

Numbers That Tell a Story

Construction and Timeline. Construction on Palo Verde began in 1976 and was completed in 1988 at a cost of $5.9 billion.[2] Unit 1 received its operating license on June 1, 1985, with Units 2 and 3 receiving licenses in 1986 and 1987 respectively.[3] Over twelve years of intensive construction, engineering, and rigorous testing, Palo Verde emerged as a revolutionary facility—one that would define the trajectory of American nuclear power for decades to come.

Generating Capacity and Performance. The scale of Palo Verde's electrical generation capacity is staggering. Each reactor has a capacity to produce 1.4 gigawatts of electric power after power up-rates approved by the Nuclear Regulatory Commission.[1] The facility's average electric power production is about 3.3 gigawatts (GW), serving about four million people.[1] To contextualize this extraordinary output: Palo Verde generates approximately 32 million megawatt-hours annually.[1]

Consider the human impact embedded in these numbers. Three gigawatts is not merely an abstract unit of power it represents electricity flowing into four million homes, powering hospitals, schools, businesses, and families across Arizona, California, New Mexico, and beyond. It means that on a sweltering summer day when air conditioning demand peaks, when industries require power to operate, when hospitals depend on reliable electricity to save lives, Palo Verde is there, generating clean, consistent power.

All three Palo Verde units are individually ranked among the top six producers in the United States, according to industry data.[4] For 2014, Palo Verde recorded its 23rd consecutive year as the largest power generator in the U.S., producing 32.3 million MWh and breaking its own record of 31.9 million MWh set in 2012.[4]

Facility and employment, the physical footprint. The facility covers 4,050 acres, making it one of the largest industrial facilities in Arizona.[5] The reactor containment buildings are some of the largest in the world.[2] Tour guides at Palo Verde famously recommend that visitors wear comfortable shoes and sturdy clothing, as the scale of the facility demands significant walking to appreciate its enormity.[5]

What's the economic and employment Impact? The economic significance of Palo Verde extends far beyond the electricity it generates. With approximately 2,500 employees at the facility, Palo Verde is estimated to have a $1.8 billion impact on Arizona's economy.[5] These are not minimum-wage jobs. Positions at Palo Verde include specialized engineers, nuclear technicians, security personnel, maintenance specialists, chemists, and other highly skilled professionals. The plant employs about 3,000 workers and has an annual economic impact of more than $1.8 billion in Arizona.[4]

For the families of Palo Verde workers, employment at the facility often represents stable, well-compensated work that supports their long-term financial security. Engineers and technicians at Palo Verde develop expertise that places them among the most skilled nuclear professionals in the world. Many workers experience decades-long careers, sometimes spanning the entire operational life of individual reactor units, developing profound technical knowledge and contributing to a culture of safety and excellence.

Palo Verder... An engineering marvel in the desert with a unique water management system. What makes Palo Verde truly extraordinary is its location. The Palo Verde Generating Station is the only large nuclear power plant in the world that is not near a large body of water.[1] This presents a profound engineering challenge, as nuclear power plants require enormous quantities of water for cooling. Most nuclear facilities globally are located on rivers, coastlines, or lakes, allowing them to access abundant water.

Palo Verde solved this challenge through innovative water reclamation. Palo Verde is the only U.S. nuclear power plant that is not located next to an ocean or other large body of water, sitting instead in the middle of Arizona's Sonoran Desert.[4] Palo Verde was the first nuclear power plant in the world and remains the largest in the U.S. to use recycled municipal wastewater for condenser and other plant cooling needs.[4]

APS concluded a landmark 40-year agreement in 2010 with the five cities in the greater Phoenix metropolitan area to provide an annual allotment of up to 26 billion gallons of treated municipal effluent to Palo Verde through 2050.[4] This agreement represents an elegant solution to water scarcity—what would otherwise be wastewater is treated, purified further at Palo Verde's own water reclamation facility, stored in an 80-acre reservoir for use in the plant's nine cooling towers.[6]

This innovation transforms a potential limitation into an environmental benefit. Phoenix's treated wastewater, rather than being discharged into rivers or the environment, becomes productive resource supporting clean energy generation. The facility itself further treats this water to meet rigorous standards, creating a closed-loop system that exemplifies sustainable engineering.

What about the environmental and climate Impact concerns. Are carbon emissions avoided? Notably, Palo Verde produces that power almost entirely without carbon-dioxide emissions. The climate impact of Palo Verde's electricity generation cannot be overstated, particularly given the escalating crisis of climate change. Since its commissioning, Palo Verde's electricity production has offset the emission of almost 484 million metric tons of carbon dioxide (the equivalent of taking up to 84 million cars off the road for one year).[1]

To contextualize this remarkable achievement: if Palo Verde were suddenly replaced by natural gas plants generating the same electricity, the carbon emissions would be catastrophic. If Palo Verde were to cease operation at the end of the original license, replacement cost of natural gas generation, the least expensive alternative would total $36 billion over the 20-year license renewal period.[1] This calculation includes only direct financial costs, not the immeasurable cost of releasing hundreds of millions of additional metric tons of carbon dioxide into the atmosphere.

Beyond carbon dioxide, Palo Verde's electricity production has offset more than 253,000 metric tons of sulfur dioxide and 618,000 metric tons of nitrogen oxide.[1] These pollutants cause acid rain, respiratory disease, and environmental degradation. By eliminating these emissions, Palo Verde protects air quality and public health across the southwestern region.

Let's about climate change and nuclear power's future. As the world confronts the urgent reality of climate change, nuclear power has emerged as a critical component of decarbonization strategy. Nuclear power plants like Palo Verde generate electricity without greenhouse gas emissions during operation. Nuclear energy generates nearly a fifth of America's electricity and accounts for half of all domestic clean energy generation.[7]

The Biden administration has explicitly recognized nuclear power's role in climate mitigation, with goals to triple the nation's nuclear energy capacity. For every gigawatt of nuclear power, equivalent greenhouse gas reduction is achieved compared to renewable sources like wind and solar, which must account for intermittency and storage challenges. Including safety, security, and operational excellence.

Rigorous oversight and safety culture is key. The facility proudly identifies itself as having earned "STAR" status with the Arizona Department of Safety and Health's Voluntary Protection Program. A top safety status whose criteria only about three dozen companies in the state have met.[5] This designation reflects Palo Verde's extraordinary commitment to safety, extending far beyond regulatory compliance to embrace a comprehensive safety culture.

Palo Verde is an obsessively secure power-generating station, with security there described as "just amazing."[5] A tour of Palo Verde requires passing through a literal maze of redundant security systems, including a background check that includes required information regarding a visitor's health condition. These measures reflect nuclear industry's paramount commitment to preventing unauthorized access and ensuring protection of the public.

Reviewing regulatory compliance. On April 21, 2011, the NRC renewed the operating licenses for Palo Verde's three reactors, extending their service lives from forty to sixty years.[1] This license renewal, following exhaustive regulatory review and analysis, represents confidence that Palo Verde can operate safely and reliably for an extended period. The Nuclear Regulatory Commission's estimate of the risk each year of an earthquake intense enough to cause core damage to the reactor at Palo Verde was 1 in 26,316, ranking it #18 in the nation according to an NRC study published in August 2010.[1]

The facility demonstrates consistently high operational performance. The average capacity factor of all U.S. nuclear power plants in June was 96.4%, the highest that it has been in six years.[4] Palo Verde routinely operates above 90% capacity factor, meaning the facility is generating at or near maximum capacity the vast majority of the time.

The Living and Working Community at Palo Verde. For the thousands of employees at Palo Verde, the facility represents far more than just a workplace. It is an institution where skilled professionals apply their expertise to generate clean electricity serving millions of people. It is where engineers solve complex technical problems, where security personnel vigilantly protect critical infrastructure, where maintenance workers ensure that equipment operates flawlessly year after year.

For a character who works at Palo Verde, the facility shapes their professional identity and community belonging. They may spend decades at the facility, witnessing the maturation of reactor units, contributing to continuous operational improvement, and taking pride in the knowledge that their work powers hospitals, schools, and homes. They understand that Palo Verde's success directly impacts the economic stability of Arizona and the southwestern region. They recognize that their professional contributions are essential to climate change mitigation and energy security.

The Future of Nuclear Power: Recycling Waste and Advanced Reactors. The challenge of nuclear waste is something to think about. While Palo Verde generates enormous quantities of clean electricity, it also produces nuclear waste. Spent fuel rods that remain radioactive for centuries. Historically, spent nuclear fuel has been stored at reactor sites in pools and dry casks, awaiting a permanent disposal solution that the United States has yet to implement. The nuclear industry has safely stored 88,500 metric tons of commercial SNF and HLW in spent fuel pools and dry casks at 76 operating and decommissioned reactor sites in 35 states.[8]

Palo Verde uses revolutionary recycling technologies, however, the future is changing. Advanced technologies are emerging that promise to transform nuclear waste from a disposal problem into a resource. For the future, the focus is on removing the minor actinides along with uranium and plutonium from the final waste and burning them all together in fast neutron reactors.[9]

Argonne National Laboratory pioneered the development of pyrochemical processing, or pyroprocessing, a high-temperature method of recycling reactor waste into fuel. When used in conjunction with nuclear fast reactors, pyroprocessing would allow 100 times more of the energy in uranium ore to be used to produce electricity compared to current commercial reactors.[10]

The implications are profound. Fast reactors and reprocessing could reduce by 90% the volume of nuclear waste that will need to be stored in a geological repository for tens of thousands of years.[11] Rather than viewing spent fuel as an intractable waste problem, advanced recycling would convert it into fuel for next-generation reactors, dramatically reducing both the quantity and longevity of waste requiring permanent storage.

The importance of Federal Investment and Commercial Development.

The federal government has dramatically increased investment in these technologies. Congress has supported the Department of Energy's reprocessing research and development program in recent years through a funding authorization in the Energy Act of 2020 and subsequent annual appropriations.[8] The U.S. Department of Energy announced $38 million for a dozen projects that will work to reduce the impacts of light-water reactor used nuclear fuel disposal.[12]

Private companies are advancing commercialization. Oklo announced plans to design, build, and operate a spent fuel recycling facility in Oak Ridge, Tennessee. According to the company, the recycling facility will be part of a $1.68 billion advanced fuel center and will reprocess spent fuel into fresh fuel for advanced reactors like Oklo's Aurora Powerhouse, which the company plans to build at Idaho National Laboratory.[13]

Fast neutron reactors, which use neutrons that are not slowed by a moderator such as water to sustain the fission chain reaction, offer advantages over existing thermal nuclear reactors. When operated in a fully closed fuel cycle, in which nuclear fuel is recycled and reused, fast reactors have the potential to extract 60 to 70 times more energy from the same amount of natural uranium than thermal reactors, thereby significantly reducing the amount of high level radioactive waste.[14]

A Vision of sustainable nuclear energy for the future. The vision emerging from these technologies is transformative. When using fast reactors in a closed fuel cycle, one kilogram of nuclear waste can be recycled multiple times until all the uranium is used and the actinides. Which remain radioactive for thousands of years, are burned up. What then remains is about 30 grams of waste that will be radioactive for 200 to 300 years.[14]

This represents a fundamental shift from viewing nuclear energy as generating problematic waste to recognizing it as a sustainable, closed-loop energy system. Spent fuel from Palo Verde and other facilities would not be a disposal headache but rather a resource to fuel the next generation of reactors. The waste footprint would shrink by 90%. The duration that waste requires secure storage would drop from thousands of years to hundreds.

Palo Verde as Pillar of American Energy... is an unknown to the masses. Palo Verde Nuclear Generating Station stands as one of America's most important and underappreciated achievements. Generating more electricity than any other power plant in the nation, serving four million people, employing thousands of skilled workers, and avoiding hundreds of millions of metric tons of greenhouse gas emissions annually, Palo Verde exemplifies what is possible when engineering excellence, operational dedication, and commitment to clean energy converge.

For families like those of Palo Verde workers, the facility is more than an industrial complex. It is a source of stable employment, community, and purpose. It is an institution that contributes to regional economic vitality and global energy security. For the residents of Arizona, California, New Mexico, and beyond who depend on Palo Verde's electricity, it is an invisible but essential foundation of modern life.

As the world confronts climate change and renewable energy sources expand, nuclear power exemplified by facilities like Palo Verde remains irreplaceable. And as revolutionary waste recycling technologies move from laboratory demonstration to commercial deployment, the spent fuel from Palo Verde and similar facilities will transform from a disposal problem into an asset, powering the next generation of reactors and ultimately creating a truly sustainable nuclear fuel cycle.

Palo Verde is not simply a power plant. It is a symbol of human ingenuity, a testament to the possibility of clean energy at scale, and a critical tool in humanity's effort to transition away from fossil fuels. It powers dreams, homes, hospitals, and futures. And thanks to emerging technologies, it will continue to power that future in ways we are only beginning to imagine.

References

[1] Wikipedia. Palo Verde Generating Station. Retrieved from https://en.wikipedia.org/wiki/Palo_Verde_Nuclear_Generating_Station

[2] Burbank Water and Power. Palo Verde Nuclear Station. Retrieved from https://www.burbankwaterandpower.com/images/administrative/downloads/PaloVerde_NuclearStation.pdf

[3] Nuclear Regulatory Commission. (2024). Palo Verde Nuclear Generating Station, Unit 1. Retrieved from https://www.nrc.gov/info-finder/reactors/palo1.html

[4] Power Magazine. (2015). TOP PLANTS: Palo Verde Nuclear Generating Station, Wintersburg, Arizona. Retrieved from https://www.powermag.com/palo-verde-nuclear-generating-station-wintersburg-arizona/

[5] Arizona Department of Water Resources. (2017). AZ water officials get up close look at one of the country's largest nuclear power plants. Retrieved from https://www.azwater.gov/news/articles/2017-27-04

[6] PNM Resources. Nuclear Power - Palo Verde. Retrieved from https://www.pnm.com/nuclear-power

[7] U.S. Department of Energy. (2024). Nuclear Energy Fact Sheet. Retrieved from https://www.energy.gov/

[8] U.S. Congress, Congressional Research Service. (2024). Considerations for Reprocessing of Spent Nuclear Fuel (Report R48364). Retrieved from https://www.congress.gov/crs-product/R48364

[9] World Nuclear Association. Processing of Used Nuclear Fuel. Retrieved from https://world-nuclear.org/information-library/nuclear-fuel-cycle/fuel-recycling/processing-of-used-nuclear-fuel

[10] U.S. Department of Energy, Argonne National Laboratory. Recycling Used Nuclear Fuel for a Sustainable Energy Future. Retrieved from https://www.anl.gov/sites/www/files/2023-09/Recycling Used Nuclear Fuel Brochure.pdf

[11] Physics Today. (2024). US takes another look at recycling nuclear fuel. AIP Publishing. Retrieved from https://pubs.aip.org/physicstoday/article/77/2/22/3230671/

[12] U.S. Department of Energy. (2024). DOE Awards $38 Million For Projects Leading Used Nuclear Fuel Recycling Initiative. Retrieved from https://www.energy.gov/articles/doe-awards-38-million-projects-leading-used-nuclear-fuel-recycling-initiative

[13] U.S. Department of Energy, Office of Science. (2025). U.S. nuclear fuel recycling takes two steps forward. American Nuclear Society Nuclear Newswire. Retrieved from https://www.ans.org/news/2025-09-08/article-7348/

[14] International Atomic Energy Agency. (2023). When Nuclear Waste is an Asset, not a Burden. IAEA Bulletin. Retrieved from https://www.iaea.org/bulletin/when-nuclear-waste-is-an-asset-not-a-burden

Maricopa County, Arizona. Palo Verde Generating Station. Retrieved from https://www.maricopa.gov/1002/PVGS

Global Energy Monitor. Palo Verde nuclear power plant. Retrieved from https://www.gem.wiki/Palo_Verde_nuclear_power_plant

Stanford University. (2016). Palo Verde Generating Station. Stanford Energy Resources Engineering Course. Retrieved from http://large.stanford.edu/courses/2016/ph241/chandler2/